UNFORGETTABLE

Colin stood behind Liesl, his gaze seeking the horizon. "I understand more than you think." He folded his arms around her shoulders and pressed her against him. The heat of her felt good.

Liesl turned in his arms, mouth open, staring, searching. Colin didn't want questions. He didn't have answers. Unconsciously, he swayed in time to an unfamiliar tune buzzing in his head. He tried to shake it away, but the melody stuck and played on like a record in a jukebox. His voice, humming the tune, echoed memories in the deep recesses of his brain. When he brought her head to his shoulder, she didn't fight him.

"You don't know me at all." Liesl stood stiff in his arms, but didn't move away.

"I know about the beauty mark on your right breast." His fingers confidently sought a spot on the navy wool covering her chest. Her head snapped up.

"I've kissed the scar on your ankle," he continued. Her mouth formed "how," but no sound came out. "The old one Grüber's mare made when she kicked you. I remember how long your hair was when we first met," he whispered. His hand flowed down to her waist, as if stroking silk. "You were only ten. I was twelve. So shy, so pretty, so fun to tease. I wanted you even then."

His skin itched with unnatural sensitivity. His heart stammered a panicked rhythm.

"No..." Liesl shook her head. Her fingers pried his shoulder and tried to push away. As helpless as a drowning swimmer, Colin tightened his hold and resumed his humming. "Sing with me, Liesl. 'Let me show you where my heart lies. Let me prove that it adores...'" When the tune ended, he stopped swaying and shifted his hold to kiss her.

W9-BFG-468

SYLVIE KURTZ

BROKEN
Wings

LOVE SPELL NEW YORK CITY

To Chuck with all my love—
for enduring, supporting, but mostly, for believing.

LOVE SPELL®

November 1996

Published by

Dorchester Publishing Co., Inc.
276 Fifth Avenue
New York, NY 10001

Printed in the United States of America.

BROKEN
Wings

Life may change, but it may fly not;
Hope may vanish, but can die not;
Truth be veiled, but still it burneth;
Love repulsed, but it returneth!
—Percy Bysshe Shelley

Prologue

Schönberg, Texas, March 1944

Dawn streaked the sky like an artist's palette with jags of red and purple. To the west billowing clouds raced toward the town while the lynch mob headed for the metal hangar near the grass landing strip. Lighted torches zigzagged across the diminishing dark with bright yellow snakes of fire. Feet slapped the craggy dirt road in disordered unison. Voices buzzed like stirred hornets with righteous justice.

Jakob Renke watched from the nearby road. He gripped the wooden fence post, and didn't loosen his hold even when a sliver of wood spiked through his skin. He'd started this. But in all his wildest imaginings, he'd never dreamed of this ending when he'd started the rumor. Now it would be finished. And there was nothing he could do to stop it, not without betraying his guilt.

For love, for a woman, he'd betrayed his best friend.

That fact burrowed a nagging feeling of guilt deep in his conscience. It ate at him like a parasite, slowly, surely, steadily. He started forward, but it was too late. Kurt had been the strong one, not him.

The angry mob tore open the hangar door. Metal ripped against metal. The rapid tattoo of their boots drummed on the hangar's cement floor. As they moved in on their target, crashes of wanton destruction splintered the air. The torches trailed black tails of smoke in the lightening sky. He swallowed hard and gripped the fence post tighter.

Jakob couldn't move.

If he did, he'd suffer the same fate. Then Liesl would be left with nothing. This way, he could console her, fill the gap that Kurt's loss would leave behind.

One day, she'd learn to love him, too.

The mob dragged a half-dressed man to the big post oak next to the hangar. Jakob closed his eyes, but the dark screen of his lids couldn't erase the bewildered look on Kurt's face, the fear in his eyes, the denial he couldn't speak.

"I vaz wrong," Jakob whispered, but he couldn't move. His hold on the post tightened, driving the splinter deeper into the palm of his hand. He welcomed the pain.

"No! Leave him alone!" Liesl's frantic voice

echoed in the dawn's cool breeze.

Jakob's eyes flew open. Liesl! What was she doing here? She was in danger. Anyone associated with Kurt was in danger.

She grabbed and pulled at the mob. They swatted her back like an insect. She yelped in pain, then charged at them again. As he raced to rescue her, Jakob's feet barely skimmed the sandy loam.

"Liesl!"

She turned and looked at him, tears of desperation streaking her face, her sleep-tousled blond hair matted in the wet trails on her cheeks. "Please, Jakob, do something!"

But it was too late, he couldn't do anything except shield her from the horror. He grabbed her and pulled her toward him, holding her safe from the crowd's fury. He tried to spirit her in the opposite direction.

"Vee have to leave, Liesl."

"No! We have to help Kurt."

"If vee try, zey vill hang us also."

She looked at him with her big blue eyes rounded and her mouth opened in disbelief. Then she tried to push him away. He held her fast, smelling the scent of Kurt's musk wedded with hers on her skin, seeing the silver band on her ring finger glitter in the dawn's light. Dreadful understanding punched him in the stomach.

He'd made a terrible mistake.

As she twisted in his rigid arms, disgust was written plainly on her face.

She hated him.

He held her closer. She fought him.

9

She'd always hate him.

The knowledge burst like a bomb in Jakob's heart. It was too late to stop. Kurt would die for nothing.

Jakob had gambled, and had lost everything. She would never love him. He would never love again.

The mob threw a rope over a sturdy branch. It held firm when they tested it. One man positioned his horse beneath the flapping noose. Two more forced Kurt on the gelding's back. Another slipped the noose around Kurt's neck. The torches' garish light stretched their shadows.

All the while Liesl's screams filled Jakob's ears. They reverberated through his bones, and etched themselves into his brain. He would hear them until the day he died.

Jakob's muscles shook from holding Liesl back. Her bare feet bruised his shins with their repeated kicks. His wrists bled from the constant raking of her nails.

Too late. His fault. All for nothing.

Gathering up their spent torches, the mob cheered, then headed back up the dirt road. Their voices, singing "God Bless America," faded as they crested the hill, leaving behind an eerie silence punctuated only by Liesl's strangled cries.

"Please," she begged between sobs, but he couldn't move, couldn't let go.

The rope's morbid creak carried to them on the stiffening breeze.

"Please, Jakob . . ."

"I'm sorry, so sorry . . ."

He loosened his hold. She sniffed and moved away zombie-like toward Kurt's limp body. While she worked with fierce determination at the knotted rope on the tree trunk, tiny squeaks like those of a pained animal's gurgled in her throat.

Jakob put a hand over her bloody fingers and pushed them away. He rasped at the rough rope with a knife from his pocket. It was the least he could do for her.

Kurt's body crumpled to the ground. Liesl ran to him, scrabbled at the rope, loosening it from his neck, and cradled his head in her lap. He opened his eyes once.

"Get help!" she cried. "Please, Jakob!"

But Jakob couldn't move.

"I love you, Liesl," Kurt croaked with difficulty. "Forever."

Then he was gone.

Liesl pleaded with him, rocked him, stroked his hair, his cheeks, his throat. She bargained with God, then stilled, waiting for a miracle. Jakob would have given anything to grant her wish.

She didn't move as morning pushed past the dawn. She didn't move when the clouds swelled, obliterating the sun. She didn't move when they burst into cold rain.

Jakob looked on, cemented helplessly into place.

As he watched Liesl's spirit die, as he watched her father and grandmother pry her from her husband's dead body, as he watched her extended family gather in a circle protectively around her, Jakob knew he would spend the rest of his life looking for a way to correct his mistake.

Giving way to tears of shame, Jakob vowed, "If it takes forever, I vill find a vay."

Chapter One

Traders Field, Texas, March 1996

"CastleAir one taking off," Colin Castle informed the small airport's dispatcher. He pushed the throttle forward, feeling the airplane's engine surge to life. The excitement racing through his veins increased in direct proportion to the revving rpm needle.

He gave a *whoop* of pleasure as the 1948 replica airplane launched down the runway. She wanted to fly, but he kept her grounded. Today he would test his machine to its limits. He couldn't afford any mistakes. Not this time. He'd made too many of those already. Everything had to be perfect for the air show.

Ten influential investors would witness the

CastleAir's unveiling at the Trinity Air Show in eight days. Five years of blood, sweat and tears would come to fruition then. And those who'd voiced their doubts would have to eat their words—including his father.

Don't get started on that line of thought. Everything has to be just right. Concentrate on the airplane, nothing else.

The joystick shuddered in his hand. The airplane demanded access to the air. Colin denied the plane's request, holding her in place. He was a good pilot—one of the best—but for this project to work, he needed to fly like the worst. If the airplane could hold up to the abuse of an overconfident, undertrained pilot, she could handle anything. Colin aimed to fly like the worst show-off, and prove he hadn't put his faith into a losing proposition this time.

The airplane groaned its protest. Colin relented, easing back the joystick. She sighed off the runway, and her *ahhh* of satisfaction echoed in Colin's heart, lightening it. His muscles unwound. His mask came off. Now it was just man and machine, muscles and metal, mind and matter. It was *him* alone in the vast blue sky.

He was free.

He never felt this way on the ground, weighted to the earth by gravity. He always had to be someone else—Jakob's serious partner, the show circuit's fearless fly boy, his father's worthless son. But the sky, that was something else altogether. There he could relax. He didn't have to pretend. He could be himself.

Colin urged the CastleAir into a steep ascent,

heading straight for the observation tower. He flew closer and closer—close enough to see the dispatcher's eyes grow wide. As Colin passed over the tower with a foot to spare, Harry ducked. Colin roared with laughter. *You'd think Harry would be used to this by now.* He raised the gear, then veered left and headed into the clear blue sky to put the plane through its paces in an unpopulated area west of Fort Worth.

"CastleAir one, zis is Traders base." The heavy German accent and the sharp, clipped tones left no doubt as to who stood at the other end of the microphone.

"What do you want, Jakob?" Colin sighed.

Jakob Renke worked metal with the skill and artistry of a master, and without his help this project would never have taken off, but lately he'd been absurdly agitated over the plane's well-being. As if Jakob's future was at stake, not Colin's.

"Come back and land zis instant."

"Can't, got work to do." Colin adjusted the power for a steady climb.

"Vee agreed. No foolishness."

"We agreed. I'm not being foolish." Colin circled the area of patched brown and spring-green pastures, checking for other air traffic and looking for a promising field should the need arise. Fields as familiar to him as every nut and bolt of his airplane, as familiar as a part of his own body. A hawk floated to his left, catching a thermal to higher altitude. Colin joined him.

"Vat do you call zis stunt?"

Colin could imagine Jakob's beet-red face with the temple veins raised and throbbing. The guy definitely needed to loosen up. "I call it the seventeen-year-old-boy-showing-off-for-his-girlfriend takeoff."

"Vee are not selling to boys! Vee are trying to attract grown investors."

"Ever heard of a mid-life crisis?"

"You are going to ruin everything vit your crazy flying. Vat good is it to us if zee airplane is crashed?"

The radio crackled in the silence that followed.

"I'm coming in." Colin reversed his position with a Cuban roll and headed back toward the airport. If they were going to have a fight, they wouldn't do it over the airwaves.

He greased his landing and parked the airplane in its spot next to the Vintage Air Factory hangar. He and Jakob reached the hangar door at the same time, but neither spoke until they were inside Jakob's workshop.

This hangar had served as Colin's home for the past five years. He slept on a cot in the back room, and lived and breathed this project every waking hour. He knew the contents of every plastic bin hanging on the wall. He knew the name and function of every scrap of metal carefully catalogued on the shelves, of every tool in the shop. He'd memorized every blue line on the plans spread over the slanted board beside the workbench.

With the public's renewed interest in history and flying museums, and a growing shortage of old planes left to be salvaged, Colin came up with the idea of building replicas—old planes from old plans with new parts.

His father had told him his plans were doomed to failure—like all his previous schemes. Then, when he'd been looking for investors, he'd met Jakob by accident at an air show in California. Jakob put up the money to build the first plane. With their combined skills, they managed to pull the project together and come up with an improved version on an old classic, the 1948 CastleAir Special Edition. When Jakob suggested this particular model, the idea intrigued Colin because the airplane shared his last name. He took it as a good omen.

Now in the wings, plans to build a Grumman F3F biplane and a Messerschmitt Me262 jet fighter waited for the right investors. Their reality hung in a successful unveiling in eight days' time at the Trinity Air Show. Colin's personal success hung on a ten-minute flight that would either make him or break him. He didn't appreciate Jakob's lack of faith at this late hour.

"Vat vere you trying to do?" Jakob asked.

A shock of stiff white hair surrounded a round face with accusing round eyes and round glasses. There was nothing round about the rest of Jakob's body. It appeared solid and wiry from the perpetual motion of eighteen hours plus of work every day for the past five years. The frustrated activity of a man laden with guilt, Colin often thought, and he'd never felt this assumption more clearly than he did now. For the first time since they'd met, he wondered at Jakob's motives. Maybe more than workmanship attracted Jakob to this project. But what? They rarely spoke of anything except the CastleAir and the odd diatribe on the physics of time.

A curl of uncertainty unfurled deep in Colin's stomach, but he ignored it. He flung his leather jacket over Jakob's cluttered workbench. "I was making sure an idiot would be safe flying our plane."

"Idiot? Vere is your head? Zese are professionals."

Colin was right. The purple veins above Jakob's temples did stand out and throb against his angry red skin. "Professionals my foot." Colin paced away from Jakob, then spun back. "Professional lawyers and doctors, maybe. But not professional pilots. These are weekend pilots with barely a hundred hours of flight time logged in their books. They hardly know an aileron from an attitude. I want to be sure our airplane is forgiving enough to see them safely to the ground should they get in over their heads."

Jakob pounded a fist on the workbench, rattling the spare parts of the electric gear motor. "But how can you risk our investment like zat so close to ze show?" Jakob ground his index finger on the workbench to emphasize each word. "No plane, no show, no investors, *nicht wahr?*"

Colin leaned his weight on his fists, and with an angry undertone he mimicked Jakob's accent. "Airplane *kaputt* after one flight by a jock

18

with more balls than brains and no more orders, *nicht wahr?*"

They stared at each other, neither willing to turn away first. Both wanting to win. Both hating to lose. Colin understood Jakob's point, but Jakob didn't even try to consider his. What did it matter, anyway? They both wanted the same thing. Success. They just had different ideas on how to achieve it.

"Listen, Jakob," Colin relented, scraping a hand through his hair. Damn, he'd forgotten to get it cut again. One more detail to take care of before Sunday.

He moved away a few paces, stuffing both hands into the pockets of his khaki pants, then turned back to face the old man. "This is my last chance. Do you think I'd do anything to jeopardize my opportunity for success? My father's in the hospital tied to a dozen tubes. The lung cancer's got him beat. The doctors don't give him more than a month. If I don't make it this time, he'll die thinking I'm a failure."

Jakob shook his head in slow resignation. "I'm not ready." He unearthed a book from beneath his bench. "Your foolish attitude is forcing my hand."

"For what?" Like the sudden silence of a failed engine in flight, Jakob's nonsense mutterings sounded off trouble.

Flicking the pages once with the back of his hand, Jakob shook his head again. "The calculations, zey are not quite right."

"Calculations for what?" Colin would know exactly what to do about a dead engine. He had no emergency checklist for a partner gone over the edge.

"For ze vindow."

Jakob seemed to wind tighter and tighter with each passing moment, reminding Colin of his wind-up balsa-wood airplane when he was a kid. The more he wound the propeller, the tighter the elastic got until one more crank either broke the rubber band, releasing the tension, or the airplane sprang free from his hand, zigzagging an erratic path across the yard. Which would Jakob do?

"Jakob, you're not making any sense."

Jakob's round glasses magnified his nearly colorless eyes, reflecting his desperation. What was going on? Why was Jakob so frantic, now of all times?

"Zis is my last chance, also." Jakob thumbed through the pages of his notebook so fast that several sheets tore partway. "If I don't find Liesl ze first time, I may never get a chance to fix my mistake. I must stop zem from killing Kurt."

"Liesl? What mistake? Who's Kurt?" Colin stood still, keeping his voice low and slow, afraid to make the wrong move and release Jakob's hold on sanity, afraid this latest failure would send him into a blind, high-speed spin into the ground. Colin latched onto a point of reference. They needed each other—at least until the air show. He couldn't give up on success so close to the mark.

"He vaz my best friend and I betrayed him for Liesl's love." Jakob wiped his brow, tugging at the corner of one eye as if to remove a tear. "Instead, I killed zem both. First, she lost Kurt."

One finger traced the outline of a girl's face scribbled in pencil on the page. A pretty girl with high cheekbones, big, sad eyes and very kissable lips. Was she the reason for Jakob's sudden madness?

"Zen she lost his dream," Jakob continued, his voice laden with regret. "She died of a broken heart. Too young to die. All my fault. I have to go back and stop zem."

He ripped the page out and threw it in Colin's direction. Colin caught the paper and absently stuffed it in his pocket.

"Stop who?" Colin asked.

He rounded the workbench and stood next to Jakob. His hands started up to comfort his partner, then fell back to his side. Colin knew nothing about the man with whom he'd spent nearly every hour of every day for the past five years—not where he'd come from, nothing about his family, nothing about his past, except his extraordinary ability to work with metal and his odd fixation on physics. At the time, it had seemed like enough. Had he missed something important?

"Jakob, I'm worried about you. You can't do this to me this close to the air show. What's wrong with you?"

Jakob lifted his gaze from the book. Tiny spider lines of red webbed the whites, and moisture magnified the pupils even more through the thick lenses. "Same zing zat is wrong vit you. I tried to impress the wrong person, using the wrong method. I paid for my selfishness all of my life. Even finding you vaz a torture of ze soul. Every day you remind me of vat I did. Looking at you every day pushed me to find ze vay. Did I ever tell you zat you look like him?"

"Who?"

But Jakob didn't seem to hear him. He pointed to disjointed calculations on an unlined page. "I'm close. So close." He turned the page. A diagram illustrated two cones joined by a narrow passageway overlaid on a map with Lake Schönberg highlighted. "Ze timing has to be perfect."

"Timing for what?" Colin spoke through clenched teeth to keep his mounting irritation in check. He wasn't going to let anyone mess with his chance to win. Not even Jakob. Not this time.

Lost in a world of his own, Jakob didn't answer.

Colin stared at Jakob. The propeller clock, ticking loudly on the wall, stretched each second into minutes. The smell of aviation gas and grease dizzied him. The distant whir of engines buzzed in his mind like crazed drones. As the background blurred, Jakob's face came into sharp focus. And the wild look in his eyes, the desperation etched in every line on the craggy face, showed Colin a man who'd lost his hold on reality.

Trying to find a grip on his anger, Colin moved away. Jakob trotted in front of him, grabbed the front of Colin's shirt and shook him with rash urgency. "You must do as vee agreed until after ze air show. I vill hold my end of ze bargain. I von't leave until you have your orders. But you must hold yours. Vee agreed. No foolishness."

Colin ground his teeth. "I'm not foolish. I'm safe."

"You take foolish chances," Jakob insisted. "Zink of Karen."

"That was thirteen years ago." Unable to stand the confining grip of the collar against his neck, Colin ripped Jakob's hands from his shirt and shoved them away. Air rasped painfully through his constricted throat. "I was a kid. Watching Karen die made me determined never to harm anyone. I'm the best damned pilot around because of what happened to Karen, and you know it. I *won't* crash the plane."

"Colin, *bitte,* like vee agreed. The maneuvers, nozing else."

A spoke of sunlight washed through the hangar's dirty windows, accentuating Jakob's age and frailty. An old man was allowed an obsession, no matter how crazy it seemed to anyone else. If Jakob's fixation on redeeming a past mistake made him work hard on this project, then so be it. The results would be the same. A successful flight at the air show would bring them both the rewards they sought.

"All right," Colin agreed reluctantly, too tired to fight. "We'll do it your way—this time. I better get back up before I run out of sunlight."

"*Ja, gut,* go back up, and do it exactly as vee planned. Do not do or touch anyzing you are not supposed to."

"Aye, aye, *Herr Kapitän.*" Colin gave Jakob a

mock salute, grabbed his jacket and jogged out to the CastleAir.

With the responsibilities of earth weighing heavily on him, and his dizzying near crash with human insanity, he desperately needed a break.

Schönberg, Texas, March 1946

"I'm leaving, Papa," Liesl Erhardt called to her father standing at the back of the general store. He lifted a hand in acknowledgment, but didn't look up from weighing out nails for a customer.

This was her favorite part of the day. Her duty done as postmistress in her father's store, she could spend what remained of the day at the airport with Kurt's airplane. Her father thought she was crazy, and lashed out regularly at what he called her morbid behavior. Her grandmother shook her head sadly, but Liesl thought *Oma* understood.

To Liesl, keeping the airport alive was the only way to make sense of all the sadness. Wearing Kurt's shirt while she worked on his plane was the only way to get through the empty days. If she could make his dream of winning the Trinity Trophy Race and starting his own aviation school come true, then he wouldn't have died for nothing, and she'd have a reason to live.

But today her steps were slow. She wasn't sure she could bear going there. Two years ago he'd died—for no reason except unfounded fear. Normally, just thinking about that day made her blood boil. But today, thinking about Kurt's senseless murder raised goose bumps all over her body and sent a dreadful snake of premonition rattling in her stomach.

She stopped suddenly and raised a hand to her throat. The air thickened, making it hard for her to breathe. She gulped hard, and blinked.

A train whistle rent the silence. The high, piercing sound, the clickety-clack of speeding wheels, the strobe-like effect of racing cars playing with the sun accentuated the sense of impending doom she'd felt all night and fought all day.

Blasting wind from the roaring train flattened her cotton dress against her thighs, and in the backwash she thought she heard her name. *Lee-ee-sl-l-l.* Long and drawn out like a lover's questioning whisper in the night.

Haunting. Like her dream.

She shivered.

As she crossed over the railroad from the German side of Schönberg to the Anglo side, a weary sigh escaped her. Liesl wiped the frustrated tears collecting at the corner of her eyes. She hated the steel tracks that gave a physical division to the town. A division that had grown more obvious, more rabid over the past few years.

Holding her breath, she tread carefully past the brick-colored plank building fronting the rail yard, and sent a silent prayer that Billy Ackley would be too busy to notice her today. She had enough on her mind without having to deal with him. About to call herself home free, she felt a hand on her shoulder. She jumped and found herself face to face with Billy.

"Hey, pretty Fräulein, I've been lookin' for you."

"Can't imagine why," Liesl said, resigned to his company until she reached the airport gate.

His white teeth gleamed, but Liesl wasn't fooled by his killer smile. She knew behind the too-pretty face, the too-blue eyes, and the too-sleek body there hid a master manipulator. She knew Billy wouldn't stop hounding her until she gave in and sold him her airport.

But she wouldn't.

She couldn't.

She had to hang on to it—for Kurt, for her sanity, for her life to have meaning.

"I've been thinkin'." Billy drew her proprie-tarily closer as he spoke. "And I think I've found a way for us to solve our little problem."

"Which little problem would that be?" Liesl shrugged his hand off her shoulder and shifted her purse until it formed a barrier between them.

"You're such a card!" He tipped back his white Stetson. "The airport, of course."

"Of course. What else?"

Like a dog on a scent, Billy Ackley had a one-track mind. One set on power. He'd been such a sweet boy, Liesl remembered. What had gone wrong? It couldn't have been the war; Billy's flat feet had prevented his participation. But some-thing had happened, because as a teenager he'd renounced his German roots—to the extent of changing his name from Wilhelm Acker to Billy

Ackley. Then once the war had begun, he'd started buying out the town piece by piece. He was now mayor, and banker, not to mention the owner of the rail yard, the Ford dealership, and most of the businesses on the south side of town.

He'd desperately wanted Kurt's airport. But Kurt, filled with an idealistic dream, wouldn't sell.

Billy had sensed success with Kurt's death, only to realize that Kurt had died one day too late. As his wife, Liesl had inherited the piece of precious land. She often wondered if Billy had engineered Kurt's death.

Which gave her one more reason to hang on to her property.

"I've been thinkin'," Billy continued, "maybe we should get married."

Liesl stopped dead in her tracks and hugged the purse to her chest. "You're joking, right?"

"I've never been more serious. We look good together. Two years of mourning is long enough, don't you think? And think how good it would be for the town. Joinin' the Ackleys and the Erhardts together might be just what the town needs to bring it back together again."

As if you care. She took a deep breath. "Not to mention it would solve your little problem."

"You're a beautiful woman, Lise," Billy coaxed. "You shouldn't have to work in your father's store. You shouldn't have to dirty your hands running an airport. I can handle all those nasty little details for you, and keep you in the style you deserve."

"I've got everything I want. And don't call me Lise."

Liesl strode purposefully forward. Billy's heavy cologne nauseated her. His proximity chilled her. Tightening her sweater around her, she counted the steps to the gate and freedom. And a different kind of hell, she thought, looking apprehensively toward the hangar. One more minute and Billy would turn back. For some odd reason, he never came onto her property and never crossed the tracks to the north side of town.

"You should be pampered," Billy said. "Wear fancy dresses, be waited on hand and foot."

"And raise a litter of your children?" Liesl laughed at the horrible image forming in her mind of a dozen little Billys yapping at her heels like hungry puppies.

"That could be arranged." His grin widened a mile. "I'd be a good husband."

Half the town's females, on both sides, seemed to think so. But not her. She didn't want a husband, especially one who would never cherish her the way . . .

Kurt's smiling face swam into her consciousness. She shook her head in rapid, short strokes and scrunched her eyes closed. She didn't want to remember. It hurt too much.

Billy touched her shoulder once more. Liesl spun to face him and break the contact.

"Look, Billy," she snapped. "We've been over this before. I won't sell before the race." *I won't sell—ever!* But Billy was too dense to realize that.

Billy's foot rose to the lower rail on the gate, hiking up his freshly pressed brown pants and showing off his brand-new tan ostrich-skin boots. He leaned one elbow on his raised knee and pulled down his Stetson, shading his eyes. "And I've told you before, you won't find a pilot willing to fly for you."

A situation carefully arranged compliments of Mr. Billy Ackley, I'm sure. "Then I'll fly myself."

"You're not licensed, sugar. You won't be allowed to fly."

As Liesl pulled the rusty metal tongue on the gate latch, it hissed. "I'll find a way."

"Suit yourself." He splayed both hands up in temporary defeat, then pushed himself off the gate. "I gave you the easy way out. For the life of me, I can't see why you'd want to put yourself through this." His mouth twisted to one side and he shook his head slowly. "It's like losing twice, Lise. First Kurt, now his airport. Why put yourself through the pain?"

As Liesl pushed open the wooden gate with its peeling white paint, it creaked. No, Billy would never understand, because Billy and his desires were the only things that existed for him. He loved himself too much to ever love anyone else. He couldn't possibly appreciate her feelings.

"I'll be seein' you, Lise," Billy called after her.

He lingered for a moment at the gate, but Liesl promptly forgot him. Her mind turned to the strange feeling of simultaneous wrongness and rightness enveloping the hangar.

Already the blue sky faded to a yellow haze

on the horizon. Golden light bathed the world in a magical glow she'd come to associate with the airport. Her mind rang with the memory of the love and laughter she'd lived there. But today, the hangar didn't welcome her. It stood dark and somber, its mouth wide and gaping, waiting to swallow her. Yet, at the same time, it drew her like a willing sacrifice with soft whispers to her soul, promising solace.

Even the bluebonnets swaying in the breeze seemed to sound a soft warning, then a giggle, as if they couldn't make up their minds either. With her heart solidly lodged in her throat, Liesl continued down the hill to the small office beside the hangar, shrugged out of her dress and into Levi's and one of Kurt's shirts.

With Billy and his purchased power stacked decisively in his corner, the odds of success stood against her. What Billy wanted, Billy usually got. Liesl slipped into army boots, tugging hard on the laces.

She needed a miracle. And despite *Oma*'s faith in them, Liesl had long given up on miracles. They didn't happen. At least not for her. *You must do better, always better.* Papa was right, the only thing she could count on was hard work. If she worked hard enough, if she loved him strongly enough, Kurt's dream would come true.

She crossed over to the hangar and, holding her breath, slid open the corrugated metal door. The air felt strange today, thick, stale, unbreathable. She dropped her head against the door, touching the cool metal to her forehead. Her swallowed sob swelled painfully in her chest. "Why did you leave me?" she whispered.

"Liesl? Are you all right?"

"Max! I didn't know you were here." Liesl jumped at her cousin's unexpected presence. Pushing herself off the door, she struggled to recover her composure. "I'm fine. I was just . . ." She couldn't help it, her gaze shifted to the oak tree, dark and oppressive against the setting sun.

"I thought about it, too."

Struck by the cracking of her cousin's voice, Liesl turned back to him. Max stuck both his hands in the back pockets of his Levi's and cast his dark eyes to the ground. Liesl smiled gently. Max would remember, too. He'd idolized Kurt, copying his dress and his mannerisms, pouring out affection he'd have showered on a father had he had one. And Kurt had given the boy the attention he sought.

Max had wrangled a promise of flying lessons as his sixteenth birthday present, a promise never fulfilled because of Kurt's untimely death. Now toward a different end, Max shared her dream of a flight school, and showed up regularly to help her keep the airplanes in flying condition.

"I know." She squeezed his arm affectionately.

Max reached in the inside pocket of Kurt's war bomber jacket and retrieved a packet of cigarettes. "I've been waiting for you. So, what happened with Matson?"

He struck a match and Liesl blew it out. "I've

told you before, not in here. It's too dangerous." Liesl sighed heavily, marched into the hangar to ease her frustration, and stopped at the racer Kurt had built. She ran her hand over the airplane's silver skin. "Matson turned me down flat. He said I couldn't pay him enough to fly for me."

Max chewed the end of his unlit cigarette, then spat out stray tobacco. "Ackley?"

"Who else? He stopped me today. Asked me to marry him."

Max made a rude noise, then leaned his back on the airplane and looked at her expectantly. "So what do we do now? Matson was our last hope for a pilot."

Liesl shook her head. "I don't know, Max. If something drastic doesn't happen soon, we'll have to withdraw."

And withdrawing would kill her as surely as the lynch mob's noose had killed Kurt. Without his dream to follow, her life would have no meaning.

"Liesl, no!" Max grabbed her arms.

Though it hurt, Liesl forced herself to smile. "We've still got a week." She threw open the engine's cowling and grabbed a wrench from the rolling tool tray beside the airplane. "Come on, we've got work to do."

For Max, she'd pretend there was still hope.

They worked side by side, but Liesl's heart wasn't in it. The air was so hard to breathe tonight, and the rattler in her stomach had started shaking its tail again. Her mind drifted elsewhere, listening, waiting. And with each passing moment, dread grew.

Slowly, softly, a buzzing noise pierced her heavy mood. She knew that noise, had heard it a thousand times. Her head snapped up. Her heart stopped for an instant, then jabbered erratically. The wrench she held dropped to the cement floor with a clang.

Without thinking, Liesl bolted for the door.

From his mansion on Schönberg's highest point, Billy Ackley stared at the triangle of his fears. Two points had already fallen to his acquired influence, their power over him remanded to the shadows of the past.

Only the land on which Liesl's airport stood remained a constant boil in need of lancing. The last piece he needed to buy back what had been rightfully his. The last ghost he needed to lay to rest.

And he could buy his peace. He'd done it often enough in the past few years to know the real power of money. He sneered. How little it had taken to buy Jakob's silence, to make him disappear with the promise of a good job in California!

He swirled the hundred-year-old brandy in the crystal snifter. Night crept its dark mantle around him, but still he focused on the dim point of light emanating from the hangar far below. Sentiments for Liesl had kept the land out of his grasp for the last two years. No more. She'd been an exception to his staunch iron will, a weakness when he'd sworn to squash them all.

He'd offered her marriage, a life of luxury. She'd turned him down. Even with all he could give her. *Him*, of all people. After all he'd gone through to create the image of a successful Southern businessman.

Now, she too would taste the magnitude of his power.

He would win the airport.

The amber liquid burned smoothly down his throat.

And he intended to appropriate her, too.

Billy Ackley never lost.

Chapter Two

Colin followed Jakob's flight plan to the letter. A smooth takeoff, followed by a touch and go, then over Lake Schönberg for basic maneuvers—a steep power turn, a chandelle, a wingover, a lazy eight. He gained altitude with an Immelmann, and followed it with a series of aerobatic maneuvers the airplane was certified to perform—an aileron roll, a loop, a snap roll.

The blue sky above, the yellow-green earth below, the live power in his hands calmed his frayed nerves, and Colin found his center of balance once more. He lost himself in the maneuvers, letting instinct and skill take over his earthbound fears. Pure joy launched him into a barrel roll. He reversed a Cuban eight. He snapped a roll at the top of a loop. He danced with the sky and teased the earth.

And through it all, the CastleAir followed like a willing and pliant partner. The phrase "better than sex" came to mind, and at this instant, Colin couldn't agree more. Not since Karen had a woman made him feel this way—so free, so exhilarated—and Colin doubted that any other woman ever would. The sky was his mistress. How could a mere earthbound woman expect to compete with such powerful chemistry?

"CastleAir one, zis is Traders base."

Colin groaned at the sound of Jakob's voice. Why did Jakob have to ruin his fantasy just when he'd finally gotten over the tension of their argument?

"CastleAir one. What do you want, Jakob?"

"She did well, *nein?*"

"She did just fine. A few glitches here and there, but nothing we can't fix in time for the air show."

"*Gut, sehr gut.* Now come in, Colin. Ze sun is too low for any more today."

"Yeah, I'll be right in."

But not before he tried one more maneuver.

The one thing that killed more small-plane pilots than anything else was an inadvertent spin. No matter what Jakob thought, Colin wasn't going to offer his airplane for sale unless he tested the ease of spin recovery. His conscience wouldn't allow him.

Gaining altitude over Lake Schönberg, he cleared the area, checked his instruments, and picked a reference point. Pretending to do a steep takeoff, he moved the stick rearward. The stall warner sounded. Colin applied left rudder and moved the stick full back to get a break. The left wing dipped while the right wing rose. The nose fell, inducing the plane into a spin.

The earth beneath him spun its mosaic pieces of blue water, brown and spring-green fields and blacktop ribbons into a wash of color, blending one into the other like a moving kaleidoscope. Watching his altitude, Colin counted the turns. With plenty of air to spare, he started his recovery.

He reached forward to pull the throttle off, brushing his knuckles accidentally on a hidden black button he hadn't noticed before. When had Jakob put that in? What was it for?

Suddenly the airplane shuddered violently. Colin pulled the throttle in the off position.

No response.

He tried again, bringing the handle forward, then back.

No change.

With cool calm, he abandoned the throttle and moved to the rest of the checklist. A power-on spin was recoverable.

Neutralize ailerons. Flaps up. Full opposite rudder. Hold. Stick forward.

Nothing budged.

All the instruments and mechanical parts were frozen into a dangerous position. The airplane's nose pointed straight into the lake. The rate of spin rotation increased rapidly. The airspeed built alarmingly. And he was losing altitude much too fast.

"*Nein*, Colin, *nein!*" Jakob's panicked voice crackled over the radio. "You fool! I told you not to touch anyzing. You are ruining my plans!"

Heat built inside the airplane. Sweat slicked his forehead, back and hands, making his grip on the stick precarious. He felt stretched like Silly Putty. His arms grew longer. The instrument panel shrank further away. And the earth narrowed to a fine dot on the windshield.

"You only have one veek to find ze vindow again." Jakob's voice sounded slow like a tape machine with low batteries. "Do you hear me, Colin? Once opened, ze vindow pinches off in one veek. You must fix my mistake and come back. Find Liesl. Save Kurt. Colin . . ." Jakob's voice splintered and fell around him in a glass-like tinkle. He could no longer make out the words from the disjointed pings chiming over the radio.

Colin fought the airplane. He fought the laws of physics. He fought the certain doom. Still he stretched until he was sure he would break apart. Unbearable heat burned him, dried him, cracked him. An eerie whistling whined in his ears. White light rushed around him.

When he thought he would hit the ground, he popped like a cork from a champagne bottle and shot into clear space. His dimensions, the plane's, and the earth's bounced back to normal. Somehow he'd gained 5,000 feet.

Realizing he still spun, Colin once more went through his recovery checklist. Thick, syrupy moves took all his concentration, but this time the airplane responded. The nose moved up to a flatter attitude. The prop stopped spinning. When the airplane ceased rotating, he neutralized the rudder and pulled out of the dive. After reaching level flight, he started the engine, trimmed the airplane into position, and blew out a long, weary breath.

That had been too close. He'd almost taken the short way to China with his death spiral, and he knew every nut and bolt of this airplane. Imagine what dire ending a beginner would have found! Jakob had been wrong. Testing the airplane had been the right thing to do. Now, they could rectify the problem before the show.

"Tra—" Colin's voice cracked. He lubricated his throat with a painful gulp before he tried again. "Traders base, this is CastleAir one."

No answer.

"Traders base, this is CastleAir one, come in."

Nothing. He waited. One minute. Two. Three.

The drone of the engine grew louder. He could hear the gas feeding the pistons, the spark plugs ignite, the air slipping over the wings. Despite the sweat pouring from his brow, a constant shiver trembled through him as he listened to the eerie clicks of the unresponsive radio.

Something was dreadfully wrong. Something more than a dead radio. But what? His skin crawled with the feeling of a thousand gnawing ants. His stomach lurched wildly. Why? Maneuvers had never bothered him before.

But this one had been near lethal.

He shook his head and forced his cramped fingers to punch in another radio frequency in the area. Nothing. He tried several more. Nothing. The tight spin must have damaged the radio. He headed toward Traders Field for a no-radio approach.

He looked for his usual reference points. Where was the onion-shaped white water tower? Highway 20? The mega truck stop, signaling the eleven mile out marker? His heart thumped hard in his chest.

Where was the airport?!

Colin circled trying to get his bearings. Eagle Mountain Lake lay northeast of his position, the train tracks ran below him, Lake Schönberg stood to the west; they were all where they should be. But where was Benbrook Lake? How did a whole lake disappear? And why couldn't he find his home base?

His muscles ached from their strained effort to get out of the spin. His dry eyes burned holes into his skull. Even his hair hurt. He was tired of working so hard with nothing to show for it, tired of the constant worry, tired of waiting. He wanted to go home, take a shower, and sleep until the show.

His single engine sputtered once, then caught again, bringing Colin's attention back to the cockpit. Glancing at his instruments, he noticed the near-empty gas gauge.

The sun, low on the horizon, splashed the sky with shades of orange. Already the moon shone dim in the darkening canopy and stars hinted at their presence. The greening fields below shifted with threatening black shadows, wooing him with their promise of soft landings, hiding their treacherous rocky ruts.

He circled once more and spotted white letters spelling Schönberg on a metal hangar roof near the railroad. Schönberg it would have to be until he could gas up again and find his way home. Flying over the field above pattern altitude, Colin checked for traffic and sought out the wind sock.

Grass? When had Schönberg reverted to grass? He entered the pattern, flared a few feet above the runway, and landed softly, careful to keep a straight track down the mowed grass path. A shadow jumped in front of him. By sheer instinct he reacted and applied the brakes, only to realize too late he'd done the wrong thing. The CastleAir didn't sport tricycle gear.

The unbalanced, tail-wheeled airplane hopped off the grass track, tail pointing skyward at an odd angle. The prop shot sparks as it bit chunks out of the ground. With a series of high-pitched groans and deep shudders, the airplane came to rest with its nose embedded in the ground.

Then silence, deep, thick, heavy. It pressed on him, squeezing him, suffocating him. He tried to move, but couldn't. So he laughed. Who would have thought it would end this way? Certainly not him. The sky had been his friend.

But then, it was the earth who'd tricked him, wasn't it?

A rapping against the side of the plane caught his attention.

"Are you all right in there?" asked a faraway, ethereal voice.

Colin cranked his stiff neck in the voice's direction and forced his eyes open. The hazy face of an angel peered at him through the dirt-splattered windshield. Jakob's drawing. In full color. Big blue eyes on fresh rosy skin, bright red lips parted to allow rapid breaths, golden hair gleaming like a beacon in the falling night, a smudge of grease on a high cheekbone. Soft hair, soft skin, soft lips. He knew they would be. He knew exactly how they would feel. He knew exactly how they would taste.

No, it couldn't be true. He must have hit his head in the crash. Slowly, stiffly, he rubbed his eyes with both leadened fists. The image refused to vanish.

You only have one veek to find ze vindow again, Jakob's voice echoed unnaturally in his mind. *Do you hear me, Colin? Once opened, ze vindow pinches off in one veek.*

Could Jakob have been serious and actually found a way to travel back in time? Colin glanced once more at the blond woman with her outdated hairdo and man's shirt. Hauntingly familiar, she reminded him of Ingrid Bergman in *Casablanca*—a colorized version. That's it, he thought, a memory of an old film; not time travel. He shook his head to dispel the shape of sheer folly his thoughts formed. Could he actually smell gardenias over the spilled life-blood of his broken metal bird?

He must be as crazy as Jakob.

A slim hand with long fingers wiped the dirty film from the window. He perceived everything in slow motion. The shadow spreading across her face, the widening of her eyes, the blanching of her skin. He'd seen them all before. Her gasp breached the plexiglass to reach his ears— an intimate, frightened gasp. One he'd heard under different circumstances. One that lingered deliciously on his mind. One that had ended much differently.

Colin tried to chuckle, grasping to the one thing that made sense. She was afraid of him. *If you think I'm scary now, honey, wait till you see me cleaned up.* Jakob had told him more than once that failure had stamped his face with a cynical look that tended to frighten people away. But Colin had learned to play the social game; he'd learned to smile and deceived many with its charm. Would it work on an angel from a distant time?

Distant time! Right! He'd bet he had one doozy of a goose egg on his head. He squirmed in his seat and found himself trapped in place.

"I'm stuck," he said to the frozen woman. He hoped his grin didn't look half as stupid as it felt.

One hand moved to her throat. A long, elegant throat. It curved white and soft into the gaping, rough material of a man's shirt.

"Help me," he said.

She didn't move. She stared at him as if he couldn't exist, as if she viewed a hallucination.

He averted his gaze to his lap and tried to undo the safety harness. His arms moved mechanically. He was weary, so weary. His fingers slipped on the buckle. Funny, he didn't remember the metal being so slick. He tried again, but his wooden fingers could only slide in the widening dark patch in his lap. His eyes drooped shut. He dragged them open. They closed once more. The heavy cloak of darkness settled on his shoulders, taking him deeper and deeper.

"Toto, I've a feeling we're not in Kansas anymore," he mumbled before darkness engulfed him completely.

Liesl stared uncomprehendingly at the stranger in the too-familiar airplane. It didn't make sense. The Castell was in the hangar, and Kurt was dead. What was going on? She ripped a nail trying to open the sliding canopy to reach the pilot.

A sense of unreality, of foolish expectations had hurried her steps to the broken metal bird. Her heart hammering, her breath erratic, she'd wiped the dirt from the airplane windshield to find her fondest dream and her worst nightmare realized.

Thick, unruly strands of brown hair danced on a gashed forehead with the same static that had stung her hands when she'd touched the airplane. But beneath the bloody river running down his face, she made out familiar features. When he looked at her she gasped. She couldn't help it. More green than brown, those were Kurt's eyes, and they pleaded for help once more—like on that dreadful morning two years ago.

She froze solid from the fear spreading madly through her brain, from the folly of her thoughts. For an instant, she connected with the strange man, in another time, another place. She felt his pull calling to her, drawing her, possessing her. She tried to yank back, to rip the invisible thread, to run away from the strange flutterings inside her, but something unexplainable, something stronger than her will, kept her rooted to the spot, looking at herself reflected through the dirty glass in too-familiar eyes.

"Liesl, what's wrong?"

Max's voice broke the spell.

It wasn't Kurt. It couldn't be Kurt. But she wanted him to be Kurt, and hated him for making her heart bleed with need. She hated him for what he'd do to her. And she wanted to yell at him, and pummel him, and hurt him before he could hurt her.

"I . . ." Liesl took a deep breath to steady her humming nerves. "The pilot's hurt. Help me get him out of here."

Max carefully climbed beside her onto the near-vertical wing, slid the canopy back, and locked it into place. He then reached down to help the pilot. "Holy Moly, Liesl, come look at this!"

With apprehension, she scooted up the wing and craned her neck to look where Max pointed. She didn't want to discuss the stranger's uncanny looks with Max. But it wasn't the stranger's face that had caught Max's attention, it was the odd instruments on the panel.

"What are those?" Max asked, his curiosity unguarded.

"I have no idea. We can look at them later. Right now, we need to get him out of here and see if he needs a doctor."

"Right."

None too gently, they managed to extricate the unconscious pilot from the cockpit and shift him to the ground.

Pressing her lips into a tight line, Liesl assessed the damage. When she reached to touch him, an audible spark zapped her hand. She snapped it back, then tried again. When she neared his body, her fingers tingled as if she reached through a prickly layer of raw cotton. As she measured the extent of his wounds, each slide of her hands fired her skin. When she removed them from his proximity, her palms throbbed with heated pain.

"Is he all right?" Max asked, watching her every move.

"I don't know. He's burning up with fever." Liesl hated the suggestion she was about to make. *No, no*, her heart pleaded. *That room is his, ours. It still smells of him. If you take the stranger there, you'll wipe out what's left of him. But*, her practical side argued, *you can't take this man to town. His face will start a riot. It's the only sensible thing to do.* "Let's move him to Kurt's room. Then you run and fetch your mother."

"Right."

As she paced the room like a wary animal, Liesl's eyes never left the stranger. No good would come of his presence. If anything, it would reopen old wounds. Wounds that had barely healed—for the town, and especially for her.

She didn't want to deal with the emotions he unleashed. Hatred, fear, all-consuming love. Dark emotions, deep emotions, emotions she'd worked so hard to quash.

Liesl tucked a wind-blown strand of hair behind her ear. After praying to die each night for a year, she'd thought she'd finally come to terms with Kurt's death, finally found a way to deal with the madness. She'd spent the last year trying to fulfill the promise she'd made to Kurt the day he'd died.

Now, this stranger, fallen from the sky, had turned her structured life into a living nightmare.

Stopping by the bed, Liesl stared into the oddly familiar face. With detachment, she noted the straight, full eyebrows, the thick lashes framing eyes set wide apart, the long, straight nose, the wide cheeks descending to a broad chin. Liesl smiled. A stubborn straight chin when he worked, but it rounded so appealingly when he smiled.

What are you doing? This isn't Kurt. To prove her point, she mentally zeroed in on the downward curve of his lips. *See, Kurt's mouth was generous and full and curved up optimistically. The stranger's lips are thin and twisted with cynicism.*

She turned away abruptly, angry at the turn of her thoughts. *Make yourself useful!* She strode out into the hangar and came back with a bucket, which she filled from the sink in the small bathroom. She jerked a white towel off the shelf and immersed it in the cold water.

Seating herself on the small wooden stool by the bed, she steeled herself. As she washed the caking blood off his face, uncomfortable tingles needled her hand. She anesthetized the pain by concentrating diligently on her task.

Fifteen interminable minutes later, Max returned with his mother in tow. Half Apache, half German, Wenona Freundlich acted as the north side's unofficial doctor. Her healing skills were recognized by many, and her confidentiality was admired by all. Liesl knew Wenona could be trusted not to divulge what she saw.

While Wenona cared for the stranger, Liesl and Max righted the downed airplane and rolled it into the hangar. Attracting attention was the last thing Liesl wanted to do.

Wenona stitched the gash on the stranger's forehead and prescribed a catnip decoction for the fever. "His body needs rest. Let him sleep. When the fever comes, give him cold tea. When the chills come, give him hot tea."

"What's wrong with him?" The fever's unnatural strength worried Liesl.

"Nothing time won't fix."

With her evasive answer, Wenona rose to leave. She paused by Liesl. "He has come a long way for you, child."

"What do you mean?" Liesl stammered, taken aback. Had *Tante* Wenona read the thoughts Liesl herself dismissed as nonsense?

But Wenona refused to clarify, leaving Liesl to wonder what her aunt had meant.

"I'll come back tomorrow." Max ran backwards to catch up with his mother. "Will you be all right?"

"I'll be fine." *If I don't go crazy first.*

It was a great relief to get away from the claustrophobic air in the hangar to go make tea on the hot plate in the office. By the time she returned, her mind whirled so fast she couldn't catch any of the individual thoughts. She counted the fact as a blessing.

All night, she dribbled the healing tea through his parched lips with a spoon. Every accidental touch was torture, every breath agony. When would the pain end?

Stoically she watched him twist and turn, soaking the sheets with his fevered sweat, and cooled his forehead with a cold cloth. She watched him shiver violently, and piled on blankets to warm him. She watched him, and willed his features to change.

Somewhere deep into the night, she heard him call her name in delirious appeal. The urgent whisper disturbed a savage need. A need so fierce it clamored against its dark, dank restraining cage, growling, shaking her to the marrow. Scrambling off the stool, she gasped. For one long, frightening moment, she was lost in time again, disoriented. His feverish whisper rolled through her mind like morning mist, light, moist, enveloping.

Holding the three-legged stool as a lion tamer might to protect himself from a beast, Liesl backed out of the room. One of his arms fell over the side of the bed, the fingers extending to reach for her. A stream of perspiration ran down his forehead onto his cheek and plopped to his neck where it hung for a moment before being launched to the pillow with the beat of his pulsing artery. His head turned. He mumbled. She dropped the stool, whirled out into the hangar, and ran, frightened by the raw, basic urge that rocked her, by the force of her anger toward him.

The stranger would be her undoing. He would complicate her life endlessly. He would plunge her once more in the roiling black river of grief she'd barely managed to escape.

Helpless doom had her seeking solace on the wing of Kurt's airplane. Perched there on the cold aluminum, she cried until dawn—for what she'd lost, for what she'd never have again, for what the stranger would make her regret. Razor-sharp loneliness engulfed her, cutting her soul to shreds, making her feel her loss as deeply as she had on that cold, rainy morning two years ago.

And when the tears were spent, she felt a psychic nudge. A nugget of an idea took root and sprouted even as every fiber of her body screamed in protest. An impossible idea, alluring, yet so reasonable. A soft seduction of the mind that appealed to her sensible nature, and wreaked havoc on her abraded heart.

She jumped off the wing to escape her thoughts and rushed out into the morning, welcoming the fresh air with great big gulps.

Could she deal with the preposterous plan her practical side had bloomed?

* * *

Colin felt her beside him, her eyes trained on him, watching him in the dark of the night. Jakob's angel. The one from the drawing. The missing part of himself he'd searched for all of his life. Her slow, even breaths comforted him. He wasn't dead—not yet.

He felt the bed beneath him, too, soft and lumpy. He felt the sweat hot and sticky on his body. He wanted to get up and take a shower. But he couldn't. His leadened limbs wouldn't obey his commands.

Then the laughter came, all sunshine and sparkle. Colin turned his head toward it. A picture formed in the gray fog of his mind. Jakob's angel lay beside him, in his bed, smiling seductively at him.

"Liesl."

He knew he was dreaming. But everything seemed so real, he reached for her.

"I love you, Liesl," he heard himself say in a voice he didn't recognize.

As he drew her against his naked body, Liesl's eyes widened. When he pressed his desire against her, her cheeks blanched. When his thumb brushed her bared nipple, she gasped and shuddered.

"I'll always love you." He drowned himself in the bliss of her kiss.

He was hot, so hot. He wanted her as he'd never wanted anybody. He needed her life after all the death he'd witnessed. He needed *her*. And she came to him willingly, unsure at first, then with a fevered frenzy matching his own. Their impassioned bodies rolled and tangled with the sheets in delirious pleasure. Her soft whispers filled his ears. Her fingers branded his skin. The scent of gardenias dizzied his mind, and one taste of her sweetness addicted him forever.

Their bodies merged one into the other until they became one. He was with her, in her, part of her. Their heartbeats, their breaths, their very blood flowed in perfect unison, drumming together stronger, louder as the pleasure of their bodies bonding grew to an unbearable pitch. Colin thought he would die from the ecstasy, then his body shook from a release as joyful as the climb.

He'd found heaven and never wanted to leave.

She rested in his arms. Her ear against his heart; her hand on his breathless chest. He kissed her hair and hugged her nearer. "Forever, Liesl."

Her blue eyes turned up to his and her smile beamed for him. "Yes, Kurt, forever."

Then the fog receded, obliterating the picture, closing around him, tighter and tighter.

Choking for breath, Colin fell out of bed. He awoke with a start when his head bumped the concrete floor. Both his hands were wrapped around his throat, and the name *Liesl* thundered painfully in and out of the tissues of his brain. He dragged himself up and opened his eyes onto a world he didn't recognize. Where was he? How had he gotten here?

Schönberg. That's right. He'd had a rough landing. He needed to find his plane and see what damage he'd caused with his error in judgment.

His head pounding, he shuffled to the hangar and spotted his mangled airplane. As he crouched beside the twisted propeller, his father's voice boomed into his mind. "Guess I'll have to bail you out of this one, too. How much did you lose this time? Why don't you just quit and come work for me?"

Colin banged a fist against the metal cowling. "No! I've still got a week to prove I'm not a failure."

Saturday

The stranger was awake.

Why she knew, Liesl couldn't say, but she knew. She couldn't hear any noise except the wind rippling against the metal building. She couldn't see anything out of the windowless office. But she felt him in her mind. Every move, every breath. The way his presence encroached on her space, he could have been standing next to her, instead of at the opposite end of a different building crouched over a crumpled propeller.

As she buttoned the fresh shirt and tucked the tails into her pants, her fingers shook. As she swallowed and rolled the too-long sleeves, her throat felt desert dry. When she ordered her legs to move forward, her knees knocked.

She couldn't stall any longer.

She had to know.

She had to end her living nightmare.

Liesl found him exactly as she'd seen him in her mind, crouched beside the bent propeller.

The dim light slashed him with stark shadows. Deft fingers probed here and there, seeking answers to questions she couldn't fathom. The white bandage stood out against the tanned skin of his serious face. Dried blood still matted a strand of chocolate brown hair. The sweat-stained white T-shirt defined shoulders used to manual work. The khaki material of his pants strained over his thighs, crimped at the knees, then flowed down long calves into scuffed, odd-looking brown leather boots.

Liesl pressed her lips tight together to keep from calling out Kurt's name. She sank her hands deep into her pockets to keep herself from reaching for him. She concentrated on the sure, mechanical placement of her feet to keep from running into his arms.

She knew every hard plane of that body, knew just how to stroke the ticklish spot on his hip to send him into a fit of bright laughter, knew the feel of his sleeping breath on her hair, the sound of his heart beneath her ear, remembered the taste of wild honey on his tongue, the feel of his skin sliding against hers. And if she closed her eyes, she could even smell the faint trace of the tobacco he liked to smoke. She knew all of him as if he were an extension of her.

Any second she expected him to turn and smile at her, and say, "Liesl, *Liebling*, come help me with this engine." As if the last two years had been a bad dream from which she'd finally woken. She'd go to him, snuggle close, safe in his arms. "You wouldn't believe the nightmare I had," she'd say, and he'd kiss her and laugh at her for being so silly. They would laugh together. The sound of his loving laughter, the sweet taste of his lips, the feel of his speeding heart against her breast would chase the dark ghosts away, and the pain would melt and vanish.

Where had the air gone? Why couldn't she breathe? Holding back tears, she clung stubbornly to her slipping sanity.

He turned and looked up at her from his crouched position. Their gazes met. For the flicker of a moment, Liesl thought she saw recognition in his gaze and a longing as deep as her own. It faded to confusion, and settled on a distant blankness before going back once more to the mangled metal.

"I don't suppose you've got an extra set of propeller blades lying around," he said.

"No," Liesl said, too shocked by his voice to say anything else. It wasn't Kurt's. It sounded too rough, too gritty to be Kurt's. She'd known all along it wasn't him. Then why did a deep sense of loss stab at her heart?

"I didn't think so."

"Who are you? What kind of airplane is this?" Liesl held her breath, and clenched her teeth for strength. She dreaded his answer. The inside of his plane with the instruments she didn't recognize, the odd cut of his clothes, the bizarre contraption on his wrist frightened her. She knew what he'd say, and she didn't want to hear. Like all those times Papa had yelled at her while she grew up, she wanted to cover her ears and scrunch her eyes closed. Instead, she crushed the material of the opposite sleeve in her hands until her short nails bit through to her palms. She focused on the dirt-streaked bent metal because she couldn't bear to look at him anymore. It hurt too much. "Please, tell me."

"It's a 1948 CastleAir Special Edition replica," he said proudly. "And I'm the King of the Castle." His mocking chuckle tripped inside her like the ground trembling before an explosion.

She couldn't help it, she had to look at the source of the detonation. He unfolded his long legs and banged his head on a jutting piece of fuselage. He rubbed his bruised flesh with one hand, sending static sparks into the charged air. "Ouch! At least I was until *this* happened."

Liesl caught the uncertainty of his last statement, as if he didn't quite know what "this" entailed. He turned his back to her, and his attention to the plane. But even as she catalogued the details of him, one piece of information stood out.

"Nineteen forty-eight?" Liesl's voice croaked out of her dry throat. She stepped back.

He stiffened. His big hands, moving along the plane's skin, slowed, then stopped. "Yes, 1948."

The air took on the consistency of gelatin. "That's impossible." She gulped through the thickness like a drowning swimmer, taking another shaky step back.

"Why?" His fingertips turned white against the green paint. His head dropped forward onto the aluminum skin.

"Because it's 1946." She crossed her arms protectively over her chest and tried to calm her shaking limbs. Battle fatigue. He had to be battle fatigued. Hadn't it happened to two of her cousins? They lost touch with reality at times. Noises made them act strange. Taking one more step back, she bumped into the hangar wall. She leaned her stiff spine against the metal, drawing strength from its tensile reality.

"Then you must be Liesl." His arms fell by his side like cast anchors. He turned and leaned in the crook formed by the wing and the fuselage. His face lay half in the dark, cutting a rigid mask impossible to read. "I'm supposed to find Kurt."

She hissed in a sharp breath. Her hand flew to her throat, and she swallowed hard. Her back slid along the wall and her tailbone smacked against the cement floor.

He reached for her, but Liesl scrambled away, the thunder of her heart booming hard against her ears. "*Who* are you? What do you want?"

His hands retreated to his sides, but he didn't move from his crouched position beside her. "I'm Colin Castle. A friend of yours, Jakob Renke—"

"Jakob? How do you know Jakob? Jakob is no friend."

With the mere mention of that name, the stranger managed to rip her heart's wound deeper. The pain flowed like warm blood, resurrecting the deepest sorrow she'd ever known. Jakob the coward hadn't lifted a finger to help his best friend. He'd slithered away like the snake he was before she could confront him.

Some said he'd gone to Florida, others insisted he'd gone to Kansas, still others argued he'd gone to California. All anyone could agree on was that he'd been hired by an aviation company as a metal worker. Not that it mattered. It didn't change any of the facts.

Kurt was dead.

And so was she.

Dead. Empty. Soulless. A body with a heart which stubbornly refused to stop beating.

A branch from the oak tree scratched the side of the building.

"He wanted me to warn Kurt—"

She fixed the stranger's shadowed eyes with lethal ferocity. How had she ever thought this was Kurt? How had she ever thought he could help her? If Jakob had sent him, it was only to make her die again. He wasn't a secret blessing sent from heaven as she'd thought for a brief, mad moment at dawn; he was an overt curse sent directly from hell.

"Kurt is dead." She scrambled further away from Jakob's monster. "He's been buried for two years." She rolled sideways and sprang to her feet. "Tell Jakob to go to hell. That's where he belongs." She spun to run, tripped the toe of one boot against the heel of the other, and fell straight into her nightmare's arms.

Chapter Three

Liesl stared at him, her big blue eyes filled with fear, as if he, Colin, were the devil himself. Two fat tears glistened on her cheeks. And seeking to regain her balance, she dug her fingers into his arms.

The calculations, zey are not quite right. The words reverberated in Colin's mind. Whatever Jakob had done to the airplane to make it travel back in time had landed him two years too late.

Now he was stuck out of his time with a broken bird. He wished he'd listened more closely when Jakob had spouted his theories on the bends, the twists, the curves of time.

How on earth would he find Jakob's window? How would he get back home in time for the air show? How was he going to prove to his father he could succeed?

"Let me go. You aren't real," Liesl cried, shaking her head.

She yanked her hands away, but he caught her wrists and hung on to her with a desperation he didn't understand. *I am real*, he wanted to shout, denying her claim. Without thinking he placed her palm against his heart, felt his lifeblood's rhythm pound against her stiffened fingers, felt the rapid pulse of her wrist against his thumb. Her skin branded him with heat and filled him with a soul-deep longing. Illogically, he wanted her with the ravenous hunger of a starved man, and he saw his need reflected in Liesl's widening eyes, saw how it terrified her. As if his life depended on it, he snagged her close and held her tight.

"I'm real, Liesl." The words spilled out of his mouth from somewhere outside of him. The intensity of his feelings frightened him. He never felt. Never allowed himself to. Not since Karen. "And I'm as lost as you are."

He released her abruptly, taken aback by his behavior, by his words, by the mad scrabbling of thoughts not quite his own. He backed away from her, from her intoxicating effect. Touching the plane's cool metal under his hands, he reassured himself that he was still solid flesh, still grounded to the earth, not lost in some misty make-believe dream. He looked at Liesl with veiled curiosity, struggling to make sense of the absurdity of his situation, of her power over his well-guarded emotions.

Through the open doors of the hangar, the rising sun bled flat rays of pink light onto the cement, encasing Liesl in a surreal aura. She stood frozen, stunned—like him.

Time travel. It didn't make sense. But he couldn't deny the facts. Liesl's hairstyle, the plane so like his own sharing the hangar with two Cub-yellow J-3's, even the smell of the air had been pointed clues. As if to accent his thoughts, several cars from a different era trundled past on the road up the hill. Cars he'd seen in museums and in the black-and-white movies Karen had been so fond of watching. He'd jokingly called her a woman out of time. They'd laughed.

Now, he found nothing funny about his flippant comment.

How could he expect Liesl to believe in time travel when he wasn't sure if it was real, or if he was merely in the midst of a superbly vivid dream?

He wouldn't even try. With a fist he worried the bandage on his forehead and reassured himself by the bruising ache. He'd fix his airplane and find Jakob's window. He could only hope the travel back through the window would put him back at the time he left. The other possibilities were simply too frightening. There was nothing he could do for Kurt, for Liesl, or for Jakob, and he had to get back home to straighten out his own messed-up life.

"Do you know where I can get new propellers?" Colin asked, slowly regaining mastery of his mind. Wariness replaced the stunned expression in her ocean-blue eyes.

"No."

Her voice was slow, soft, sweet, and replete with guarded caution like a rabbit with a bobcat blocking its warren. If she only knew the bobcat suffered an unnatural urge to protect, not to devour. An urge that grated against his survival instincts.

"Where'd you get yours?" With his chin he pointed to the silver plane so like his own in the corner. But she didn't seem to hear his question.

"Did Jakob build the plane? What did you call it?"

The quivering shirt collar gave the only indication that she wasn't in perfect control. Soft steel, he thought as he watched her study him with intensity.

"A CastleAir Special Edition. We built it together."

Her nostrils flared for a breath, showing another fissure in her cracking control. "Killing Kurt wasn't enough, he had to steal his plans, too." She spoke calmly, but her hands bunching into white-knuckled fists gave away her anger. "Why don't you call *him* and he'll bring you the parts you need?"

"Can't."

"Why not?" With an irritation-tensed flick of her wrist, Liesl tucked an errant strand of hair behind her left ear.

As much as he hated to complicate his life, Colin had no choice. He had no idea who to call in 1946 for spare parts, and with Jakob's window threatening to pinch him out of his time, he didn't have the luxury of wasting days looking for the parts himself. He'd have to win Liesl's trust, if only for a little while. "Because no one can make a phone call to a time fifty years into the future."

Her face flushed red and her lips thinned into a straight line. "Why do you lie? Why would Jakob want to hurt me this way?" She whirled away and strode toward the hangar door.

"No," Colin said, running after her. Catching her arm, he spun her back to him. "Jakob doesn't want to hurt you. He wanted to help you. He wanted to come back so he could stop Kurt from dying."

"You lie!" Her chest heaved with her restrained sorrow.

"No, look." Still holding her by one arm, Colin reached into his pants pocket. Damn, why was it so important she understand? He didn't care. He couldn't afford to. He smoothed out Jakob's drawing on his thigh and handed it to her. "It's you."

She gasped at the picture. It wavered in her hand. "Where did you get this?"

"Jakob drew it. He cares for you. See how it shows in the picture." He traced a finger over the penciled lips on the paper, around the eyes, over the cheeks. His finger slid down the nose drawn straight and smooth. He lifted his finger to Liesl's face and touched the bumpy ridge Jakob had missed. Her nose was skewed off center like Karen's. Karen had earned her broken nose in a fall trying out a new cheerleading stunt. Absently he wondered how this woman had gotten hers.

"Except for the nose, it's just like you," he said, his voice thick and gruff.

Her mouth parted in a silent sigh; she closed her eyes. He licked his dry lips, remembering the taste of something he'd never had, something he wanted very much. His head started down as his thumb moved to cup her jaw. With barely more than a whisper of skin on skin, she flinched and turned away, leaving him starving for more.

"Jakob is a fool." She mashed the paper into a ball and launched it across the room.

"Jakob is an old man—"

"He's twenty-six, no, twenty-eight by now," Liesl said, shaking her head and scrunching her eyes closed.

"He's seventy-eight, alone, tired, and obsessed with finding you and fixing some sort of mistake."

"No!" She covered her ears and hunched forward. Her hair fell like a golden curtain, obliterating his view of her face.

Dragging his wallet from his back pocket, he walked forward a few paces. He extricated his driver's license from its plastic window and extended it to her. He touched her arm with it, and felt a zing of energy stab his hand. Ignoring the confusion in his brain, he pushed the card between her resisting fingers. "Look. Look at the picture. Look at the date."

He had to give her points for spine, Colin decided. Apart from the small lurch when he could have sworn her heart stopped for a beat, she kept her cool. She touched his colored DMV mug shot with the tip of her index finger, and retracted it immediately. Singed by undeniable facts, or by the same strange energy he felt swirling in the hangar's stale air?

The red of her lipstick, a bright slash against her too-pale skin, moved, then stopped. A frown wrinkled her forehead. As she handed him back his license, her hand shook.

"How?" she pleaded on a deep exhalation. "How is this possible?" Her eyes desperately searched his face for a sensible explanation.

He had none.

He reached for the license, and they stood for an endless moment, joined by the three inches of plastic, and separated by a gulf as wide as time.

"Can anyone join this party or is it private?" a young voice boomed from the hangar door.

Startled, they both jumped. Liesl let go of the plastic and turned to face the gangly young man. Her face softened and her shoulders slumped in relief. "Max!"

The young man sauntered into the hangar. He was dressed in a checked shirt—tails untucked—and rolled-up Levi's, with a brown leather bomber jacket flung over his shoulder. A cigarette dangled from his lips. His jet hair was cropped short on the sides and a bang hung long in the front, covering part of a dark eye. His smile lit his whole face. He draped an arm casually around Liesl's shoulders and gave her a friendly hug.

"I came to see how our patient's doing. Up and about, I see. How's the head?" Max asked, looking Colin up and down.

Reflexively Colin reached toward the bandage. "Could be worse."

"Yeah, looks like you'll live." Max flicked his half-smoked cigarette onto the hangar floor. Grounding it out with a foot, he looked expectantly at Liesl. "Have you asked him yet?"

He watched Liesl, eyes wide and breath held, look from one man to the other. Why would the prospect of asking him a question make her look as if she were trading her soul to the devil?

"Asked him what?" Liesl said to gain time. She didn't want to hear Max voice her thoughts.

"Well, isn't it obvious, cuz? He's a pilot. We need a pilot. It's perfect."

It didn't surprise her that Max had reached the same conclusion she had somewhere between dawn and day. They shared the same dream. And to reach step one, all they lacked was a pilot—a logical fact in this murky nightmare.

Colin Castle with his patched head and broken bird was the answer to their prayers. Her practical side understood this.

But his looks, his tug on her suppressed memories, were a bane to her soul. His mere presence made her feel too vulnerable, and the raw wound on her heart recognized the damage he could wreak.

How could God be so cruel? He'd sent her an angel, but why dress him with the face of the man she'd loved? He has His reasons, *Oma* would say. But Liesl found no comfort in her grandmother's accepting faith. Only the devil would choose this disguise.

But she had no choice. No matter how bewildered he made her feel, she had to face the hard facts. He was a pilot. She needed a pilot. She'd find a way to deal with the nagging uneasiness his presence had on her.

For her future, she had to.

"Ask me what?" Colin said, leveling his gaze on her. The green-brown of his eyes delved deep, reaching her soul with arrow-straight accuracy. She lowered her lashes against the intimate invasion.

Something wasn't right. He shouldn't be able to reach her. He shouldn't be able to move her. He shouldn't be able to make her feel so much. Not this easily.

"To fly the Castell in the Trinity Air Competition next Saturday," Max said, beaming a smile as if he'd just bestowed upon the stranger the greatest honor.

Colin's gaze never left her, and Liesl couldn't escape the burr-like feeling that his coming here was no coincidence. There was too much at stake, and she didn't believe in miracles. Who would gain except Billy?

"Castell?" One of Colin's thick eyebrows curved up, and his arms rose to cross over his chest.

"Yeah," Max said with the vibrancy of a puppy. He pointed to the silver airplane in the corner. "It's one of a kind. And it's going to win. I just know it."

The way Colin looked at the airplane disturbed her. His eyes, clouded by the shortening shadows, were unreadable, but the straining of his T-shirt along his shoulders and the slight backward sway of his body filled her with a sense of wrongness.

The oak branch scratched against the building in a tense, irregular rhythm, accentuating Liesl's mounting irritation, flaring it into anger.

She could handle anger. Anger was much better than all those buried feelings Colin Castle unearthed. And with the anger came the dawning of understanding.

Billy wanted her airport. Billy would stop at nothing to get it. Billy knew she wouldn't stop looking for a pilot, and he had one week to stop her. Had Billy sent her this devil in disguise?

Like a puppy begging for a treat, Max cocked his head at Colin. "Say you'll do it."

Colin looked at her, then at the plane. His jaw twitched. He was hiding something. But what?

Liesl stared at him with new eyes. Was his uncanny resemblance to Kurt supposed to unnerve her until it was too late? Would he play along until race day, then disappear? Would he fly and lose on purpose? Billy had always discounted her ability to think.

She'd show him; she'd beat him at his own game.

"I can't," Colin said. His body stiffened as if he steeled himself for a blow.

Refusal? Liesl hid her surprise. She'd expected easy acceptance. What sort of game was he playing?

"Why not?" Max asked.

"Stay out of it, Max," Liesl said, studying the

Broken Wings

whirling kaleidoscope of Colin's eyes, watching him watch her with the same daunting intensity. He ruffled her insides to no end, but she shielded her soul from his too-knowing glare. For now, she was safe. "He doesn't want to do it."

"So you're going to let him walk out of here?" Max pivoted to her with a disgusted look on his face. His arms flew wildly as he spoke. "What's wrong with you? You wanted a miracle. Now you got one, and you're just going to let him go!"

"It's none of your business, Max." She didn't need the extra pressure of Max's outburst in the already thick atmosphere. What she needed was time. Time to think, time to weigh her options, time to make a logical decision.

And she wasn't going to get any.

"Hey, bud, it's not her fault," Colin said, disconnecting their live-wire link and turning to Max. "I've got to fly elsewhere or lose five years' worth of work."

Max glanced over at the CastleAir and shook his head. "Well, it doesn't look like you'll get very far with it, so why not help us? Maybe we can help you in return. Liesl's not a bad mechanic, and I'm pretty good at banging metal into shape."

"He's right, you know," Liesl said. Why was he here? What did he want? "That airplane won't be going anywhere for a while."

"I can't." Colin's jaw tightened, highlighting the taut ligaments beneath the tanned skin.

"But—" Max started.

"Stay out of it, Max."

69

Max glanced from her to Colin. His mouth pressed into a thin line and his eyes grew cold. "*Mutti* sent some breakfast for him. I'll go get it."

"Good idea," Liesl said.

She waited for Max's retreating footsteps to fade, then she looked Colin straight in the eyes, challenging him. "What are you afraid of? The accident? Billy Ackley?"

"Hey, Liesl," Max called from the hangar door. "Sam Jenkins is coming up the walk."

Panic, sure and swift, made Liesl's head snap up. She ran to the door to see for herself. Sure enough, Sam's portly figure swung the gate open. "You didn't tell anyone about the pilot, did you?"

Max blushed a deep red and scuffed the toe of his boot on the soft earth beside the door. "Only Stefan and Anton."

"Max, no! Now everyone knows."

"Sorry, I didn't know he was a secret."

"Nobody can know he's here. It's too dangerous." Didn't Max realize what he'd done? Once Billy found out about Colin Castle, they'd have no chance of getting him to fly for them. And with Sam Jenkins, Billy's right-hand man, waddling down the lane, Billy had to know. She'd have to bluff her way through this and hope Billy himself didn't decide to breach his rule of no trespassing.

"Who's Sam Jenkins?" Colin asked, joining them. His hands on her shoulders sizzled her skin through the material of her shirt, irritating her already raw nerves.

"Trouble," Liesl said, drumming her fingers against the gray metal of the building. "He's a little snoop who reports directly to a man who thinks he's above the law."

"What's that got to do with me?" Colin asked, gliding his hands down her arms, causing an internal combustion.

Hands on hips, she spun to face him. "Spout that time travel stuff in front of this man and you'll find out what trouble really means. Others have died for less."

"Time travel?" Max questioned, raising both eyebrows in naked curiosity.

"Forget it, Max," Liesl said, brushing him aside. Over her shoulder, she spotted Sam halfway down the road. She didn't have much time. So what else was new? "Run home and get *Oma* to let you in the attic. Bring me some of Kurt's clothes, some soap and some scissors. We'll have to make him fit in until he can leave."

"Anything else?"

"A razor," Liesl said, glancing at Sam Jenkins's determined ruddy face. "Some good luck wouldn't hurt, either." She gave Max a light shove and sent him on his way.

"Back in a flash." Max jumped on his bicycle and pedaled at top speed, tipping his head in greeting as he passed Sam.

Now that the town knew Colin was here, how would they react? Liesl shivered as the possibilities rolled through her. With his odd instruments and his singular likeness, the fear would revive. Then what? A repeat performance? She had to keep him out of sight before they saw him and drew their fearful conclusions. The air competition would be soon enough for his unveiling, and he'd leave before they could act.

"He can't see you here," she whispered.

"You want me to stay out of sight while you deal with him?" Colin whispered back, a touch of amusement tainting his sandy voice. His firehot breath singed her ear. A needy quiver rippled through her.

"It's no joking matter." Her voice cracked, but she didn't have time to sort her tangled feelings. Sam Jenkins was too close.

Liesl crossed the wide hangar opening and tugged at the sliding door. "Go back to the room and stay out of sight until I come back. Please," she added as an afterthought.

"This time."

He winked at her as she closed the door on him. He didn't take her seriously. Couldn't he see she was doing this for his own good? Why did she have to do all the thinking around this place?

Liesl stepped toward her office and waited for Sam to arrive. Despite the cool breeze blowing, he removed his tan Stetson and mopped his perspiring forehead with a rumpled handkerchief.

"Mornin', Miz Erhardt." The graying handlebar mustache twitched as he attempted a smile. His damp salt-and-pepper hair retained the shape of his hat.

"What brings you here, Mr. Jenkins?" Liesl asked, looking down at the balding circle on the little man's head.

"Well, I've heard you got a visitor." He chuckled dryly. "I came to give him a big Schönberg welcome."

"I guess you heard wrong. There's no one here but me now that Max has left."

"Well, you see, Miz Erhardt." He rolled the brim of his hat with his sausage fingers. "It just so happens that your cousin Max is the one who's spreadin' this joyful rumor."

"You know how kids are." Liesl shrugged her shoulders. She hated to lie, but Kurt's death had made her face a lot of the ugliness of this world. She'd lie to insure the survival of Kurt's ideals. Especially after what people like Sam had done to him. "He's upset we haven't been able to find a pilot yet. Some of his friends were teasing him, so he made one up."

"Just like that . . ." Round and round went the hat. Stab and feint, stab and feint went Sam's small, pearl-shaped eyes.

"He's just a boy."

"Yes, well, I simply wanted to offer my welcome to the stranger."

"And we all know how hospitable you can be." Liesl hid the sarcasm behind a smile. She reached for the office doorknob and turned it. "Is there anything else, Mr. Jenkins?"

"No, no, I'll be on my way," he said, eyes darting to the hangar door.

"Say hello to Billy for me." Liesl entered her office and turned back to close the door.

"I will, Miz Erhardt, I will." He returned his well-fingered hat to his head, crammed it down with one hand, and waddled back up the hill.

Liesl let out her caged breath, knowing the relief was temporary. Leaving the door partially open so she could keep an eye on Sam's progress, she slid into the hardwood chair and propped her ankles on the desk. Hands splayed over her abdomen, she thumped the toes of her boots together in a steady rhythm.

The preliminary rat should be giving his report any minute now. How long would it take Billy to send someone with more brass? He practically owned the Parker County sheriff, and she wouldn't be able to stop the sheriff if he wanted to have a look-see around her hangar.

The thing about nightmares, Liesl decided, was that they tended to feed upon themselves and grow. She sighed. Leaning her head back and closing her eyes, she wished someone would pinch her awake before this one got out of control. But no one did, and she still had her belligerent pilot to deal with.

She had to convince him to stay. She had to convince him to keep out of sight until next Saturday. She had to convince him to fly for her. And somehow, she had to keep her own emotions under control. If she cracked under Colin Castle's preternatural physical pressure, she wouldn't do Kurt's dream any good.

Resigned, she sighed and eased herself out of her chair and out of the office. Right into the lion's mouth, she thought as she slid open the hangar door.

She spotted him by his airplane, striped by the morning sun through the high barred windows. He hadn't listened to her. Helpless realization stalked her. He wasn't going to make this adventure easy.

She almost wished her prayers hadn't been answered. This devil with an angel's face was going to be the death of her.

"So," she said, stopping near enough to observe him, but far enough to miss the static envelope that seemed to surround him. "How bad is it?"

"Nothing a good mechanic can't fix." He looked up at her from his crouched position. "Are you really good?"

Her stomach feathered at the suggestive gleam in his hazel eyes. "I've had a good teacher."

Even this far away, his magnetism drew her. She crossed her arms to shield herself and took a step back. She had to stay in control. Why was it so easy for him to expose her vulnerable underbelly? Acid bubbled in her stomach. Yes, anger. That was much better. "Why won't you fly for me?" With a flick of her wrist, she flipped her hair back. "Are you *afraid?*"

His eyes narrowed. His body unfurled like a cobra from a snake charmer's basket. He advanced toward her. Impossible to read him through the thick ice of his eyes. Cold terror drenched her sharp and fast, raising goose bumps along her arms and tying her stomach into a series of hard knots. What vipers' nest had she disturbed?

Liesl backed away, and trapped herself against the CastleAir's wing. She spun to escape and found herself corralled by Colin's arms.

"What are *you* afraid of?" Colin's gritty voice sandpapered her skin.

The heat of his presence shimmered toward her, sending slow curls of earthy musk her way, and an unnerving sense of familiarity.

"What have I got to be afraid of?" *Except you and the trouble you'll cause.*

"I don't know," Colin said, reaching for the stray strand of her hair that had popped free once more. He rolled it between his fingers before tucking it behind her ear. She braced herself for his touch, and felt the maddening zap anyway. "You tell me."

His proximity prickled her skin. Coiled energy radiated from his taut muscles straight into her bloodstream, speeding the flow. She shifted closer to the aluminum, but it didn't help. Her blood was on fire.

"I don't trust you, Mr. Castle. Not one bit."

Half his mouth quirked up, but his attempt at a smile didn't fool her one bit, not with the cold ice frosting his eyes.

"I'm not afraid of anything," he said, but Liesl didn't believe him. Something ate at him. Something deep. Something strong.

Liesl leaned forward into the buzzing field around his body. Brown swirled into the green of his eyes. Green swirled into the brown, taking her back in time, choking her with memories. She fought them, latching onto her anger for survival. "Prove it. Fly for me."

"I don't have to prove anything to anybody." His lips were close, close enough to taste if she dared, close enough to see his clenched teeth as he spoke, close enough to hear the slight catch in his voice. Had she hit the bull's-eye? What did Colin Castle have to prove? To whom?

"How much did Billy Ackley pay you to put on this charade?"

Colin dropped his arms and made his way to the mangled propeller. He stroked a blade. She felt the echo of his touch along her skin, and bristled at her easy disloyalty.

"Believe it or not, my colorful landing was an accident. I didn't come here to bother you. I didn't come here to sabotage your chances of winning the competition. I just want to fix my plane and go home."

Prodded by the gusting wind, the building's thin walls popped and snapped. She may not trust him, but he was her last hope for a pilot, her last hope to win the race for Kurt. Wherever he'd come from, he was all she had. The time had come to deal.

"You want propellers, and I've got propellers," Liesl said from her safe vantage.

The scritch-scritch of the oak branch against the building increased.

"Fly for me on Saturday and I'll give you the blades."

"Win or lose?" Colin looked at her sideways over the bent metal.

"Win." Liesl smiled as she shook her head. "It's the only guarantee I have that you won't run out on me." She released her crossed arms, at ease for the first time today. "So which will it be, Mr. Castle?"

"The girl needs a hero," Max said from the hangar door. "Come on, man, be her hero."

Colin's hands gripped the metal blade until the knuckles turned white. The blood drained from his face. And his eyes turned murder black.

Come on, Colin, be my hero. A blinding smile. A flash of golden-brown hair. Pleading amber eyes. Colin squeezed out the memories threatening to flood him with remorse. Failure weighed on him like a cement jacket, choking him. Steeling his features, he hardened his weakness away from view. He sucked the dense air through the narrow straws of his lungs.

"I'm nobody's hero."

"Sure you are," Max said as he deposited a huge paper bag on the tool cart. "Anybody who flies a plane like yours has to be a hero. By the way, I've been meaning to ask, where'd you get those instruments?"

Behind Max, Liesl shook her head and her wide eyes pleaded for his silence. Who could blame her? Speaking of time travel was the shortest way to a straitjacket and a long vacation in a mental institute. The easiest thing to do was to play along.

"They're prototypes I'm developing," Colin said. His left eye twitched as he lied, but Max didn't notice.

"For the government?" Max asked, practically panting with enthusiasm.

"For private investors." At least that part

wasn't a lie. Liesl tucked her stray strand of hair behind her left ear. He remembered the silky feel of her hair, the deep hunger that touching it had aroused. The way it incited memories he couldn't possibly own.

"Yeah, Kurt was doing that, too." Max sighed longingly. "He was trying to open a new, safer pilot training center. He saw a lot of people die during the war, but he knew aviation was the way of the future."

Max walked to the trainer. "One day, people will have airplanes like they have cars. That's what he said, and I believe him. He wanted everybody to feel safe in the sky. This is his prototype. A two-seater cuz he was going to use it as a trainer, too." He patted the aluminum wing gently as if it were the head of a favorite dog. "He was going to win the Trinity Trophy with it and make a name for himself. And name recognition would bring him investors." Turning back to Colin, he cocked his head. "You're our only hope to win the competition. No one else will fly for us."

"Why not?" Colin asked. He leaned against the fuselage and crossed his feet at the ankles. He didn't care. He really didn't. He was simply being polite, using the proper social manners his mother had drilled into him.

"Because," Liesl said, "Billy Ackley wants my airport. He owns half the town and wings a lot of influence. If I don't put in a good showing at the competition, no one will want to invest in my center. I won't make a name for myself. I won't be able to open the innovative pilot training center Kurt dreamed of. So you see, you're being very selfish."

Her long fingers rubbed her rolled-up shirt sleeve in short, jerky strokes. For a moment he envied the threadbare garment.

"I've got dreams of my own that I'll lose if I don't find my way home by Saturday."

"I'll help you."

Her voice was gentle, too gentle. And the gentleness pierced through his armor, striking a rusty chord deep in a place he'd forgotten existed. Hating her for seeing his weakness, he still let the soft seduction of her deadly siren song lure him. Unexplainably, he gained comfort from her steady blue gaze. Like a cloudless sky on a warm, sunny beach, it relaxed him. His mind slowed, allowing logic to soak through.

Colin raked a hand through his hair and paced away from her. He had less than ten dollars in his pocket, and couldn't use any of it because it was minted post-1946. His bank account wouldn't exist for another forty years. He couldn't remember if credit cards were in use in this day and age. Not that it mattered, it would be declined anyway.

Bone-deep weariness swamped him. He didn't want to be anybody's hero. Especially hers. Not with all those unnatural feelings she cajoled straight out of his soul. But what choice did he have? If he wanted to find his way home, he needed an airworthy plane. And without Liesl's help, he was doubtful he'd have it fixed in time. Whatever time meant when traveled through.

"What events did you enter?" Colin asked, delaying the inevitable.

"Power-on precision landing, power-off precision landing, and the Trophy race." She paused for a moment, cocking her head to one side. "Are you up to the challenge?"

She wanted the fearless fly boy; he'd play the role. Slipping on the expected mask, he flashed her his famous smile. "Lady, I can land on a dime and give you change."

"So you'll do it?"

"Yeah, I'll do it."

Max gave a whoop of victory and slapped him on the back. Liesl let out her breath with a whoosh and relaxed her stiff shoulders.

Capitulation—another sign of weakness. Colin swiveled away to the hangar door, unable to watch the glow of triumph Liesl surely sported. He leaned on the frame and gazed at the horizon. Away to the south, a front rolled in. Gray clouds puffed and billowed. Roweled by the warring winds, they grew taller, darker, until a whip of lightning struck the tossing flank. Seconds later, thunder bucked its response.

"Max brought you some clothes," Liesl said somewhere off to his right. "I'm afraid there's no bath here, and going into town is out of the question. There's some soap in the bag and towels in the bathroom." She hesitated before she continued. "And we'll have to cut your hair."

His fingers ran through the matted mess, brushing his T-shirt's neckline. He'd meant to get it cut weeks ago and never got around to it.

Looking at Liesl over his shoulder, he shot her a suggestive smile. "Will you be my Delilah?"

She swallowed hard, and Colin realized he liked her off balance, liked knowing she wasn't perfect.

"I won't betray you," she said. "Will you betray me?"

"That's not what I had in mind."

She blushed, and walked away. Suddenly tired of playing games, Colin became aware of the jackhammer rattling away in his brain. He rubbed the back of his neck. "Do you have any aspirin?"

"In the bathroom."

"Listen, it's been fun," Colin said, pushing himself off the door frame, "but my head is pounding and I need to rest for a while."

"We'll leave you alone." She reached for Max's arm. "Come on, Max. I'd better make an appearance at home before Papa comes looking for me."

Colin watched them go up the rutted road and wondered why he felt so bereft. When they rounded the hill, he dragged his tired carcass to the tiny bathroom and scrubbed himself clean with the frigid water. He shaved his ashen, distorted face in the fractured mirror, and tried not to think. Ignoring the food Max had brought, he fell exhausted onto the bed.

Be my good little boy. Be my hero. Echoes of the past teased his fatigued mind.

As he closed his burning eyes, a somber thought hovered on the edge of his consciousness. It flickered and buzzed like a broken neon sign in a bar. And as he tripped into the darkness of sleep, he remembered.

Each time he'd heard those words, someone had died.

Chapter Four

"She's hiding something," Sam Jenkins said, perched on the edge of his chair, small eyes bright with anticipation, rolling the brim of his hat between his stubs of fingers. "I can smell these things."

His nose twitched, making him look like his rodent nickname. Billy had never liked the man, wouldn't dare turn his back on him, but he had no qualms about using Jenkins's talents. The man could dredge nuggets of gold from sewer sludge and never have a speck of dirt showing on his well-fed body.

"Want me to call the sheriff and have him smoke her out?" Jenkins panted with ferine delight.

"No, let her think she's won for now. Stick to the hangar like a tick on a dog and report what shows up." Billy tapped the solid gold tip of his pen on the stack of papers before him. "If she has managed to snag a pilot, he'll have a price. They all do."

Winded from her hurried walk and the frantic thoughts churning through her mind, Liesl stepped into the kitchen of their living quarters behind the family store. *Oma*'s ever-present pot of soup steamed on the stove, wafting solace into the air. Light from the noon sun slanted through the window and illuminated her grandmother's bread bowl at the edge of the counter. A few feet away, *Oma* prepared batter for one of her famous *streusselküchen*.

"Zere you are, *Liebchen*. Dinner is still hot." *Oma* smiled, dimpling her rosy cheeks, and wiped her floury fingers on a sack cloth. White wisps of hair escaped from her tight braid wound in a crown at the nape of her neck.

When Liesl saw her father still seated at the plain wood table, her answering smile died. He should have been back at the store by now, revived by dinner, ready for an afternoon's work.

Jürgen Erhardt pushed his plate toward the center of the table and leaned back in his carved walnut chair. "Where have you been?"

"At the airport." Liesl stood stiffly by the table.

Her father was a tall, thin man whose eyes and mouth curved downward in a permanent state of sadness even on those few occasions when he smiled. Now his stern face and hard eyes showed no tenderness and made Liesl feel like a disobedient little girl. She drew in a shaky breath and fought the urge to fiddle with her hands and stare at her shoes. She wasn't eight years old, for heaven's sake. She was a grown woman; she didn't have to explain herself.

"Come sit and have some dinner, *Liebchen*," *Oma* said as she busily piled slices of beef and chunks of potatoes and carrots onto a plate. Liesl understood this was *Oma*'s attempt to diffuse her father's sour mood, and scraped back the chair in her usual spot across from her father.

"*Oma*'s been worried sick about you. She had to take your place at the store today. You know Saturday is her cleaning day. You know she has food to prepare for tomorrow. What do you have to say for yourself?"

As she sawed a slice of bread from the dark wheat loaf on the cutting board, *Oma* made disapproving noises. But a man was the head of the household even if he was her son, Liesl knew, and as such *Oma* couldn't defy him in front of a child, even an adult one. After fifty years of living in America, the people of Schönberg still followed the ways of the old country. On the north side anyway, Liesl thought, remembering Billy's disgusting proposition. Was it only yesterday afternoon? It seemed a lifetime ago.

"I'm sorry, Papa." Liesl stabbed a potato but didn't lift it to her mouth.

"You need to apologize to your grandmother, not to me."

"I'm sorry, *Oma*."

"Ze change did me good, *Liebchen*. Do not vorry about it." *Oma* hugged her to her ample apron, and Liesl smelled the comforting scent of cinnamon and flour dusted upon it, glad to have one ally in this world that often seemed more cruel than good.

"Why do you waste your time there?" Her father pulled a brown ceramic jar from the sideboard behind him, retrieved his pipe and filled it with a measure of tobacco. "Kurt is dead." He brought a match to the pipe's bowl and puffed on the stem. "You can't bring him back."

Papa might change his mind if he saw the man hiding in her hangar. Like a ghost he would haunt Schönberg with its past and revive the hatred and the fear for the townspeople, just as he'd haunted her with the memories he'd rekindled. She shivered involuntarily. She didn't want to think about Colin or the way he made her want things she could never have again. She berated herself for her disloyalty. Colin was just a pilot. Nothing more. She almost choked on the piece of meat she tried to swallow.

"I can make him live by making his dream come true," Liesl finally managed. Why couldn't Papa understand that simple fact? Why had he never tried to understand her feelings? Why had he never loved her?

The answer was easy—because her birth had caused her mother's death, and he'd never forgiven her for it. The sadness etched on his face was her fault. She'd tried to make up for his loss all of her life and hadn't yet succeeded. She would try harder.

"What about you, daughter? When will you start to live?"

Her head snapped up at his unexpected concern. "I'm happy living the way I am, Papa."

A sob caught in her throat at the lie of the words. She wasn't happy. She would never be happy again. Not without Kurt. Tears burned her eyes and threatened to spill. Her father didn't approve of shows of emotions. She rose abruptly, heading toward the hall stairs.

"Liesl."

She stayed her flight, muscles trembling at the effort to show control. Her fingers gripped the door jamb, biting into the soft wood. She looked at her father over her shoulder. "Yes, Papa?"

"I want you at church tomorrow and the picnic afterwards, not hiding at the airport." He turned his pipe upside down in the glass ashtray and tapped it several times. "It's too much for *Oma* to handle alone."

"But, Papa, I have to—"

"Tomorrow you stay here."

"But—"

"Enough! You will do as I ask. Is this understood?"

"Yes, Papa."

Liesl started for the stairs again and sank to the bottom step. Her hands, knotted in tight fists, pounded on the stairs' faded runner, her teeth clenched, and her rapid breaths puffed through her nostrils. She wasn't from the old country. She wasn't a child anymore. Why did she let him treat her like one?

"Leave ze girl alone, Jürgen," she heard *Oma* say.

"I tell you, *Mutti*, it's just not natural."

"Vat's so unnatural about a broken heart? You of all people should understand."

"No, the mystery is why a pretty twenty-three-year-old girl isn't married. Even soiled, someone would have her if she'd let them."

"I do not see anyone varming your bed!"

"It's not the same."

"Umph. And thistles bear no grapes."

"Are you saying I have failed as a father?"

"I am saying you need to look in ze mirror. You are too hard on ze child."

Soiled! The word cut straight to Liesl's heart as she ran up the stairs to her room. Papa had never approved of what he called her infatuation with Kurt. But infatuations faded, and Liesl had loved Kurt since his family had moved to Schönberg when she was ten.

Nothing she had done with Kurt had been wrong. She sank onto her bed and fingered the silver chain around her neck, slipping the two silver bands dangling from it onto her left ring finger. They'd been in love. They'd been married.

But Papa couldn't accept their hasty marriage because he hadn't been there to give his blessing, and their union had been officiated by a justice of the peace in an impersonal courthouse instead of their minister at the local church. Papa had always thought she could do better. Kurt's gypsy ways didn't fit in with his plans for his daughter. He hadn't accepted her choice then. He didn't understand her choice now.

No, she didn't feel soiled and never would. Nor could she forgive her father for his refusal to accept her choices.

As memories of her wedding day came flooding back, pain filled her heart. She bit her trembling lower lip to stop the tears. From beneath her bed, she dragged out a shoebox and settled it on the quilt. Lovingly she swept away the dust from the cover, feeling the constricting ache, feeling the love, feeling the emptiness swell in her heart.

He'd loved her. He'd told her so a thousand times. She'd loved him. He'd known she had. She'd shown him in a hundred different ways. But she'd never dared voice the words—not even on their wedding day—fearing that if she did, he would turn away from her, the way Papa always had, and shatter her grown-up heart, the same way Papa had broken her young one.

She lifted the cover and with ritualistic precision took out the letters Kurt had written to her while he was in England. A rush of emotions overcame her, and she pressed them against her heart.

Between dealing with Colin, her father, and her memories of Kurt, Liesl's emotions felt wrung to their limit. A warm bath relieved her knotted muscles, but did nothing to untangle her thoughts as they wove and meshed around Colin and Kurt, one becoming the other, melding into one. What was she supposed to feel? *Forever, Liesl.* What was she supposed to do?

What was she supposed to think?

She forced herself to work all afternoon in her father's store, wearing a false smile to please the clients despite the rain pouring outside, managing to keep thoughts of Colin at bay until she could deal with them sensibly. She kept the idle chatter to a minimum, and sighed with relief when it came time to close the post office window.

After supper Liesl insisted on doing the cleaning up by herself, sending her grandmother to join her father in the living room. She put aside a plate for Colin and wrapped it with a cloth.

"I'm going to bed," she announced, stepping into the living room to snag a book from her father's bookshelf.

"Good night, *Liebchen*," *Oma* said, looking up from her embroidery for half a moment.

Her father grunted but didn't look up from his book.

Silently she left the book on the kitchen table, grabbed the plate she'd prepared, and headed for the airport.

I can handle seeing him again. He's just a pilot. He'll get me what I want. I can handle it. I have to.

A car backfired on Main Street. Her shoes squished into a puddle, and the cold rain-freshened air zinged her cheeks. From the gate, Liesl could see the hangar door gaping open. Dim light from the bedroom shone yellow into the hangar, spilling into the night.

She pressed her lips tight and gripped the plate's edge harder. He'd disobeyed her once more.

Why couldn't he understand the danger his foolishness would cause for everybody? Her steps lengthened with her determination to once and for all get this stubborn pilot of hers under control.

About to call out his name, Liesl saw him outside, leaning against the death tree, dressed in Kurt's shirt and pants. She stopped abruptly and choked down a gasp.

In the moon's light, she saw Kurt again. How often had he leaned against the tree that way, gazing out at the far horizon, picturing his dream? The plate shook in her hands. She brought her attention back to the red and blue flour logo on the cloth, concentrating on the flower design to keep herself from walking to her illusion and putting her arms around his waist; to keep herself from sinking her head onto his back and breathing in his scent; to keep herself from wanting him so badly.

I'm sorry, Kurt. I don't mean to be disloyal, but he reminds me so much of you, and I miss you so much. I keep wishing he were you. I keep wishing . . .

Try as she might, she couldn't ignore him. Like scattered needles drawn to a magnet, her gaze returned to the familiar stranger. The night breeze ruffled his hair as it whispered through the oak's leaves. The moon's light accentuated the creases of unhappiness lining his face. His closed eyes were blind to the nightscape around him. He looked so lost, so vulnerable. Was he remembering his world?

For an instant, a deep protective urge flowed

through her. She'd been so selfish, thinking of herself and her problems. But what would it be like to find herself lost in time? How would she feel were she faced with the prospect of never going home again? Her heart softened. She'd tell him. She'd make him understand that he had a friend in this unfamiliar world he found himself in.

Plate still in hand, Liesl approached Colin. Gently, so as not to startle him, she touched his arm. Her fingers prickled uncomfortably and she snapped them back. "I brought you some supper. I'm afraid the sausage is on the cold side."

He turned and smiled at her, the way Kurt had done so many times, taking her breath away. "That's okay, I'm not hungry anyway."

He made it so difficult to keep focused on the present, instead of drifting into the past. His eyes, his mouth, his hands as he reached out for the plate replayed scenes from her memory, bringing a longing so deep, Liesl thought her heart would bleed from the need. She closed her eyes and scrunched them, willing Kurt's ghost to disengage itself from Colin's face. When she reopened them, the illusion persisted. Could she stand this devastating pain for one more week?

The plate fell from her grip.

Colin caught the plate in mid-fall. "Hey, you should warn a guy before you hand him his dinner like that!"

Her hand shook as it rose to her throat. "I'm sorry. It's just . . ."

Her pale skin bleached in the moonlight, her blue eyes widened with fear, her body strung itself taut with tension. She should be smiling, Colin thought, wrapping her arms around his waist, tilting her face up for his kiss. He'd seen her in his mind's eye doing just that moments before she touched his arm. He could still feel her warmth, taste her sweetness. It had seemed so real—as if she'd done it a hundred times, as if he'd stood by that tree a thousand times waiting for her, as if it were natural for her to mold herself intimately to him, for him to feel such comfort in her presence.

"Just what?" he asked, shaking his head to clear the cobwebs of fantasy. The ride through time sure had scrambled his brain.

She stared at him for a moment. The white buttons down the front of her navy sweater rose and fell in an erratic rhythm. "In the moonlight . . . when you turned, you looked . . ."

"Looked how?" He desperately wanted to hear something from her, but what? As he waited, his breath ripped through his tightened lungs.

She shook her head and lowered it, averting her soul-reaching gaze. "We need to go in before anyone sees you."

Liesl started toward the hangar, but Colin caught her arm. Gripped with unexplained fear, he looked deep into her eyes. What did he want her to say? What did he need to hear? "I looked how?"

"Like a ghost from the past."

Her whispered words skittered like an icy

wind across his skin, raising the hair along his arms. Her pale eyes looked hollow in the moon's watery light. She stared at him, right through him as if he didn't exist. An unnatural disappointment washed over him. The ice of hope melted into the water of regret. Not right, those words. What had he hoped for, anyway?

Play the role. She wants the fly boy, remember? Colin chuckled. "I realize I'm no Mel Gibson, but no one's ever described me as a ghost before." One more press, one more stab at . . . what? "Do I look that bad?"

"No," she said simply, without amplifying.

Part of him wanted her to, part of him feared her answer. And all of him ached for her to reach for him as she'd done in his dreams.

"Who's Mel Gibson?" she asked.

"An actor—from my time."

The sounds of night surrounded them—the whispering breeze, the rasping crickets, a coyote's plaintive howl. A thin cloud slid over the moon, playing shadows on Liesl's face as she stared at him, asking her own silent questions. He was falling under her spell. Maybe he could talk her into coming home with him. Then he'd have time to explore just what about her caught his fancy. He shook his head. Crazy idea. If he kept losing himself in fantasy dreams, he'd never get back home. He'd fail again. He didn't have time to play the fool or the lover, much less the hero. Scrubbing his hand through his hair, he turned away from her gaze.

"How's your head?" she asked, glancing at his forehead.

He reached for the stitched raw spot. "Better."

"Do you . . . are you . . ." She let out a sigh of exasperation and tucked a strand of hair behind her left ear before crossing her arms under her chest. "What are you doing outside? I told you to stay out of sight, didn't I? What if someone saw you?"

"Would it be so bad?" After five years of almost nonstop work, this forced inactivity drove him crazy. As the rainy afternoon had dragged on, the hangar had felt like a prison.

All his attempts at bringing logic to his situation had failed, leaving him with a pounding headache that surely could have registered a six on the Richter scale. Facts weren't supposed to be wishy-washy. That's what feelings were for, and he'd managed to curb those after Karen. Facts, figures, logic had sustained him. But now they only added to the confusion, because the facts didn't add up, and logic insisted he couldn't be here.

When the clouds had lifted and the sun disappeared over the horizon, he hadn't been able to resist the temptation to leave his cage and breathe freely from the cool night breeze. At least the earth and sky still existed.

"If someone saw you, it would ruin everything," Liesl said.

"Why?"

"We would never get the chance to get ready for the air show, and the race must come above all." She uttered the last part as if it were a reminder to herself more than a warning to him.

She grabbed his arm and pushed him forward. "You must eat and get strong. I need you . . . to fly and win."

They sat at the small table in the cramped bedroom in the hangar. Colin forced himself to eat the cheese, sausage, bread and fruit she'd brought him. She'd made coffee in her office and sat sipping hers across from him—as far as politely acceptable, he noticed and almost smiled.

"Why are you afraid of me?" he asked, ripping off a bite of bread.

"I'm not." The answer came too fast, too sharp to be true. The white bow at the prim and proper collar of her white blouse shivered. In her nervous hurry to steady her hand, she sloshed coffee from her cup to her hand.

Colin reached across the table and wiped the spill with the cloth he'd used as a napkin. Soft, so soft. She tried to tug away, but Colin held fast to her hand, stroking the reddened skin between her index finger and thumb. Without taking his eyes from her face, he lifted her hand to his lip and kissed the hurt flesh. Her pupils dilated until only a small ring of blue surrounded the black. A zing of awareness traveled through his arm and settled low in his belly, inviting sweet pictures of surrender.

"A kiss to make it better," he said, smiling, knowing he wanted much more than a kiss, regretting he couldn't.

As she pulled her hand away, her nostrils flared. This time he let her go.

"We're going to have to cut your hair," Liesl

said, hands primly set in her lap.

"Sure." He'd let her change the subject, if that's what she wanted. He sure as hell didn't understand how he could want her so much, and he didn't have time for entanglements. Not with only six days to find Jakob's window before it pinched him out of his time forever. He smiled at her. "But you'll have to promise me you won't cut my strength along with the hair."

"Let's go in the hangar." She rose to hide her blush, and picked up a comb and scissors from the bag Max had brought that morning.

Carrying a chair, Colin followed her into the wider space. If she thought she could dilute the strong current between them with the added space, Colin knew she was wrong. It was there, to be ignored or answered, but there nonetheless. "Where do you want me?"

"There by the door."

From his position, he could see the stars twinkling in the inky sky, but the metal wall kept him from feeling the cool caress of the breeze. "Have you done this before?"

"Many times. I cut my father's hair and Max's."

She tested the scissors with a few snips of air. He heard her long intake of breath before she reached to touch his hair.

"I know that being here must feel strange to you," Liesl said. Her fingers touched his hair.

"I've lived in a hangar for the past five years."

"No, I mean being here, out of time." Warm and soft, her fingers shot tingling sparks into his scalp and sent slow, erotic waves rolling through his body. He shifted in the chair. She jerked her hands away.

"Don't move or you'll end up with a nasty cut." She resumed her cutting. "What's it like in your world?"

How to explain progress since the forties? He didn't have the energy to try. "The same, only more complicated."

"Do you have family?"

"Just a father who's dying. One of the reasons I have to get back."

"No one else?"

"No." Why did the answer ring so hollow? Why did it hurt to know that no one would miss him should he stay stuck in this time?

"You said your airplane was a 1948 replica. If you live in the nineties, why do you fly such an airplane?"

"Nostalgia."

"I don't understand."

A lock of hair fell into his lap. He brushed it aside. How could he explain something he didn't quite understand himself? He'd been born to fly. He had known from his first remembered thoughts that he would fly.

"I've always loved airplanes. All kinds of airplanes. I've been going to air shows since I was old enough to sneak away from home. The maneuvers, the precision, the excitement of it all. I wanted to be a part of that."

Colin crossed his arms over his chest and lifted an ankle to his knee. "My father owns an air freight business. He's wanted me to join him since I graduated from college. But . . . I wanted something else. I didn't want the routine."

He started to shake his head, then remembered Liesl's warning. One set of stitches was enough. "I was a bush pilot until I lost my plane in a crash—mechanical failure. I flew medevacs for a children's hospital until I couldn't meet the payments on my plane anymore, and it was repossessed. I taught flying for a while. I told a snot-nosed kid he was too dangerous to fly. His daddy took offense and I got canned. The worst part is the kid went and killed himself the very next month on his first cross-country solo."

Cut hairs slid down his shirt and prickled the back of his neck. Liesl's proximity grated like a new shoe on a heel blister.

"But I always came back to the show circuit," Colin continued. "Flew whatever I could, whenever I could. Then I got the idea of making replica airplanes for flying museums. And that's what I've been doing for the past five years. I like to fly the older planes because they have so much character. It's like a partnership—you give, you take, you compromise. Throw in a healthy dose of respect and you can do anything. You can be free—"

Colin cut himself off, embarrassed at having said so much. What was it about this woman that made him act so out of character? Only Karen had been able to draw him out that much since his mother's death. And she was dead, too. Both because of him. He slapped his foot back on the ground.

Liesl stopped cutting. "Kurt felt that way about flying, too. It was something strong inside of him. That's why he wanted to start a pilot training center."

Paper scratched against fabric. Over his shoulder, Liesl handed him a picture of a man dressed in a World War II Air Force pilot's uniform. "This is Kurt. He sent me this picture from England. He flew B-17s for the Eighth Air Force at Bassingbourn. He flew thirty-four missions before he was shot down."

He stared at his own face on the black-and-white photograph with the ragged edges. As Liesl spoke, her words faded. They were replaced with feelings and images deeper than human memory. *Suddenly he sat in that B-17, the bulky flight suit weighing down his body, the oxygen pumping through his rubber mask, the freezing and sweating of his body at the same time. Thick, black smoke swirled outside the airplane's window. A whine and bump came from the wing. The number three engine died. The console lit up, the plane grew heavier. His muscles quivered from the force of holding her in the air. Eight men depended on his skill to return them home safely.*

His flight engineer returned to his post.

"How's it looking, Johnny?"

"Not too good, Kurt. The tail's like Swiss cheese. Hydraulics are out. No flaps. No brakes."

A second engine died.

"Tell the crew to get ready for a crash landing."

Fighting the wounded plane every inch of the way, he flew back to Bassingbourn, skidded onto the runway at 135 miles an hour, and looped into a manure pile.

Half of the co-pilot's face swam in blood. The radio man had taken a bullet in the leg. Two of the gunners suffered broken legs and arms. One walked away clean, as did the bombardier. The engineer got out with a dislocated shoulder. Not a pretty sight. But they were all alive.

The impact had driven a loose piece of metal straight through Kurt's right knee, shattering it instantly. Running on adrenaline, he hadn't felt the pain until all his crew had made it safely off the plane. As he walked toward the jeep waiting to take them back to base, his legs buckled beneath him and the whole world went black.

"Colin?"

Liesl's voice snapped the vivid film running through his mind. His arm muscles quivered, and he realized he gripped the side of the chair like a vise. His right knee throbbed with phantom pain. Kurt's picture stared back at him from the cement floor. He loosened his fingers and brushed away the uncomfortable moment with a chuckle. "You sure have a way with words. I felt like I was really there."

"There?"

"In England. You were talking about Kurt crashing."

"No, I was talking about the fear the war brought and how it killed Kurt."

A bead of sweat rolled down his forehead, angled away at his brow, slid down the side of his face, and plopped onto his collar. His whole life was slipping through his fingers and he couldn't seem to hang on to anything long enough to make sense of it. He had to get a grip on himself.

Fear. He'd lived with it most of his life. Like a shadow it followed him everywhere. He'd managed to control it, harness it, and make it his friend. But now, like a rabid dog, it seemed to turn on him and threatened to bite him. He couldn't let it.

"What about the fear?" he asked, concentrating on the movement of her fingers in his hair instead of the empty dark pit inside his stomach.

"Schönberg used to be one small town. All Germans who'd come from the old country together fifty years ago. *Oma*—"

"Who's *Oma*?"

"*Oma* is German for grandmother. *Oma* said they were all tired of drinking life with a coffee spoon." Liesl chuckled. "*Oma* loves maxims. They wanted freedom and found it here. Over the years Anglo families settled here, too."

The snip snip of scissors cut a relaxing rhythm. "Then the war came," Liesl said sadly.

"What happened?"

"The whispers started. The people remembered the hatred they'd lived through in the first war, how they'd suffered because of their roots. They were afraid. It didn't take much for the people to believe the rumors, to want to protect themselves from them, to do *something* about them before they suffered again."

"What kinds of rumors?"

"After the war started, we all stopped speaking German in public. We all planted Victory

103

gardens. We all bought war bonds. We didn't want anybody to mistake us for anything but American. We sent our men to battle. Many didn't come back."

Liesl moved in front of him, her knee brushing against his. His stomach tightened. Awareness crisped between them. She carefully edged away, leaving a breath of space between them. As she swallowed, her throat convulsed.

"When the rumors of a spy among them started, the people panicked," she continued.

Her arms rose, bringing the scissors and comb to his hair once more. His arms twitched with the need to hold her, to inhale the perfume of her skin, to drown in the sweetness of her kiss until the fear, the confusion, left him. "What did they do?"

"They decided they had to find the spy before it reflected on the whole community. Everybody suspected everybody. The Anglos refused to associate with the Germans. It divided the town in half. Then Kurt came home and started working on his plans, building his airplane, talking about the future. And the whispers grew louder."

The scissors' snips stilled for a moment. Her breasts were so close, so tempting. He wanted to take each soft peak in his mouth, to feel them harden on his tongue. He was going crazy, stark raving mad. He closed his eyes and concentrated on her words.

"Wasn't he a war hero?"

"Yes, but that didn't protect him. He couldn't survive his reputation. Before the war, he'd been the town's 'bad boy.' He played too many practical jokes, rode motorcycles, flew airplanes. He didn't act the way people expected a well-bred person to behave. That's what they remembered. They didn't understand how living through so much death had changed him. He'd found his focus, but they didn't give him a chance."

The hairs on the back of Colin's neck rose straight against the chill rippling through him. She could have been recounting his own life.

"He'd told several people he wished he didn't have to go back to finish his tour of duty," Liesl said. The steady rhythm of her scissors calmed his speeding pulse. "After his leg healed, he was to work at the American Air Force Training Command. Fuel to the fire, so to speak. Only a spy would want to turn his back on his country in its hour of need. They didn't understand his love of flying, his desire to train pilots safely, how a desk job would kill him. And when the scandal of stolen documents erupted just after he visited the local air defense plant, they felt they had to protect themselves from being linked to Kurt."

She moved away from him. He opened his eyes and saw her leaning against the metal door, staring into space. "I was too in love to notice anything wrong. I never heard the buzzing."

The metal walls popped and creaked against the breeze.

"We were going to get married when his assignment was up," Liesl continued. "Then we decided we couldn't wait and eloped. That morning, they came."

"Who?"

"The townspeople—Anglos mostly, but the Germans didn't stop them. United in fear." Liesl gave a short, bitter laugh, then paused for a moment. "They hung him on the oak tree outside." Her voice croaked, and her eyes shone with unshed tears.

His head dizzied. His heart beat faster. Sweat beaded on his forehead. His throat constricted. He couldn't breathe. Pain and fear ripped through him like a plane in a spin. *I love you, Liesl. Forever,* a voice, not his own, echoed in his mind.

"To save themselves from a possibility, they killed an innocent man." She shook her head. "Your friend Jakob Renke could have told the truth, but the coward disappeared."

What's happening to me? Breathe in. Breathe out. That's it. Control. Concentrate.

"When the real spy was caught," she continued, unaware of his struggle, "they blamed each other, cementing the rift between them. Kurt's death was ruled an unfortunate accident."

Breathe in. Breathe out. A measure of control returned, but his head still felt caught in a strange current.

"So you see, if you show your face, you will bring out the guilt, the pain we're all trying to forget. Peace is so fragile."

"I'm not afraid of the townspeople."

"I'm afraid for you." One of her hands rested at her throat, slim fingers splayed. The other, holding scissors and comb, was wrapped around her waist. She swiveled her head to look at him, her blond hair catching a moonbeam. Her eyes hid in the shadows, but he could feel their pleading. "I'm afraid for me. I have to win. Can you understand that?"

He stood and joined her at the door, standing behind her. His gaze sought the horizon. "I understand more than you think." He folded his arms around her shoulders and pressed her against him. The heat of her felt good against him. His breath stirred the spun gold of her hair. "I understand about loss, about the unfairness of death, about failure. I understand *you.*"

She turned in his arms, mouth open, staring, searching. He didn't want questions. He didn't have answers. Unconsciously, he swayed in time to an unfamiliar tune buzzing in his head. He tried to shake it away, but the melody stuck and played on like a record in a jukebox. His voice, humming the tune, echoed memories in the deep recesses of his brain. His mind wasn't his own. When he brought her head to his shoulder, she didn't fight him.

"You don't know me at all." Liesl stood stiff in his arms, but didn't move away.

"I know about the beauty mark on your right breast." His finger confidently sought a spot on the navy wool covering her chest. Her head snapped up. Where was this surging tide of impressions coming from? He erected a barrier, but the pictures burst through as easily as if it had been a sand dam.

"I've kissed the scar on your ankle," he continued. Her mouth formed "how," but no sound came out. "The one old Grüber's mare made when she kicked you." So real, those images flashing through his brain like an incoming tide.

"I remember how long your hair was when we first met," he whispered. His hand flowed down to her waist, as if stroking silk. "You were only ten. I was twelve. So shy, so pretty, so fun to tease. I wanted you even then."

His skin itched with unnatural sensitivity. His heart stammered a panicked rhythm. Had time travel rearranged his brain cells and mixed them up with someone else's? What was happening to him? The scissors and comb Liesl held clattered to the floor.

"No . . ."

Liesl shook her head. Her fingers pried his shoulder and tried to push away. As helpless as a drowning swimmer, Colin tightened his hold and resumed his humming. "Sing with me, Liesl. 'Let me show you where my heart lies. Let me prove that it adores . . . '" When the tune ended, he stopped swaying and shifted his hold to kiss her.

The heady taste of her sent what remained of his sanity spinning into a dangerous whirlpool. His hands molded her to him, explored remembered curves, and cursed the clothes coming between the soft heat of her skin and his desperate need to touch her. He left her mouth to taste the throbbing pulse at her throat, losing himself deeper in the mirage of his mind. So real, so right, but not him.

"Kurt . . ." she whispered, hot and husky, in his ear.

Kurt. The name echoed and reechoed in his brain. His throat constricted and his panting breath couldn't fit through the opening of his lungs. Dizzy, he let her go abruptly, turning to hide his weakness. Hunched over the rolling metal tray, he forced air into his lungs, swallowed the panic, and slowed down the madness with sheer willpower.

Colin heard Liesl sob behind him. He turned to apologize, but couldn't make the words come out. With tears streaming down her face, she ran from him. He watched her race up the hill, watched the gate swing back and forth from the force of Liesl's push, watched the darkness engulf her. He stared long after she'd disappeared.

He'd never meant to kiss her. He'd never meant to make her cry. He'd never meant to feel.

Would he ever find himself again in all this madness?

Liesl ran. She ran as fast as she could. Air burned through her overburdened lungs. Her legs ached from the unaccustomed stress. She didn't bother to mask the sobs bursting from her. She didn't try to stop the tears.

How could anyone be so cruel? How could he pretend he knew her? How could she fall for his trick?

No matter how fast she ran, she couldn't escape the feeling of being trapped, of falling prey to a master hunter.

For a mad moment, she'd let herself believe. She'd let him weave his illusion. *How could you be so stupid?*

Even his voice had softened from a sandy grit to a purring rumble. He tasted like Kurt. He felt like Kurt. In that instant when he'd kissed her, he was Kurt, and the two tortuous years since his death had melted away. And she'd fallen for it.

Tears blinded her, but still she ran. She didn't know where she was going, didn't care.

How could he have known all those details? Who had told him? How could he have known that "Star Eyes" was the song Kurt had sung for her on their wedding night? *How could he know?*

She pushed herself further, wanting to feel her lungs burn, her legs ache—anything to take the pain away from her heart. Betrayal, hers, his, Colin's lashed venom through her brain.

When she couldn't move another pace, she bent over to gulp oxygen into her lungs and found herself outside the cemetery. Had her guilty conscience brought her here?

"Kurt."

Rasping breath through her overworked lungs, she opened the wrought iron gate and wound her way through the tombstones and trees to the far end of the park. She stared at Kurt's grave marker. Numbly, she knelt on the damp grass by the stone and ran a finger over the carved letters.

"Kurt." A fresh wave of tears assaulted her, and she crumpled on the grave. As deep sobs racked her body, her fingers dug into the grass.

When the stream of tears finally slowed and faded, she lay feeling the cool, wet earth beneath her, the wind ruffling her skirt, the night sounds surrounding her. No one could have known the details of her life that Colin knew. The inflection of his voice, the feelings, the touch, he couldn't have known about them. And how could he possibly fake the taste?

He has come a long way for you, child. Tante Wenona's words echoed in her mind. She sat up with a gasp. Her whole body shook from the idea forming in her head. Her trembling hand reached for the cold stone.

"Kurt?" Was it possible? Could a spirit project his essence onto a different body at a different time? Could it be Kurt's spirit in Colin's body?

A train whistle tore through the night. The train's wheels clicked and clacked on the tracks. As the freight cars chugged by, the ground rumbled beneath her. Again she heard the eerie whisper of her name in the backwash. *Lee-ee-sl-l-l.*

She looked up at the post oak's shaking limbs. A lingering raindrop swooped the curved leaf, hung on its end long enough to catch a glimmer of moonlight before it fell to the puddle beside Kurt's grave, stirring its surface in a series of widening circles. Her fingers pressed into the stone.

"Have you come back to me, Kurt?"

Said out loud, the words sounded ridiculous.

She shook her head. Of course he hadn't come back. Ridiculous. As farfetched an idea as time travel.

And yet . . . evidence seemed to point out that Colin *had* traveled through time. No. She stood up and brushed the dirt from her dress. *Enough!* She wiped the tears from her eyes, and sniffed as she flipped a strand of hair behind her ear. These thoughts were merely her broken heart's wishful thinking. Dead people's souls went to heaven or hell; they didn't come back to earth.

Colin's face made her vulnerable. Colin's face had brought back the painful memories she'd so carefully stored away. Colin's face muddled her senses and made her forget her goal.

He was a dangerous man, with his own agenda. She had to remember that.

If she wanted to win, she couldn't underestimate him.

Chapter Five

"I need a drink," Colin said to the empty night, staring at the black space where Liesl had disappeared from what seemed like hours ago. Maybe through the haze of alcohol he could figure out what was happening to him. Logic certainly wasn't working. Liesl had gotten coffee from her office, maybe she kept something a little stiffer there, too. He didn't hold much hope, but headed in that direction, anyway.

Action, any action, had to be better than standing around letting himself fall over the edge of insanity.

It didn't make sense. None of it. Not what he'd seen, not what he'd felt, especially not what he'd known. He rubbed the back of his aching neck, cursing the shakiness still trickling through his limbs. It was crazy. Maybe he'd gone mad.

Whatever, he didn't want to think about it anymore. Maybe in a while, but not now.

Colin found the door unlocked and entered, stumbling in the dark until he found the switch to the light on her desk. A battered metal desk, a set of metal filing cabinets in the same bedraggled condition, a wooden swivel chair, and a small table with a hot plate to make coffee stood on a perfectly swept wooden floor. The desk top was neat. Not a speck of dust marred any of the furniture. Two spoons rested neatly beside two shiny mugs near the clean coffee pot. Colin opened the desk drawers and found them in perfect order. He went through the file drawers and found them in the same condition.

So much for the idea of a stiff drink.

Pinned on the wall, he saw a blueprint of a plane. Upon closer inspection, it looked an awful lot like his CastleAir. Had the Castell been a forerunner of the CastleAir? How come he'd never heard of the Castell? With Kurt dead, maybe it had never gotten off the ground. Had Jakob really stolen Kurt's plan as Liesl had accused him of? No, that didn't make sense. CastleAirs had had a reputation as great pylon racers for a few years before the racing fad had all but died in the fifties.

As Colin sank into the chair, it groaned. Absently he toyed with the pencils in the organizer on top of the desk. Loose coins jingled at the bottom of the container. He emptied the container on the green blotter. How much did a beer cost in 1946? From among the spilled pencils, he plucked two dimes and six nickels.

Surely fifty cents would be enough. The more he thought about it, the better the idea of a beer sounded. He brought out two quarters from his pocket and placed them where he'd found Liesl's coins.

He wouldn't be gone long. Slip out, drink his beer, come back. He arranged his hair to cover the neatly sewn flesh on his forehead. Quick. Easy. Fast. No one would notice him. Couldn't get drunk with fifty cents. Not even in '46. Before he'd thought through all the consequences, he walked out the door and up the hill.

He hesitated at the gate, not knowing which way to go. Closing his eyes, he pictured his version of Schönberg and, avoiding a large water puddle, headed left toward the Anglo side of town. Liesl would have a fit if she found out he'd left the hangar. But she wouldn't. Just one beer. He deserved it after all he'd gone through.

Schönberg's rutted main street looked like a movie set for a period film. Packards, old Fords and a few old Buicks lined the street. It wasn't so much the buildings with their boxy brick and wood construction that looked out of place as the window displays and the ads—the old-fashioned gas pump with gas for fifteen cents a gallon, the clothing with mannequins dressed in styles that had long gone out of fashion, the record shop announcing the newest Frank Sinatra and Benny Goodman 78s.

Thinking he might have traveled in time and actually seeing proof of it were two different things. Neither sat well on his stomach.

The Saddle and Spur Saloon hadn't changed

much in the past fifty years. The same metal cowboy tried to rope the same metal calf, only the red paint wasn't peeling and the white neon light worked. Avoiding eye contact with anyone, he headed straight for the counter at the back of the room.

"What can I do for ya, fella?" asked the basset-hound-faced man behind the counter. As he spoke, he polished the wood surface with a cloth.

"Give me a beer."

"Carling or Grüen?"

"Grüen," Colin said, wondering if it came from the same local brewery it did in '96.

The man filled a tall glass and placed it in front of Colin. "Ten cents."

He pushed the coins across the bar and chuckled silently. Maybe fifty cents was enough to get drunk. Half turning on his stool, he observed the occupants of the room. Light from shaded bulbs hazed the faces in red. Most of the men wore jeans, boots and work shirts dirty from a day's work outdoors. A few wore cuffed pants and dress shirts with the sleeves rolled to their elbows. A few even wore narrow ties. A game of poker played itself out at a corner table. The smell of smoke and stale beer stained the air. Except for the World War II posters still lining the walls, Colin didn't feel out of place.

A gale of raucous laughter erupted from another table—the same table he'd spent so many evenings talking over his plans with Jakob. Colin shook his head. No, he'd never been here with Jakob.

As he returned his gaze to the foam in his glass, Colin noticed a small, squat man scurry out the door. *Probably married to a nag.* Colin laughed silently. Enjoying the feel of the cold brew slipping down his throat, Colin sighed and let himself forget he was far from home.

"Passin' through or stayin' longer?" asked a smooth voice, startling Colin from his daydream.

"Just passing through." *I hope.*

When Colin turned to greet the man, the intruder's wide smile twitched for a minute and Colin could have sworn the tanned skin blanched one degree. Had the man mistaken him for Kurt in that moment? With his crisp white shirt, pressed brown pants and freshly steamed Stetson, the man looked like a magazine ad, and Colin took an instant dislike to him.

"Good, good." The man turned to the bartender. "Give me a Carling. Thanks, Brett." As if regaining his composure before he resumed his conversation, he drank a long swallow from the glass. "Where are you from?"

"Here and there. Is there a problem?" Colin found it hard to choke down the irrational animosity he felt toward the stranger. The side of his jaw clicked from the tension of clenching his teeth.

"No, no, Schönberg's a friendly little town." The man's smile showed off a brilliant row of white teeth. Yet the flatness of the smile belied any of the pretended warmth. "I'm Billy Ackley, the mayor of this town, and I like to greet everyone who passes through." He extended a hand toward Colin.

Billy Ackley. The name rang a bell. Ah yes, the man Liesl mentioned who thought he was above the law. That smile and those golden good looks were familiar, too. How could that be possible? They'd never met.

"Pleased to meet you, Mayor Ackley," Colin said, extending a hand. When their hands touched, Billy's face swam before him, and Colin found himself staring at a younger version of the same face.

Oh, no. Not again! Colin fought the drowning images and lost.

"Come on, Willy, stop being such a baby. This is the shortest way."

"But we have to go through Grüber's woods," eleven-year-old Willy said, holding on to his fishing pole with both hands. "There's ghosts in there. Mama says there are. Ghosts of men hung for cattle rustling."

"They're just stories. I'm going." Kurt trotted off through the path carved between the post oaks, thorny mesquites, and saw-toothed vines crawling over both, his own fishing pole held forward like a jousting knight's lance.

"Hey, wait for me!"

Kurt slowed his pace and waited for Willy to catch up. They walked deeper into the woods. The moon slipped beneath a cloud, darkening their path, but Kurt knew the way.

"Are you sure you know where you're going?"

"What's the matter, Willy, scared like a girl?"

"Am not." Willy brandished his pole about like

a sword. "One day I'm going to be stronger than you."

"Oh, yeah?" Kurt chuckled, two years older and twenty pounds heavier. The prospect of little Willy Acker with his pretty golden hair, freckled nose, and ratty clothes whipping him in a fight didn't seem too likely.

"Yeah, and you'll be sorry you ever laughed at me."

Suddenly a terrible thrashing came up from ahead. The earth shook beneath their feet. Branches cracked. Leaves protested.

"What's that?" Willy asked in a hushed whisper, drawing closer.

"Don't know. Maybe it's a ghost!" Kurt laughed and kept walking boldly forward. He knew what it was. Had heard it dozens of times as he'd cut across Grüber's farm to reach town and Liesl's house. It had scared even him when he'd heard it the first time. But he'd let Willy suffer. Scaring him was so easy and so much fun.

The thrashing noises got louder, closer, more ominous like the stampede of a chariot escaping Hades. Kurt counted silently, then without warning shoved Willy into the prickly brush. A second later, a cloud of dust exploded in front of them and Grüber's gray mare pounded down the path, spraying them with dirt and lashing them with her waving tail. She looked like a white ghost in the dark night. After feeding time, she always headed hell-bent for the pond where they'd been fishing.

Willy screamed. Kurt laughed.

"I'll get you, Kurt Castell! You mark my words, one day I'll get you."

As he released his grip on Billy's hand, Colin shook his head to clear the intrusive memory. One that couldn't be his, yet had seemed so real.

He had no control over these netherworld invasions. What did they mean? Were they real or part of this nightmare he'd trapped himself into? Was it possible to share someone else's memory? He'd learned to accept stranger things over the past few days. Time travel wasn't possible, yet here he was. Why not memories?

"What brings you to our fair town?" Billy asked, settling more comfortably on the stool next to Colin's.

"Just passing through." Colin took a sip from his beer. His fingers shook against the glass's sweating sides.

His gaze fixed on a poster above Billy's shoulders. Two men leaned on a bar with mugs of beer between them. The artist had drawn the bottles behind the bar with faces. "Be careful what you say and where you say it!" one man whispered to the other. Big letters across the bottom spelled out the warning "Careless Talk Costs Lives."

"There's a rumor goin' around you're a pilot," Billy continued.

A stranger in a small town like Schönberg would attract attention, and draw this unwanted conclusion, given that Billy had made it next to impossible for Liesl to hire a pilot. Billy had to eliminate the possibility that she might actually have found one despite his interference.

"What if I were?" Colin said. Had little Willy grown up and become the dangerous man he'd promised? Liesl seemed to think so.

"Well, then, being such an aviation aficionado, I'd be curious and ask who's your lucky employer?"

"And I'd have to say I'm self-employed." Despite his easy, friendly manner, Colin didn't trust Billy. His vision had shown him that little Willy had much to be angry about, and angry boys often grew up to be angrier men.

"Is that so? What kind of flyin' do you do, Mr. . . . I'm sorry, I didn't catch your name."

"Castle. Colin Castle. I fly whatever I can get my hands on."

"Is that so? Do you race?"

Oil-slick and brandy-smooth, Billy's voice had Colin wondering where the man was headed. "Sometimes."

"If you're lookin' for work, I've got somethin' that might tempt you."

"What's that?"

The glint in the man's eyes told Colin that Billy sensed impending victory. "A Mustang I've just acquired and been thinkin' of racin' in the Trinity Trophy. It's stripped and powered for speed, and hotter than hell."

"Um." Colin pretended disinterest, waiting for Billy to get to the point.

"I'll pay you a good salary and give you a cut of the winnings besides."

"Why me? For all you know I might not know

the difference between a wartime Mustang and an old gray mare." Colin couldn't resist the hidden jab.

The corner of Billy's mouth twitched. "Now, I very much doubt that."

Colin returned his attention to his glass. He didn't have time for politics. He just wanted to get back home with as little fanfare as possible. Whatever war Liesl and Billy had going, they would have to settle on their own. "Not interested."

"Somebody give you a better offer?" The smile stayed in place, but a note of antagonism crept into Billy's voice.

"Nope."

Billy downed the rest of his beer and signaled for another. "Well"—he cleared his throat—"I feel I ought to warn you about somethin'. You know, man to man."

"What might that be?"

"There's a woman by the name of Liesl Erhardt." Billy tipped the front edge of his Stetson down, shading his eyes, and crossed his ankles as he leaned back against the counter. "She's lookin' for a pilot. Seein' as you're not interested in flying in this race, this won't matter, but I just feel I ought to warn you about her just the same."

Billy leaned his head to one side and shook it as if he were talking indulgently about a child or an aging aunt. He chuckled. "Now, don't get me wrong. She's a purty little thing, but she lost her fella in the war, and she's been a bit touched since then. She's been goin' around botherin' people, askin' them to fly for her, makin' promises she can't keep. She hasn't got any money or a prayer of winnin'."

"Why not?"

Billy leaned forward and shielded his mouth with a hand. "It's an experimental airplane. Never been in the air before."

"Sounds like a challenge."

Billy's eyes hardened and his shoulders rose as he straightened on his stool. The bright smile faded to a stiff crease on one side of his mouth. "I think it would be best for everyone concerned if you just left town." Not a drop of brandy left in his hard voice.

"Um." Colin drained the last of his beer. "I don't take too kindly to threats, Mr. Ackley."

"What'll it take?" Dead serious now. The smile vanished from Billy's face.

Colin twirled his empty glass on the polished wood. *Swish swish. Swish swish.* If Billy had as much influence as Liesl feared, here was his chance to get back home sooner.

"A set of Curtiss three-blade constant speed propellers," Colin joked, then realized he meant it. Finding his way back to Jakob's window in time and getting home got top billing on his list of current goals. A pang of guilt somersaulted in his stomach, but he ignored it. Liesl would survive.

"It can be arranged." Relief spread over Billy's tense features and the smile returned.

"Next week'll be too late." Colin pushed his glass away. "I've already got a set promised to me straight after the race."

"I wouldn't chance it, Mr. Castle. It's a small town and word travels fast. These are peaceful people, but when one of their own is threatened, well. . . ." Billy shook his head for emphasis. "Even her daddy wants her to be left stranded without a pilot on Saturday. He wants her to quit all this nonsense. You can understand that, now can't you, Mr. Castle? A father's love for his little girl?"

Colin swiveled on his stool to face Billy. "Sure. I can also tell a con when I hear one. What's in it for you, Mr. Ackley?"

He felt her then. Her eyes trained on him, staring at him, through him. Liesl's anger pummeled him as if she'd punched him. He looked at her through the open bar door, and her feeling of betrayal jabbed him like a heavyweight's uppercut. She'd gotten it all wrong. Colin slid off his stool and headed toward the door, irritation making his movement jerky.

"I'm warnin' you, Mr. Castle—"

Colin slowed his pace and glanced over his shoulder. Sitting there so regally on his stool, Billy made a perfect target for his rising anger. "Are you still afraid of ghosts, *Willy?*"

Well, he'd done it now. He had the whole bar staring at him and whispering. So much for anonymity. He hoped for Liesl's sake that their interest would fade quickly. No mistaking Billy's reaction, either. Payback was written all over his red mottled skin and narrowed gaze.

Liesl heard footsteps behind her and hurried her pace.

"Liesl!"

She ignored Colin's call. When he trotted up to her and touched her arm, she recoiled automatically. She breathed in the damp night air, filling her lungs with the cold to keep the pain of betrayal from stinging. She'd believed him.

Wanting to take the shortest way home from the cemetery and the icy chill permeating the air, she'd decided to cut across the Anglo side of town.

Suddenly she'd walked through a wall of static. She'd tried to ignore the pull, but couldn't. As if an invisible hand guided her, she stopped, turned, and looked inside the Saddle and Spur. The shock of seeing Colin inside hurt more than she could have thought possible.

He'd said he'd help her, fly for her, win for her. She'd trusted him, and he'd betrayed her. Why hadn't she trusted her instincts? Hadn't she suspected all along that he was one of Billy's peons? This was all a game to him. A sick, cruel game.

To her it was life itself.

"It's not what you think," Colin said, his breath rasping in and out loudly at her side, making him impossible to ignore.

"I'm not thinking anything," she lied, wrapping the edges of her sweater tighter around her. Cold and numb, she pressed her pace. She didn't want to think. Maybe if she walked fast enough, it would take days for her thoughts to catch up with her.

"Listen to me!"

She brought her hands up to her ears, forging ahead. "I understand."

"Listen to me!"

Colin grabbed her hands and pried them away from her ears. "I'm sorry." Now that he had her attention, he seemed at a sudden loss for words. "I'm sorry I left the hangar after you told me not to. After . . . I couldn't stay there. I needed to get away. I . . ."

Her hands in his tingled with awareness, reminding her of how he'd lit her body on fire hours earlier, and anger flared from those embers, consuming her. She snapped her hands from his and walked away, the soles of her feet hurting through her shoes from the force of her steps.

"You must think I'm stupid." She shook inside from the fury of her own foolishness. "How long did you think you could string me along before I figured out you worked for Billy?"

"I don't work for Billy. I don't work for anybody."

The anger in his voice fueled hers to rage proportions. Her breaths came faster. Her stomach stormed. Her fists balled. "Then how did you know about—" Unconsciously, a hand went to her breast. "About the scar? How did you know about the song?"

Colin kept pace with her. His arm brushed hers accidentally. She moved one step sideways. He didn't follow.

"Why are you so willing to dismiss me like that?" he asked.

"Why? *Why?*" Her arms waved about wildly.

"Because I know Billy. I know his power. I know what his money can buy." What it had already bought. "I was raised to believe a man's word was sacred. What happened to yours?"

"Why can't you trust me?"

She laughed a bitter laugh and felt its acid trickle all the way to her belly. "Because I just saw you sitting nice and cozy in a saloon with Billy Ackley." She stopped and faced Colin. "I wanted to trust you. I wanted to believe in you."

Colin shook his head. "You've never trusted me. And no matter what I say or do, you'll go on believing the worst. That's easier for you to swallow than the truth, isn't it?"

His voice was soft. His warm finger touched her cheek and hooked a loose strand of hair behind her ear. Her heart twisted, aching.

"What do you know about the truth? Making plans with Billy. You never had any intention of winning the race." Crossing her arms under her chest, Liesl walked away from Colin.

"You've made up your mind about me and you haven't even heard my side of the story," Colin said, striding in step with her.

"Why should I listen to lies?"

"Because maybe, just maybe, you'd hear the truth."

She stopped abruptly, and Colin had to turn to face her again. Their gazes met. His eyes were honest and open; she saw no attempt at deceit, but then, she couldn't seem to trust her instincts lately. Her anger flickered and faded.

He was right. She wasn't being fair. But why should she? When had the world been fair to her? She'd played by the rules, and had her life snatched away from her. She'd counted on him, and found him talking with Billy. She needed him in ways she didn't want to examine, and couldn't examine if she was to win the race.

If she couldn't trust him, she'd lose her only chance at her dream. If she trusted him, she might lose anyway. When had everything gotten so complicated?

"What were you doing in the Saddle and Spur?" She raised her chin and straightened her spine, dropping her arms by her sides.

"I was having a beer." Colin stuffed his hands in the back pockets of his Levi's. "Then Billy showed up and started asking me all sorts of questions."

"And?"

"And I answered them. Questions about me, Liesl, not questions about whatever scheme you think I'm cooking up with him. Although he did warn me about you."

His smile teased her. She took the bait. "What did he say?"

"He said you were a little touched."

"Touched! Umph! He thinks any female who doesn't swoon at the sight of him is touched. If he thinks I'm touched now, he hasn't seen anything yet." She paused for a moment. "I'm going to find a way to win—with or without you."

Colin reached for her shoulders. "He offered me a set of propellers, Liesl."

Her breath stuck in her throat. Her heart stopped beating. A sinking feeling plummeted through her. She closed her eyes so she wouldn't have to read his eyes. He was right; she didn't want to know the truth. The truth hurt too much. He was going to leave, and she'd be left alone once again. Without him, without her dream, without anything at all. But could she blame him? In his place, she would move heaven and earth to find her way back home.

"I think you should take it," she finally said, opening her eyes.

"I . . ." Colin scraped a hand through his hair. The moonlight accentuated the lines of anxiety wrinkling his forehead. "I've been waiting to prove to my father that I'm not a loser since I was seven years old."

"I understand." Hadn't she tried to make up her mother's loss to her father for most of her life? "The race is my dream, not yours. You've got your own dream to follow. I'll manage without you." Pure ice flowed through her veins. As she dragged herself forward, her feet shuffled along like lead. "I can't make you the same offer."

His hand settled on her arm, stopping her. She looked at the fingers curled on the blue wool of her sweater, liking their feel, their look. With a finger of his free hand he hooked her chin and looked deep into her eyes. For a moment she saw nothing of Kurt in Colin's hazel eyes, only the look of a lost man, fighting an inner battle only he could understand, and she knew she wanted him to find his way home.

"You've got a lot to offer the world, Liesl," Colin whispered, his gritty voice rasping over her gently, softly. "I'll stay. I'll fly for you."

"I can't make you stay."

"You can't make me go. I'll keep my promise."

Liesl had no tears left for the joy spilling through her, no words left to express the emotions filling her. She left him standing alone in the dark as she made her way back home. In one breath she thanked the heavens she wouldn't have to give him up just yet. In the next, she sent up an apology for her infidelity.

Alone in the dark, Billy paced the confines of his office.

Where had this stranger come from? Billy had recognized him even before the man had shown him his face. He'd recognized the antagonistic tension he'd always felt in his friend's presence. The different name didn't fool him. After all, he himself had changed his name to escape the past. Why wouldn't Kurt, after all the trouble he'd caused?

But how had Kurt managed the flesh and bones? The ghosts Billy usually saw were ephemeral.

Billy stopped in his tracks and thoughtfully tapped his front teeth with a finger. Why had he come back now? Because of Liesl? Because of the airport? It would be just like him to try and spoil his success.

Jakob's guilt and shame had turned him into a ready puppet. He hadn't had the courage to show his face in this town and swear to his friend's innocence. Every man had his price. Jakob's had been traveling expenses and a job. Kurt had stated his as being a pair of propellers.

But Kurt couldn't be trusted even to stay dead. It would take something more. Something stronger.

Billy had beaten back all the ghosts, the hapless thieves of his childhood, his father. Kurt would be no different. And this time, he would know what it felt like to be squashed by power. Billy had the perfect medium to cleanse away this condemned specter.

He spun on his heels and headed for the telephone. "Jenkins, I've got a job for you."

Sunday

Colin struggled with a particularly stubborn bolt, holding a mangled propeller blade in place.

"Need any help?"

Disappointed that it wasn't Liesl standing there, Colin looked up at Max's lanky frame leaning against the hangar door, a cigarette dangling from his lips. "Sure. Hold this."

Max crushed the cigarette beneath his boot and entered the hangar. Colin handed Max the wrench holding the bolt head and put all his weight behind the wrench holding the nut.

"How old are you, Max?"

"Seventeen." He straightened and puffed out his chest.

"Hasn't anyone ever told you smoking's bad for you?"

"All the hot flyers smoke."

The nut creaked as it moved. Encouraged, Colin redoubled his effort.

131

"The smart ones don't. Not only does smoking ruin your lungs, it interferes with your ability to fly. You want to fly, don't you?"

"Sure." In Max's eager nod and shining eyes, Colin recognized the signs of a love affair with flight. "As soon as Liesl starts her center, I'm going to be the first student."

"Not if you keep smoking." Colin grunted with effort. The nut moved again, and turned more easily with each crank of the wrench. "It clouds your brains, slows your reflexes, and the effects of altitude start affecting you a lot lower."

"You're joking, right?"

"I'm dead serious." Colin finger-turned the nut the rest of the way off. "Cigarettes are why my father's tied to a dozen tubes, dying in a hospital."

"How old is he?" Max removed the wrench and the bolt while Colin held the cuff and the blade. Colin carefully placed the parts on a piece of canvas on the ground.

"Fifty-six."

"He's old." Max leaned back against the cowling and took the pack of Lucky Strikes from his pocket.

"He had to quit flying in his thirties and take a desk job. Have you ever been up in an airplane?"

"Kurt took me up a few times," Max said, glancing fondly at the two yellow Piper Cubs in the corner.

"Then you understand that to a pilot, being grounded is the worst thing that can happen."

Max stared down at the pack of cigarettes in

his hand. With a rapid rise of both eyebrows, he stuffed the pack in his jacket pocket. "Liesl sent you some breakfast."

"Afraid to come down herself?" The angry jab came out before Colin could restrain it. That wasn't fair. He'd been the one to act out of turn, not her. After he'd betrayed her confidence, she'd generously offered to let him back out of their agreement even though it would certainly cost her the race.

Colin wiped the grease from his hands with more vigor than necessary. Then he remembered Jakob's words, *First she lost Kurt. Then she lost his dream.* He'd felt guilty—as if he'd let her down a second time. For reasons he didn't quite understand, he felt loath to disappoint her. If he timed things right, he could race for her and still find his way home.

"Why would she be afraid of you?" Max asked. "You're gonna make her dream come true. She's got to help her grandmother get ready for the picnic after church. She hates those things, but her father's making her go. He wants her to get married again. He thinks if she does, she'll forget Kurt and be happy. But he doesn't understand."

"Maybe he thinks he's doing what's best for her. Maybe if she explained how she felt." He was a great one to give advice. His own relationship with his father was past strained and barely hanging on by a thin thread. Putting his frustration into his work, Colin removed the second blade from the propeller hub.

"You don't explain anything to Uncle Jürgen.

He's right about one thing though. Liesl's not the same since Kurt died."

"Maybe she misses him." Colin carefully laid the parts on the canvas, trying to keep Karen from edging into his mind.

"Yeah, but she's making herself sick with it. If the Castell doesn't win, I'm afraid it'll kill her. Getting this plane ready for the air show has been all that's kept her from giving up living." Max shook his head as he handed Colin a second wrench to remove the third blade. "You should've seen her after the funeral. She let herself go to nothing. She was like a zombie until Billy Ackley tried to take her airport away from her. Then she started living again—part of her anyway. I wish she could be like she was before . . ."

"You like her a lot."

"Yeah, she's like a sister."

Colin's own feelings for Liesl were as far removed from sisterly as possible. Every time he looked at her, he didn't see the sad mask she wore. He saw her smile for him, saw her mold herself to him. He yearned to breathe in her gardenia-scented hair, to taste the heady sweetness of her skin, to lose himself in loving her in the most elemental way.

When he thought of Liesl, he forgot about home.

Lust, pure and simple, and dangerous as hell.

If he didn't find his window home in the next week, he'd be stuck here forever. Would he grow to resent her distraction? Would he grow to hate her for keeping him a failure? Could she agree to follow him to the future? No, that was as crazy as him staying. She had her own dreams to follow, her own goals to reach. He couldn't let himself get sidetracked by the feelings of tenderness she stirred. He needed to ground himself. He needed to fly.

"Are the J-3s operational?" Colin asked.

"We start them once a week. Liesl lets me taxi them on the runway. It drives me crazy. I just want to push that throttle full open and take off."

As Max spoke, he mimicked the actions, and Colin's blood revved in anticipation. He needed the sky to make him forget this woman on earth.

"How about if we take one up for a spin?" Colin asked, wiping his hands clean on a rag.

Max's eyes rounded in open anticipation. "You mean it?"

"Got to keep my flying skills sharp."

Max helped Colin push one of the fabric-covered J-3s onto the apron, then proceeded to jump into the front seat.

"Hey, what about your walkaround?" Colin called to Max.

"Walkaround?" Max cocked his head and gave Colin a questioning look.

"You've got to make sure the equipment's safe before you take off. When you're in the air isn't the time to find out you've got a clogged pitot tube or a stuck aileron." *Or a little black button that'll jolt you out of your time.*

"Man, you're as bad as Liesl," Max said, dragging himself out of the airplane.

"What do you mean?" Colin leaned inside the cabin and checked the ignition switch in the "off" position, the fuel valve in the "on" position.

"Everything's got to be perfect with her."

Colin walked around the airplane checking the condition of the skin, the rudder and elevator's freedom of movement, the condition of the hinges and retaining pins. "Nothing wrong with perfection."

"Yeah, but she tends to go a little overboard with it sometimes, if you know what I mean."

"There's a saying that goes, 'There are old pilots. There are bold pilots. But there are no old bold pilots.' Safety starts on the ground, son." He finished checking the stabilizers, then let his gaze drift to the clear, blue sky above him. "The sky's a tough mistress. To play even, you've got to act smart. And that means making sure you and your equipment are in top shape."

Colin completed his walkaround, explaining to Max what he was looking for as he went along, then eased his body into the J-3's cramped cabin. Going through his mental checklist, he started the engine.

It was good to feel the power rumble through his hands, to feel himself coming alive again, to feel the call of the sky. Maybe up there he could forget for a little while the nightmare he faced on the ground.

Liesl left the church service early to finish the preparations for the picnic. A long table was laid out behind their home between the two freshly hoed gardens. One of her grandmother's lace tablecloths graced the battered wood table-top. Piles of utensils, plates and cups already sat, weighing down the cloth against the stiff wind. One by one, Liesl brought out the platters of food her grandmother had spent a week preparing, and the ones other family members had dropped off before heading to the service.

Though she couldn't see the airport from where she stood, Liesl's gaze kept wandering in that direction. She wanted to ignore Colin and his invasion of her mind, but even a night of jagged sleep had done nothing to resolve her mixed feelings toward Colin or her attraction to him.

If she didn't keep a diligent guard on her thoughts, he crept in, then took over. And when she thought of him, she couldn't keep longing from storming her body. She hated him for that. Hated the way he brought back the loneliness she thought she'd accepted. Hated the way he filled the airport with life and made her miss Kurt with such desperate desolation.

And she detested the way her mind could easily accept him as Kurt. Rationalization, she knew, but soothing to the soul to think he might have come back to her. Was the feat so impossible? What did anyone truly know about death?

Liesl sank into a chair and placed a hand over her heart. It felt so empty, so dark, so dead. Tears tightened her chest. Every time she looked at Colin, she wanted to pretend he was Kurt, to fill herself with his life, to drown in his strength. She wanted to forget. But every look reminded her of her loss, every touch of her emptiness, every kiss of her helpless hunger. He was so much like him, it was hard to believe he wasn't.

Shaking her head, Liesl stood and dragged chairs from the kitchen to the yard. She couldn't give in to her craving. She couldn't yield to satisfy her hunger. If she did, she'd betray her memory of Kurt, she'd betray their love, she'd betray their vows. She couldn't allow that to happen. She'd already let too many people down.

"Zey are coming," *Oma* announced as she rushed past Liesl into the house. "Is everyzing ready?"

"Almost. *Onkel* Aldo will stop to get beer from his brewery. And here comes *Tante* Wenona."

"Have you seen Max?" Wenona asked after exchanging greetings.

Liesl glanced into the house and, seeing her grandmother disappear up the stairs, she said, "He went to bring Colin some breakfast. I told him to come right back."

"How is Colin's head?"

A low buzzing sound interrupted their conversation. Shading her eyes with a hand, Liesl looked up into the sky to see one of her Cubs zipping through the air. She gasped. "No!"

"Is that Colin?"

"Who else?"

She unknotted her apron and threw it down. Wenona's hand gently covered hers. "Time is a precious gift, Liesl. Don't squander it with your stubbornness."

"He doesn't listen. He doesn't care."

"And you, do you listen?"

Listen to what? The logic in her head? The impossibility offered by her heart? Liesl didn't have time for her aunt's troubling questions, she had a race to win and a pilot to keep under wraps.

"I listen too much," she said as she stomped away.

"Liesl!" *Oma* said as she stepped out carrying a plate full of *Kartofellpuffer*. "Vere is zat child going?"

"Don't worry, Ulla. I'll help you," Wenona said.

"Liesl, your father vill be here soon."

"I'll be right back," Liesl called over her shoulder. *As soon as I give a certain someone a piece of my mind.* Flying over the town was not the way to remain inconspicuous. Hadn't Colin learned anything from his outing last night?

She held her breath while she skirted Billy's rail yard building, and groaned when she heard the front door open. She didn't have time for a word duel with Billy this morning. But it wasn't Billy that emerged, just his right-hand rat.

Sam Jenkins tipped his tan Stetson in greeting. Despite the cool morning breeze, his face shone with perspiration. "Mornin', Miz Erhardt."

"Mr. Jenkins."

Liesl nodded in return, then rushed past him onto the dirt road leading to the airport, not giving him a chance to retain her. She swung the gate open, and didn't bother to secure it behind her.

As Liesl hurried down the hill, Colin brought the yellow plane around into the traffic pattern. It shone in the sun, its shadow racing ahead, then falling behind with each different turn. With a precision that impressed her, he turned for his final approach, crabbing against the wind.

Watching the airplane glide with such beauty, Liesl felt a pang of . . . what? Jealousy? She shook her head trying to dismiss the thought, but found she couldn't. She wanted to be the one in that airplane with Colin. She wanted to feel the power and the joy that Kurt had never dared to share with her. He'd shared everything with her but the sky which held his soul. After all the loss he'd suffered, he couldn't bring himself this final intimacy. Just as her own fears had kept her from telling him how much she loved him. *Tomorrow*, he'd always promised. *Tomorrow*, she'd silently vowed. But tomorrow had been stolen from them.

Hearing the sigh of rubber on grass as the airplane touched down for a picture-perfect landing, and Max's joyful laughter above the roar of the engine, and smelling the gasoline mixed with the wild flower-scented breeze amplified the riot of feelings boiling inside her.

While the airplane taxied, Liesl walked onto the field to meet it. Something out of the corner of her eye caught her attention. She focused on the moving shadow as she turned to look, and stopped dead in her tracks. Her heart lurched, then raced in time to the beat of her feet rushing toward the hangar. "Oh, no!"

Her dream was in there, her future. And thick black smoke curled around the open hangar doors.

Chapter Six

Liesl raced toward the hangar. "No!"

Her dream was going up in smoke. She had to stop the fire.

As she drew nearer, intense heat assaulted her. Hot, acrid air filled her lungs. She coughed, placed a hand over her mouth, and kept going. When she crossed the threshold, thick smoke enveloped her. Coughing, with hands splayed before her, she tried to find the fire's origin through the blinding smoke.

Nothing, she could see nothing. Where was the fire?

"Get help," she heard Colin call to Max behind her, then solid arms jerked her back and propelled her outside.

"Stay out!" Colin ordered, and rushed past her to the hose on the side of the building. He flung down his leather jacket, took off his T-shirt, wet it, and wrapped it around his nose and mouth. Dragging the hose, he disappeared into the smoke.

Bent over double, Liesl wheezed fresh air through her irritated lungs. The Castell, she had to save the Castell. Without it, there would be no race. Without the race, there would be no future. Still breathing hard, she staggered back toward the hangar.

Held back by the heat, Liesl saw Colin crouching low, sweeping the fire's edge with the stream of water from the hose like a ghost in a murky nightmare. Suddenly the water seemed to ignite around him.

"Colin!" Liesl yelled. She stepped in. Nausea dizzied her, pushing her back.

"Stay out!"

Colin retreated, throwing the hose out before him, sending a stream of cold water down her Sunday dress. He looked around him frantically. He grabbed the shovel lying near the hose outlet, took up a shovelful of dirt, then disappeared inside once more. Liesl hurried behind him to help, but the smoke watered her eyes and started a new wave of coughing spasms.

The flames taunted him, rising and falling like snakes in the foggy darkness. With total disregard for his own well-being, Colin valiantly fought the flames alone. Feeling helpless, Liesl could do nothing but watch while panicked fear ran rampant inside her.

With a final shovelful of dirt, he knocked the

fire down. Only a few forked tongues of glowing red remained.

Colin moved in on the dying fire. Shaking out dirt from the shovel at the blackened mass at his feet, he pulled apart the pile of rags on the floor with his booted foot. He turned them over and over, covering them with fresh earth until the last ember died and the smoke started to recede. He pushed the mess outside and piled more dirt on the bits of charred rags until no hot spots remained to smolder up again.

His chest glistened with perspiration. His Levi's clung limply to his body. His hair hung in wet strands, plastered against his head. Even with the black ashes, carved with runs of sweat covering his forehead, he looked good.

And he brimmed with life.

Not until that moment did Liesl realize how great a risk Colin had taken to save the airplanes. He removed the T-shirt from around his nose and mouth and mopped the sooty mess from his face. His labored breathing matched her own.

He could have died! As if a fist had slammed into her, she gasped. *He could have died, and she could have done nothing except watch helplessly.*

A trickle of blood ran from his stitched forehead.

"You're hurt," Liesl said, her voice hoarse. She took a handkerchief from her dress pocket and applied pressure to the wound. As she held the white linen square in place, her fingers shook. The stress of the fire, she argued with herself, not guilt, not Colin. "Are you feeling all right?"

"I'm fine." Colin tried to push her hand away, but she wouldn't let him. For saving the Castell, the least she could do was care for his wound. It would ease her conscience. What else could she do? What else could she say?

"The airplanes?" she asked, groaning inwardly. How trivial a concern after he'd risked his life! She couldn't make more of a fool of herself if she tried.

"The fire didn't reach them. We'll have to wait till the smoke clears to be sure."

She lifted the handkerchief and nodded awkwardly. The flow of blood had stopped. She'd ask Wenona to look at the stitches just in case.

Her apprehension about Colin's motives had been wrong. If she spent all her energy from now until the race worrying about Colin and his trustworthiness, she'd have no energy left to tune the Castell to perfection. At one point she'd have to take a leap of faith, as *Oma* was so fond of saying, and trust him.

The deep breath she took hurt. The time was now. He'd promised to help her, and she would have to accept his word as honorable.

He'd taken a big risk for her, yet the thank you she meant to offer stuck in her throat.

"You could have gotten yourself killed." Liesl folded the stained handkerchief and stuffed it in her pocket. She swallowed, lubricating her raw throat.

"My ticket home is in there." He coughed and bent over the running hose, taking a deep drink, then washed his face in the cool water.

Yes, of course. Why had she thought he'd done it for her? Just because in a moment of weakness last night she'd had this crazy notion that part of Kurt resided in his body? Just because she found herself melting under his touch? Just because losing him in a week would hurt as she'd known it would ever since he crash-landed on her runway? He wasn't Kurt. She'd better get her emotions under control and her thoughts straightened out in a hurry before she made a complete fool of herself.

"Your ticket home, and my ticket to the future," she said. "Thank you for saving them both."

"Yeah, both." The cold distance in his voice and the scowl on his face gave her the distinct impression she'd hurt his feelings.

Before she could analyze his reaction further, Liesl heard the clang of the fire truck's bell and turned in time to see it crest the hill. Max pedaled madly down the road behind it.

The fire chief and his volunteer crew examined the site and declared the fire beaten.

"Be more careful where you put your cigarette next time, son," the chief said, looking straight at Colin. A personal friend of Billy's, Chief Gardner didn't bother to hide his dislike for Colin.

"I don't smoke. Never have. Never will." Colin stared back, challenging.

Cigarette! Liesl's head jerked sideways, seeking Max. His gaze was directed at the ground, watching the toe of his boot dig into the dirt.

She bit her tongue to silence it.

"Well, someone did," the chief said, shaking his grizzled head. "The whole hangar could have gone up in smoke, if you hadn't acted so fast to put it out. Trouble is, it should never have happened in the first place. Cigarettes and oily rags don't mix. You were lucky. You might not be as lucky next time."

The fire truck climbed the hill and left. Hands on hips, Liesl spun to face Max. "How many times have I told you not to smoke in the hangar?"

"I didn't."

"Then explain to me how one of your cigarettes found its way to a pile of rags!"

Like a hurt puppy, Max's features sagged. "I didn't smoke in the hangar. Tell her, Colin. I gave up smoking this morning."

"That's right." Colin walked over to his jacket and extricated Max's Lucky Strikes from his pocket. "We made a deal at fifteen hundred feet. He got his first flying lesson today in exchange for the pack." Colin threw the pack in Liesl's direction and she caught it swiftly.

"Don't you know I'd never do anything that would hurt the airplanes?" Max asked, his face twisting with indignation. "After all the time I've spent helping you, don't you know that?"

"Max . . ." Liesl started, filled with guilt once again. She couldn't seem to do anything right today.

Max ran to his bicycle and pedaled off.

"Max!" Liesl followed for a few paces, then lagged.

"Let him go," Colin said. "He'll be back." He walked over to the pile of dirt and bits of burnt rags. "It wasn't Max who started that fire. He didn't light up inside today. There were no rags on the floor when we left, either. I don't think it was an accident, Liesl. I think someone deliberately set fire to your hangar."

Liesl gasped in shock. "Who would do such a thing?"

But she already knew the answer. If Colin had told the truth and didn't side with Billy, he'd been branded as an enemy to be conquered by their esteemed mayor. If Billy couldn't buy Colin, he'd find another way to keep him from flying. The race was too close; the stakes were too high. There was no time left to play mind games.

Which left only action. Violence, she corrected.

Her mind took her back two years, and she shivered involuntarily.

What would be Billy's next move? Was she in danger? Was Colin? How far would Billy go to win?

"From my talk with the mayor last night," Colin said, "I'd say he's a prime suspect. What is it between the two of you?"

"It's not me." Looking at the flat strip of mowed grass in the gently rolling fields, Liesl sighed. "It's the land. He wants it; I won't sell."

"How much is the land worth to you?" Colin asked. His voice, low and gritty and so close to her ear, shivered down her skin.

"My life," Liesl said breathily, turning to face him.

Colin's intense gaze made her edgy. She twisted her hands behind her and shifted her weight from one leg to the other. "Do you think we can go in and see the damage?" she asked to break the tension of his stare.

"Let me get the ladder and open up the windows first."

As they rounded the corner of the hangar to reach the side windows, they heard an angry screeching from the ground. Trying to take off with one wing cocked at an odd angle, the sparrow flailed and warned them away.

Liesl rushed to help the injured bird. It pecked at her hands. "She's got a broken wing."

"She probably hurt it trying to protect her eggs. I see a nest in a branch near the window."

Colin set the ladder securely, then disappeared, coming back moments later carrying a bucket. "I'll put the nest in here, then we'll put the mother in and take her to a vet."

"*Tante* Wenona will know what to do. I want her to look at your stitches at the same time."

"I'm fine."

"She'll decide."

Liesl wrapped the mother bird in a towel and settled her in the bucket in her nest with her eggs. Colin opened the three small windows on the side of the hangar. The smoke soon dissipated. The smoke's stench, on the other hand, still permeated the air, and Liesl found it hard to breathe. Colin got her a wet cloth to keep over her mouth and nose.

The remaining Cub's skin had blistered in the heat, but the Castell and the CastleAir had sustained no visible injury.

Out in the fresh air once more, Liesl removed the cloth from her face. "You can't stay in there. You'll poison yourself with the smoke."

"Can't leave the airport unattended either."

Liesl sighed. Colin was right. But Colin also needed to have his forehead doctored, and after his heroic efforts to save the airplanes, he deserved a bath and a hot meal. "We'll lock the doors and come back later. I don't think Billy will try anything more until this incident's hush dies down. I'm taking you home."

Between the slats of his office window blinds, Billy watched the smoke die. When he snapped his hand away, the slats clanged together before bouncing back into place. Damn! The fire hadn't burned long enough to cause any real damage. Soot washed away easily.

Billy strode to his corner cabinet and poured himself a healthy dose of brandy. He downed half the drink in one swallow. Glass in hand, he paced the length of his office.

Kurt had always been lucky. How many times had Billy been blamed for Kurt's wrongdoings? How many times had Liesl stared at him with disgust when Kurt had been the one to put a frog in her lunch bucket or tie her braids to her chair? But Billy had learned. Kurt's smile had let him get away with much too much. One flash and he'd be forgiven. So Billy had practiced in front of his mother's black-veined mirror. He'd practiced until he'd outmastered the teacher. Kurt's dead body in a casket had shown Billy that his power was greater than his teacher's.

Now, the teacher's ghost had come back, luckier than ever. Billy would have to pull out all the stops to prove he was better than him.

He gulped the last of the brandy and threw the glass across the room. It crashed against the door, falling in a soft tinkle to the carpet.

Willy might have been a fool, but the same couldn't be said about Billy. He wasn't beaten. Not by a long shot. Soon Liesl would come begging to him. And soon he'd show them both how he'd mastered the game of power.

Outlined by a neat row of white picket fences, a dozen cottages stood rooted at even intervals on both sides of Main Street. Open gates and freshly swept walkways invited a visit. Glazed flower pots lounged empty on windowsills, but soon Colin imagined they would spill with color. His mother had had the same habit. In spring, purple pansies had decorated her windows, followed by red begonias in the summer. She'd fussed at the flowers, talking to them while she plucked finished blooms and watered the new buds. The same tender care she'd fostered on him.

On the corner, a pitiful patch of land seemed out of place. Weeds ran wild. Its weathered fence drooped and sagged in mournful pieces like the decayed grin he'd often seen on old homeless men in the city.

The strains of violins competed with the low umpah of a tuba, filling the air with the lively sounds of the strangest polka Colin had ever heard.

As they turned onto the treeless street where Liesl's father's store stood, laughter rose and dipped, a dog barked playfully, and children shrieked. When the tempting aroma of roasted meat and sweet desserts wafted their way, his stomach grumbled a complaint. Last night's cold sausage seemed an eternity away.

"Is there a party going on?" Colin asked.

"No," Liesl said. "Every Sunday after the church service, we get together for a community picnic. A different family is host every week. We eat, sing, laugh. In the afternoon, the men show off their shooting skills in Grüber's field, then they drink a keg of beer and brag about their efforts. The women gossip over coffee and cake. It keeps the community together. *Oma* calls it organized fun. *Gemütlichkeit.* Any excuse is good to get together, eat and drink. Doesn't your family have get-togethers?"

"No." Colin thought of all the lonely holidays he'd spent over the years. Packages left on placemats celebrated Christmases and birthdays. No bows, no ribbons, no cards—only unspoken wishes and an empty room. His father had worked twelve-hour days every day of his life until the cancer finally floored him—escaping, Colin had often thought, because of me.

Colin shook his head and jammed his hands into his jeans pocket. "I don't think I've ever heard a polka done on a violin before."

"That's *Onkel* Karl." Liesl chuckled and shook her head gently. Her hair caught a ray of sunshine and winked a sparkle despite the dusty film tarnishing the gold. He wanted to brush the soot away until her hair shone brightly again. "He'll play anything, any time. *Onkel* Aldo plays the tuba. He puts on quite a show. That's probably what everybody's laughing at. Usually *Tante* Irma joins them on the piano, but she hurt her hand tending the stock last week. Be thankful *Onkel* Wolf's accordion is broken. He has no sense of rhythm at all."

"Must be nice to have so much family around."

"Not always. They all like to interfere too much."

And he knew all about interference, didn't he? All about loneliness, too.

Liesl paused and looked down the side of the building. Colin leaned into her to catch a glimpse of the festivities, absorbing wisps of her sweet fragrance through the acrid scent of smoke. A dozen adults dressed in their Sunday best slapped their hands on their knees and laughed, watching Aldo's wild antics while he blew his tuba. A few couples polkaed into a cleared patch of grass. Children zipped and ran in the courtyard. A gaggle of teenage girls in bobby socks giggled by the lone pecan tree, and stared at a group of teenage boys busy pilfering from the food table.

Liesl shifted the bucket with the bird from one hand to the other and turned her head, bringing her lips close enough to kiss. Colin's

153

stomach tightened in response to the swift desire trampling through him. He swallowed and pushed himself back before he gave into the impulse.

"You'll have to be quiet," Liesl said, pushing awkwardly away from him. "My father can't see you here."

"Why not?"

"I'll get in trouble."

"Aren't you a little old for that?" Colin teased. He twirled a strand of loose hair around his index finger, giving in to his need to touch her, and watched her blush before she swatted his hand away.

"He's very strict. I'm living in his home. I must live by his rules."

Liesl grabbed his hand and shoved him into the house through a side entrance.

As a teenager, in a last-ditch effort to narrow the growing gulf between them, his father had taken him to Disney World. The interior of Liesl's house looked like something from the GE Theater of Progress—the early years. If he'd doubted the change in time before, he didn't now. A new-looking Wedgewood stove with its gleaming white enamel stood in prominence. A small refrigerator with a rounded top hummed noisily in the corner. A pantry door left ajar revealed familiar brand names dressed in unfamiliar labels—Arm & Hammer baking soda, Quaker Oats, Hershey's cocoa; and other brands he didn't recognize—Nunsig corn starch, Hoesum molasses, Lyons green label tea, as well as rows and rows of home-canned fruits and vegetables.

After settling the bird in the kitchen, Liesl led Colin to the staircase. His hand brushed against a tray on a small table at the foot of the stairs, starting an avalanche of tumbling glassware. He rushed to catch the falling tray.

Too late.

The black metal tray, painted with a bright design of fruits and flowers, clanged on the wooden floor. The glasses crashed around his grasping hands.

The music stopped abruptly.

"Leave it," Liesl said, grabbing at his shirt. "Come on. Go upstairs. Second door on the right. And don't come out until I come get you."

As Liesl directed Colin, a man came through the kitchen door. Tall, thin and dressed in black, he filled the doorway. His dour expression reminded him of Jakob's pained, somber face. The man glanced first at Liesl, then at the mess on the floor, then at Colin perched guiltily halfway up the stairs.

"What is the meaning of this, daughter?"

"Papa—"

"Who is this?" Hatred hissed between the sharp-spoken words.

As he advanced steadily, Liesl's father's gaze focused unwaveringly on Colin, taking in his dirty clothes and unkempt appearance. Colin probably looked anything but proper, but he didn't flinch. He stood up straighter, and stepped back down the stairs. He'd done nothing wrong.

"I'm—"

"By what right do you enter my home?" Liesl's father ignored Colin's proffered hand.

"Papa, I—"

Eyes wide and full of fear, Liesl tried to get between them, but they stood toe to toe. Liesl's father glared at Colin like a bull about to charge. What sin had he committed to warrant such anger?

"Listen," Colin said, "I don't know what I've done to offend you, but—"

"Go upstairs, daughter. Now!" The old man's cheeks rippled with suppressed rage.

"Papa, don't—"

"Go!"

"No, Papa. He's a friend."

As Colin watched Liesl fight for him, he took in her sooty dress, ripped stockings and muddy shoes, and understanding dawned on him. Had he been standing in her father's place, he'd have killed anyone who might have harmed his daughter, and asked questions later.

A group of curious relatives gathered in the kitchen, pushing and shoving for a good view of the unfolding scene. Whispered questions floated up. Once or twice, Colin heard the name Kurt mentioned.

"I'm her pilot," Colin said, trying to defuse the tension. "That's all."

"Pilot! What good are pilots? Gypsies with no sense of duty. Why do you prey on a vulnerable girl?"

"I'm not preying on anybody. She's the one

who begged me to fly for her. We made a fair deal."

"Beg! No child of mine has to beg for anything. And what does a biscuit like you know about fair? You look too soft to have ever done a fair day's work."

The crowd guffawed. Colin cringed. Past failures gnawed at him. *When are you going to give up your schemes, Colin, and come work an honest trade with me?*

"You tell him, Jürgen!"

"*Ja,* let him have it!"

"Papa—"

"I asked you to go upstairs, Liesl. Obey me!"

Liesl stood her ground, despite the fear visibly plaguing her. Colin almost smiled at the touch of spice beneath the cream.

"What do you consider a fair day's work?" Colin asked, crossing his arms over his chest.

"Providing for your family every day with honest sweat, not fly-by-night enterprises doomed to failure."

The old man had pushed the wrong button. Fingers hooked through belt loops, elbows splayed out, Colin crowded into the other man's space, taking in the deep lines bracketing Jürgen's mouth, the crow's feet by his eyes, the painful ripple across his forehead. "I'm no soft biscuit."

"There's gonna be a fight!" a girl squealed.

"Zere will be no fighting in my house," an old lady said, pushing her way to the crowd jammed at the door. She stood by Liesl and gathered her in her ample arms. "Jürgen—"

"You can't back down," launched an anonymous voice from the pack. "Challenge him, Jürgen."

"*Ja*, a work duel, like Hans and Josef last year," offered another. "I've got a fence that needs mending."

"I've got a field that needs to be plowed."

Laughter exploded around them. Offers of work to be done poured glibly from the crowd.

"Hey, there's that fallen tree in your yard that needs chopping, and you've got no son."

"Work makes life sweet, young man," Jürgen said, his dark expression unchanged. "Do you know how to swing an ax?"

Surrounded by the determined crowd, Colin felt at a distinct disadvantage. Liesl begged him silently to decline. The liquid blue of her eyes melted his insides, but he'd never backed down from a fight, and wouldn't now. Not even Jürgen's age and tired features could dissuade him. Without being told, he understood that this "duel" had nothing to do with work and everything to do with honor—and Liesl.

"I can do anything you can do." Colin leaned forward, leaving barely an inch of space between his face and Jürgen's. "Better."

"Quartered and stacked."

For an instant, Colin imagined he'd seen a slight crinkle of amusement in Jürgen's pale blue eyes, but he'd been wrong. They stared back at him cold and determined. Good thing they weren't dueling guns, because a stare like that could kill at less than ten paces.

The crowd piled into the hallway laughing

and hooting. Several people took Colin's arms, some pushed from behind. A twinge of panic twisted his gut. Bits of a disjointed picture fractured in his mind. He was at their mercy. The claustrophobic crush of the crowd pushed him outside into the open courtyard.

As the crowd buzzed around him, placing him into position by the chopping block, he looked for Liesl, but couldn't find her in the blur of people. Where had she gone? Two men set up a second chopping block while the rest of the men piled logs between the two blocks. Jürgen took off his jacket and shirt. The defined pecs and biceps surprised Colin. For a man who spent his day tending a general store, he had a lot of muscle to show for it. Colin followed suit and removed his leather jacket and stained T-shirt. The cool air raised goose bumps along his exposed skin.

"Aldo will give the signal," a rotund man said. He stood on a chair and held a wrinkled handkerchief in one hand.

Following Jürgen's lead, Colin placed a log upright on the block. He picked up his ax, tested its sharpness with his thumb, then balanced it in his hands, trying to get a feel for the foreign object.

The man on the chair lifted his hand high. At Aldo's loud tuba blurt, he dropped his arm.

As Jürgen raised his arms to swing the ax, the crowd cheered for Jürgen and jeered at Colin in a mixture of German and English.

Colin swung the ax. It landed beside the log, bringing a rowdy round of comments. His second attempt embedded the ax head halfway down the log. The crowd hooted. Frustrated, Colin jammed the log lodged on his ax down on the block, splitting it in half. Jürgen had already quartered three logs.

"Look at him. He's never done this before," said a voice from the crowd.

"He's a biscuit all right."

"I think he's kind of cute, don't you, Emma?"

Colin stopped his untrained action and watched Jürgen's smooth movements. He'd found a rhythm and let momentum carry him. No wasted effort in the old man's manners. A glimmer of admiration penetrated Colin's frustration.

"Look, he's not even trying!"

"Uncle Jürgen's gonna beat the pants off him."

"Bet you he doesn't," challenged a female voice.

"How much?"

"I'll bring you lunch for a week. If you lose, you milk the cow for a week."

"You're on."

Taking a deep breath, Colin picked up the ax once more and mimicked Jürgen's actions. Back and up. Down and split. The landed blow smarted his hands. The blow's concussion rang all the way to his elbow. Right the log. Back and up. Down and split. Push off. He soon found his own rhythm.

As the competition went on, the camp divided in two. The women cheered Colin on while the men sided with Jürgen. Before long, a few teenage boys defected to the women's camp. A warm feeling spread down Colin's chest, and it had nothing to do with the sweat pouring off his face. A new feeling he didn't have a word for. Disturbing. For a half a movement his rhythm broke, but he found it again and charged ahead with renewed energy.

Every time he placed a log on the block, he looked for Liesl, but couldn't find her among the animated crowd. Disappointment wavered through him, but he couldn't let it break his rhythm. He'd explain later. He'd make her understand about honor and success.

Liesl sat beside her grandmother at the table. She'd taken *Tante* Wenona aside and shown her the sparrow. Wenona had fashioned a splint for the wing and pronounced that the bird would live to fly again in no time. Liesl was left with no excuse to ignore the duel between her father and Colin.

Oma bustled about the table, replenishing platters and bowls of food. The crowd's cheers and jeers fell around Liesl like rain. Running away would feel so good about now. She needed solitude to think. But she couldn't leave Colin at her relatives' mercy. They worked hard all week, and they played equally hard on Sunday. From what Colin had told her, she doubted he would know how to handle these overzealous people. She didn't even want to think about how Papa would mince him to pieces.

"Why doesn't Papa ever listen?" Liesl asked,

twirling a silver fork on the table absently with one hand.

"Because he has to be right. It's as hard for him to be wrong as it is for you." *Oma* settled in the chair next to Liesl's and patted her hands gently. "You are so much like him. He only vants vat is best for you."

"But if he asked, he'd know." Tears burned Liesl's eyes. From the fire, she thought, dismissing them. "He'd know the airport and the training center are what's best for me. He'd know I can't be the perfect housewife he wants me to be." Liesl stood up and paced from the table to the doorway. "And why did Colin have to act like such a child? Why did he have to take Papa up on his challenge?"

"Men, zey can be such babies," *Oma* said, shaking her head. "Zick-headed ones. It has to do vith pride. Let zem go. Jürgen vill accept Colin on his terms, not yours."

"So if Colin is too proud to let Papa win, what will happen?" Liesl asked, flailing her arms about. "Will Papa lock me up in my room like some Rapunzel and throw away the key just because of pride?"

"You are upset for nozing, *Liebchen.* Colin is putting in a good effort. Your *Vater* vill have to respect zat. Your *Vater* is not ze only one zere."

Putting both hands on Liesl's shoulders, *Oma* turned Liesl toward the spectacle. Above the crowd surrounding the men, Liesl saw the red and iron-gray ax heads rise and fall like obsessed hens pecking at grain.

"Look for yourself," *Oma* said. "Look at ze

crowd. Zey are cheering for both men. Zey recognize his vorth. Your *Vater* is zick-headed, but not stupid. He may never like Colin, but he vill accept him. He has no choice. The challenge vaz ze easy vay out of an error in judgment."

Oma led Liesl to the edge of the crowd. Dragging her feet, Liesl let herself be led. "Look how vell he is doing. Um, and look at zat body! If I veren't so old, I might flirt with him myself."

Liesl chuckled, and swatted her grandmother softly on the arm. "*Oma!*"

The crowd's cheers rose to a new heightened pitch. Liesl caught a glimpse of Colin's sweaty chest glistening in the sun, muscles flexing and extending like taut cords in rhythm to the sounds of splitting and falling wood. And God help her, she would like nothing better than to run her hands over his slick skin.

"You like him, don't you?" *Oma* cocked her head in that knowing way of hers. Liesl wanted nothing more than to escape the grasp of her grandmother's gaze. She didn't want to answer questions. She didn't want to put her mixed feelings for Colin into words.

"I can't, *Oma*." Liesl tried to turn away from her grandmother, from the crowd, but *Oma*'s iron grip around her waist didn't let go.

"Vy not?"

"Because . . ." The fire of a blush crept up her cheeks. *Because of Kurt. Because of our vows. Because of our dream.* She couldn't let anything interfere with that—especially not disloyal feelings about another man.

163

"Foolish girl. Don't get stuck in ze past. Life is meant—"

"I know. I know. Life is meant to be drunk by the cupful, not tasted with a coffee spoon. But, *Oma,* haven't you noticed how much he looks like Kurt?"

"*Ja,* and so has everybody else."

"Aren't they . . . Don't they . . ." The words choked in frustrated gulps down Liesl's throat.

"Zey do not forget, *Liebchen.*"

"After what Kurt's death did to the town, how can they accept him?" How could he not revive their fears the way he had for her? How could he not revive their guilt?

"How can zey not accept him? After vat happened to Kurt, zey must. Ze war is over, Liesl. Zey do not forget, but zey forgive—zemselves and each ozer. You must also."

Liesl shook her head. The tears brimmed, blurring her vision. How could they forgive so easily when their mistake had cost a young man his life? She simply couldn't fathom their heartlessness. "How can I forgive murder?"

The tears fell in hot streams down her cheeks. Her heart, bruised and heavy, quivered in her chest. She reached for the pain, unconsciously curling her fingers around the cotton of her dress. A deep, raw ache invaded her mercilessly like a plundering enemy. The emptiness, the hole—they hurt so much.

A raucous shout caught her attention. The chopping stopped. The stacking started. Colin moved with animal-like fluidity, muscles shifting, straining the worn Levi's against racehorse-sleek thighs and rump. As he smiled at her father, tired pleasure shone on his face. Kurt's smile. Her chest pinged, rubbing more pain into the needy soreness. "How can I forget Kurt when he looks so much like him?" The question came out in a whispered sob.

Oma hugged her fiercely. "You do not forget, *Liebchen*. You enrich."

"But you and Papa, you didn't 'enrich.' Neither of you loved again."

Oma took Liesl's chin between her thumb and index finger. Her white eyebrows and forehead wrinkled with sadness. "And ve are two crotchety old people. Ve have done you no favor. Live while you have a chance, Liesl. I leave you now." She patted Liesl's arms. "You zink about vat I said."

Her grandmother headed back toward the food table. "*Oma?*"

Oma turned to look at Liesl. Before her courage failed, Liesl blurted out her question. "Do you think it's possible for souls to come back?"

Liesl fidgeted in *Oma*'s silence. How could she have asked such a stupid question? Her grandmother's piety would never entertain such foolish notions.

Oma slowly looked toward Colin. "Vere love is concerned, I zink anything is possible."

Colin's last log hit the stack one second behind Jürgen's. His hands burned red from the friction of the ax's shaft. Splinters riddled the insides of his palms. His forearms still reverberated from the concussion of the ax hitting

165

the wood. His shoulders screamed with fatigue. His lower back spasmed with pain. But pride kept him from showing any signs of weakness. Amid the sounds of congratulations, he headed toward Jürgen and shook his hand.

"You have never chopped wood before," Jürgen said. His face showed no expression. He reached for his shirt and jacket.

"Never." Colin pulled on his dirty T-shirt.

"You learned fast."

Colin realized he would get no other praise for his effort, and no apologies for Jürgen's burst of anger when they met. The fact that it didn't matter surprised Colin. What was wrong with him? He'd lost and he didn't care. Success, no matter how small, had always meant everything.

The crowd enveloped them both and led them to the table. Liesl's grandmother offered them chairs. Acceptance. Community. In all his years growing up, he'd seldom felt them—except with Karen and while flying. Now, they were offered to him without reserve, without question. Colin wasn't sure how to react.

"Somebody get these thirsty men a beer," Aldo ordered. Red still stained his cheeks from straining to shout.

Two mugs appeared filled to the brim with dark liquid. Tan foam dribbled down the sides. A young girl, smiling shyly at Colin, placed plates heaping with food in front of them. A lively discussion of their efforts flew around them like a bird caught in a whirlwind. It moved away. Aldo took up his tuba, Karl his violin, and soon a disjointed polka filled the air.

"What are your intentions toward my daughter?" Jürgen asked. He took a long swig of beer, freezing Colin with a steady gaze.

"I have none." *None I can act upon, given the circumstances. Don't you know? Time travel is hell on relationships.* "We're just friends." *But I want to make love to her with a craving that borders on madness. A craving I don't understand. A craving that will drive me crazy before I leave.* "I'll fly for her on Saturday, then I'll be going home."

"Where is home?"

Colin hesitated, thinking of the temporary window separating his time from this one. "Far away."

Why did the words make him cringe so? Surrounded by this lively bunch of people, his lonely home paled in comparison. Far away. And looking farther all the time. "She's safe. I promise. I won't hurt Liesl. The last thing I want to do is hurt anybody."

"I'm glad to hear that. Liesl has suffered too much already."

"I know."

They ate their meal in silence. Fat sausages, slices of beef and pieces of chicken edged out mounds of potatoes, broad wiggly noodles, carrots and asparagus. A slice of dark bread piled on top of the meal threatened to fall onto the table. Everything tasted heavenly and felt good as it filled his empty stomach. He pushed his plate away with a satisfied sigh, earning him a smile from Liesl's grandmother. Liesl seemed to have completely disappeared. He dared not ask her whereabouts. He didn't want to break the tentative truce between him and her father, but her absence troubled him. Was she angry?

Jürgen excused himself. "Come join us when you are ready." He walked toward a group of men checking hunting rifles.

Liesl appeared from the house, and his heart lifted. She'd changed from her soiled dress to a navy and white checkered shirt dress with long sleeves cuffed at the wrists, a full skirt, a row of navy buttons down the front, and large cuffed pockets on the sides. She'd brushed her hair until it shone like polished gold and pinned it back behind her ears, rolling the hair on the side to form a long coil from ear to collar. Bright red lipstick accentuated the luscious curve of her lips, and dark mascara magnified the light blue of her irises. But none of the feminine adornments pleased him as much as her presence.

"How is our little sparrow faring?" Colin asked, not knowing where else to start the conversation.

"*Tante* Wenona says she'll be flying again soon. She'll take the sparrow home and take care of her until her wing mends."

"I'm glad to hear that." Colin shifted restlessly.

"I've run a bath for you," Liesl said. No ice, no sunshine in her voice, just distance, long and impenetrable.

"Thank you." He hadn't taken a bath since he was six. "Baths are for girls," his father had informed him. "Real men take showers." But just about now, a hot bath sounded like heaven. The only thing that could make it better would be having Liesl join him, and the chances of that happening stood at nil. Not with this protective bunch around to guard her virtue.

Colin followed her up the same stairs that had started the whole wood-chopping incident. Her steps rang hollowly in the corridor. The material of her dress fell smoothly against the rise of her buttocks, swishing against her nylons as she moved. Enticing. He'd like to peel all the layers off, peel the distance, peel the mask.

His stiffening muscles protested in time to the confused whirling of his thoughts. He wanted her soft and warm against him. Yet he didn't want her that close. She would thaw that cold, hard place inside him he didn't want disturbed. He would feel again. And he couldn't afford to feel. Not for her. She belonged here. He didn't. She couldn't leave her world any more than he could stay. Right place. Wrong time. Even if he could have the woman without losing his heart, he'd be foolish to take the chance. His luck hadn't run too well lately.

"I've laid out some fresh clothes for you," Liesl said. "There are clean towels behind the door."

Hot water in an old-fashioned clawed tub steamed the room, promising soothing relief for the stiffness threatening to rust him in place as surely as the tin man after a good rain. "I'm sure everything's fine."

Liesl nodded and grasped the doorknob to close the door. Her painted face was as stiff as a China doll's. Her remoteness chipped at him. He had to explain.

"Liesl . . ." Foreign emotions warred inside him and words failed him. "I had to."

"I know."

She closed the bathroom door softly behind her. Colin stripped off his clothes. He'd be gone soon enough, her distance wouldn't matter. He slipped into the warm water, sighing his contentment. As he closed his eyes, her smiling image formed in his mind. He slipped further into the tub, submerging his head and blowing frustrated bubbles.

Fifty years wouldn't be far enough.

Chapter Seven

Wednesday

Colin and Liesl ambled down the road to the airport, replete from one of *Oma*'s dinners. He couldn't remember the last time he'd eaten so much so many days in a row. His meals usually consisted of coffee for breakfast and sandwiches slapped together haphazardly or fast food caught on the run for the rest of his meals. He'd miss *Oma*'s cooking when he left.

The thought of the window bridging his time with this one had him glancing at the sky. In less than four days it would close. He shook his head. There was nothing he could do until he got a set of propellers. And that wouldn't happen until Saturday. If he worried about it too much, he'd drive himself nuts, then he wouldn't be any good to anyone, least of all himself. He might as well enjoy the time he had with Liesl.

The sun shone warm despite the chill in the air, a few birds trilled in the distance, and fat clouds drifted aimlessly above. As the slow measure of country life beat lazily around him, a languid feeling permeated Colin's limbs, and the utter contentment of the moment had him unconsciously reaching for Liesl's hand. Soft and warm, it felt right in his palm. He answered her strange look with a slow smile. When she left her hand in his, he felt sure the day could only get better.

Colin had spent the rest of Sunday joining the family fun. He'd taken a crack at target shooting in the razed field which had once been Grüber's woods, drunk his share of beer, bounced half a dozen toddlers on his knee. And ate, and ate, and ate until he thought he'd burst.

After she heard about the fire, *Oma* ("Call me *Oma*, everyone else does") had insisted he spend the night at the house, and warned him if he didn't show up for meals she'd come get him herself. Liesl assured him he didn't want that to happen. The fuss alone would drive him to punctuality.

Amid the fuss and bother around him, he understood what Liesl had meant by interference, and her definition and his differed completely. He grew to like her family—and their interference—more than he'd expected. Colin found himself laughing and relaxing in a way he hadn't done in years.

Even Liesl had thawed, her distance decreasing in the warm folds of her family. She'd negotiated a reprieve from her father, and for the rest of the week, her cousin Emma would take her place at the store. But being near her without being able to hold her still ached like a bruise that wouldn't heal. The confines of the hangar on Monday and Tuesday had heightened the feeling to near agony. To ease the torture, he'd used every excuse possible to brush his fingers against hers, to drag her scent into his lungs, to draw close enough to hear the gentle rhythm of her breathing.

The Castell was almost ready. A few tweaks here and there and he could take it up for a test ride this afternoon. Over the past few days, they'd overhauled the whole engine. Liesl had proved to be a more than able mechanic, and her knowledge of the Pratt & Whitney radial engine had been invaluable.

When Liesl abruptly stopped walking, Colin, lost in his thoughts, suffered momentary confusion.

"No!" she screamed and took off toward the hangar. Colin ran after her.

A pall-like silence blanketed the hangar. Someone had hacked the lock off the door, and inside lay utter carnage. The destruction slammed into him like a Mack truck without brakes.

One hand over her mouth in horror, the other on her stomach, Liesl shook her head in denial and walked stiffly to the Castell. As Colin drew close, he saw her limbs trembling. Without thinking, he pulled her against him and held her tightly.

"How could he? *How could he?*" she asked in a low, creaky voice. Colin had no answer.

Someone had taken an ax and butchered the Castell's exterior. Pieces of metal jutted everywhere like a half-plucked chicken, flattened tires supported the mangled bird, a wing hung almost severed from its body, and oil and various other life-giving liquids spilled, darkening the cement like blood. The violation stung as raw as if it had wounded his own flesh.

"It's ruined, Colin. There's no time to fix it." Her arms tightened like a vise around his waist, stirring protective instincts deep inside him. "What am I going to do?"

Failure. He couldn't accept it now any more than he ever had. Colin looked around for a solution. The carnage hadn't been confined to the Castell. Both Cubs' skins hung in tatters. Scattered tools littered the ground. Supplies lay in ruin all around him. Even his CastleAir hadn't been neglected, but minimal damage marred the structure.

Liesl extricated herself from his arms. Spine stiffened and eyes dry, she squared her shoulders and lifted her chin. She rounded the Castell with a zombie-like gait, touching the torn metal here and there as if she could heal it by laying on her hand. Colin fought the feeling of helplessness paralyzing his limbs.

"We'll fix it, Liesl," he said, putting his hands on her drooping shoulders.

"There's no time." She shook her head, looking at the mess around her. "No supplies. No money." Her voice faltered. "I've lost, Colin. I've lost everything."

He spun her around and forced her to look at him. He wasn't ready to give up yet. "We'll find a way. Do you hear?" He shook her shoulders to jar her out of her defeatism.

"How?" Her wide eyes begged him to find a way, but the deepening crease along her forehead accepted her loss.

The answer was too simple. Colin argued and counter-argued with himself, but the solution didn't change. If he followed this course of action, he'd take the risk of losing his ticket home. But what else could he do? His piloting skills ranked above average. He'd have to trust himself to come out of the race safely. "We'll use the CastleAir."

"No!" She pushed him away and marched outside.

Colin followed her, stunned by her refusal. "Why not?"

"Because."

Did she really think he'd skip out on her as soon as the Castell's props were attached to the CastleAir? "I gave you my word, Liesl. I won't go back on it."

"That's not it." She shook her head, lips pursed in a brave stemming of the emotions which played themselves so vividly on her face. "I have to use Kurt's plane."

He grit his teeth in irritation. What difference did it make? A win was a win. She didn't want a racing career, she only wanted the recognition the win would get her. "Do you want to race or not?"

"Of course I do." She flipped a strand of hair and tucked it jerkily behind her ear.

"You won't be able to with the Castell. I'm offering you a chance to win. A chance to make your name, to build your training center. Isn't that what you want?"

"But it would be *your* plane, *your* name, *your* win."

The soulful look in her wide blue eyes almost undid him. He couldn't let it, he couldn't let *her* get to him. Not with his ultimate failure looming high before him.

"So pass it off as the Castell," he said, more gruffly than he'd intended. "Their looks are similar enough, and you'll be able to rebuild the original with the prize money."

She shook her head and lowered her gaze. "It's not the same."

"What do you want, Liesl?"

As she turned away from him and walked to the oak beside the hangar, her shoulders hunched. "I promised."

Liesl slid her back along the oak's trunk until she sat beneath the deep green canopy of leaves. She plucked an errant dandelion and rolled the stem between her fingers. Her gaze drifted to the horizon. "The view is beautiful here."

"It is," Colin answered, looking at the forlorn woman beneath the tree and not the distant vista. The breeze ruffled the leaves, speckling her skin with moving light and shadows.

"This is where they killed him." Her low voice

held not a trace of emotion, but the whirling current in her eyes denied her composure. She lifted her gaze to the branch above her, grazing her head against the trunk. Her hair clung like a golden spider web to the rough bark.

As Colin followed her gaze skyward his chest tightened. His throat constricted. Air grated through his windpipe like pumice. A painful spasm shafted the back of his neck. He fought the sensation of a vision creating itself from the shreds of mist fogging his brain. He battled—and won.

Breathing deeply, he cleared the gray clouds. He cleared his throat and found his voice once more.

"I would have thought you'd have chopped the thing down," Colin said, leaning a hand on the trunk, feeling the bark bite into his palm. Inane chatter was infinitely better than the serious turn this conversation was headed for.

"I tried." Her fingers ran along the deep cuts scarring the base of the tree. "But it shades the hangar in the summer and it gets so hot in there."

How did one respond to such a comment? What strength of character had it taken to quell the fury of injury and think logically? Respect for her courage flowered.

"They left him hanging." Liesl shredded the dandelion's yellow head in her hand. The pieces fell from her fingers like the tears she couldn't shed.

Words failed him once again. What could he say? What could he do? He wanted to ease her pain. He didn't want to get involved. He couldn't help her. Discomfort built a whirlpool in his stomach. The taut muscles of his legs and arms threatened to shatter if he continued to stand unmoving. He sank beside her, resting his back on the trunk, letting his shoulder touch hers, lending her silent support.

"He died in my arms."

I love you, Liesl. Forever. The voice not his own echoed in his mind. Colin closed his eyes, fighting the fog. He cleared his throat and reached for her hand, twining his fingers with hers. He drew as much courage as he gave. "I'm sorry."

She leaned her head against his shoulder. "I promised him."

He rubbed his cheek on her hair. Her loyalty touched him deeply. He extended his arm around her shoulder and squeezed her gently. In the face of her courage, how could he let her give up? He still had time, didn't he? "Then we'll just have to put the Castell back together again, no matter what it takes. If we have to, we'll miss the landing competition on Friday. The qualifying rounds won't be flown until Saturday morning. The race is the important event."

"You forget. We don't have any supplies left."

"Can you buy more on credit and pay them back with the prize money?"

She frowned as she thought. "I can try."

Loath to let her go, Colin nonetheless realized time was of the essence. "What time is Max supposed to show up?"

"After school."

Her warmth saturated his side. He pressed her closer, imprinting the curves of her body on his, before he pulled his arm away and stood up. "That gives me a couple of hours to clean up the mess and you some time to line up supplies. When Max gets here, we'll start putting some skin back on your bird."

Liesl latched the garden gate behind her and stepped purposefully into the street before her house. The last few hours had proved near useless. Not only had her supplier laughed in her face when she'd asked for credit, he'd told her he'd be a fool to accept her offer of prize money as collateral. She wasn't expected to place, let alone win.

The man's response had so horrified her, she'd almost given up. Then she'd thought of Colin, his determination, his gentleness by the tree. For a wonderful few moments, it had been like having Kurt by her side. And she knew she couldn't let him see her doubts. Like Kurt, he would expect her to be strong, to keep her promise, to be . . . perfect.

If he only knew how far from perfection she was!

At least he'd made her see that she couldn't give up until the race was finished. On her way back from the supplier's, she finally realized she'd have to reach beyond Billy's circle of influence to make any headway at all. She'd talked a Kendall Oil representative into donating six cases of oil in exchange for placing a sponsor sticker on the bottom of the Castell's wings.

She'd struck out with Texaco, but Mobilgas had promised 400 gallons of fuel for the race. They'd put their sticker on the tail.

The last of the war bonds she cashed would go toward the rest of the supplies. All she missed now were the sheets of aluminum needed for the skin. And Billy, knowing her need, held the latest shipment hostage at his rail yard. No supplier—friend or foe—could get to it. She had no time left to go elsewhere. She'd have to negotiate with Billy.

She smoothed the straight skirt of her brown tweed suit, took a deep breath, and knocked on Billy's office door.

"Door's open," came the muffled reply.

Liesl squared her shoulders and entered. Billy's smile widened a mile when he saw her. The pleasure in his bright blue eyes seemed genuine, but Billy had grown into a consummate actor over the years. Hard to know the real from the fake. The fact he smiled at all sparked her anger. How could he dare smile at her after what he'd done to her airplane?

"Liesl, what brings you here?" He rounded his desk and drew out one of his leather-covered chairs, inviting her to sit. Liesl ignored the gesture.

"As if you didn't know." She hadn't meant to launch her anger at him. She'd meant to sweet-talk him into releasing the shipment. But, oh, that confounded smile of his had her hackles up in fighting position.

"Hey, sugar, don't jump all over me like some kerosene cat in hell with gasoline drawers on."

"You deliberately sabotaged my airplane."

"I've never set foot on your land, sweetheart." He grinned, showing off his perfectly white teeth, sending another round of acid bubbling up from her stomach. "Why don't you sit down, and I'll pour you a nice cup of coffee." Billy lifted the silver carafe from the low table between the two leather chairs and poured coffee into a gold-trimmed cup.

"Of course you didn't come on my land." Liesl stood her ground. "You don't have the guts to do your own dirty work—"

The carafe paused in mid-pour. "Now just hold on a minute here. Before you go makin' accusations, you'd better have somethin' to back 'em up. Do you have any proof?"

"Of course not, you're too smart for that. You've paid off everybody that could pin you." He had the nerve to chortle gleefully! It took all of Liesl's control not to smack that smile right off his face. "You're right, it's just my penny word against your dollar one. But we both know you'd do anything to see me lose."

Billy handed her a cup, then sat on the edge of his desk. "Was there a point to your visit, Lise? If not, I'm a busy man."

"Yes, there was a point." Liesl swallowed the tirade she had prepped to launch at him. She'd have to calm down or she'd antagonize him into holding the shipment until it would be too late. With precise care, she sat down and placed the cup on the table beside her. A slow curl of heat twirled above the cup, and she watched it for a moment while her anger cooled. The smile she pasted on felt as if it would crack her skin. "I thought you were a reasonable man. I came to ask you to release the aluminum shipment you're holding back."

He splayed his hands up in a helpless motion. "I'd like to oblige you, princess, but it's got a whole mess load of paperwork problems."

"But someone as important as you could probably untangle that whole nasty mess in no time at all." The sugary sweetness of her voice nauseated her.

"I s'pose I could, but you see, I sense a little desperation on your part." He crossed his arms over his chest and cocked his head sideways. "To me, that's a sure signal there's some profit to be made."

"Is that all you think about, profit?"

His eyebrows knit in mock despair. "When you keep denying me, Lise, what else am I supposed to do?"

She leaned forward, pushing the sugar factor up a notch. "If I mean so much to you, then why don't you release the shipment as a personal favor to me?" She'd have batted her eyelashes if she'd thought it would help.

"Because I'd still be here alone and you'd still be on the other side of the tracks."

Billy reached to touch her cheek and rubbed the side of his thumb along her cheekbone. The coldness of his fingers sent a shiver down her spine. As slowly as she could, she leaned out of his reach.

"Okay," she said, "let's say I understand your need to profit. In exchange for releasing the shipment, I'll give you the prize money I win on Saturday."

Billy guffawed and slapped his thighs until tears ran from his eyes. "I don't need your prize money, honey. I've got more money than I know what to do with."

"Then what'll you take?"

The laughter stopped. Not even a smile graced his pretty face. "I'll take a promise of marriage from you."

Liesl's shocked gasp remained stuck in her throat. She reached for the rings beneath her suit jacket and her fingers curled around the skin-warmed, fabric-covered silver circles. "That's out of the question. I can't marry you."

He looked so handsome, so polished. The admiration in his eyes should have warmed her, but instead it left her cold. Why couldn't she feel for him what he wanted? Why couldn't his touch set her on fire the way Colin's did, the way Kurt's had? Why couldn't she pretend? But just the thought of Billy's well-manicured hand on her skin made her want to vomit.

Marriage shouldn't be a convenience. Marriage meant a blending of souls, the kind of deep comfort she'd felt with Kurt, not the cardboard advertisement to be displayed that Billy wanted. Even the zinging connection, the unnerving awareness she felt around Colin came closer to her idea of a relationship than the charade that Billy proposed.

"Then I'll front you a loan for the material you need and take the airport as collateral," Billy said.

"What?" Still unbalanced by his proposal, Liesl couldn't make sense of his words.

"You win, you keep the airport and accept the aluminum as my gift. You lose, the airport's mine."

"The whole shipment of aluminum isn't worth the price of the land!"

"I thought you were certain of winnin'."

"I am."

"Then what have you got to lose?"

A chill went down to the soles of her feet. What had she gotten herself into? He'd left her no way to win. If she accepted, she'd put him on the defensive. How far would he go to make sure the Castell wouldn't cross the finish line? Was she asking for another attack on the airplane? Was she putting Colin in danger's way?

Liesl sighed wearily. Maybe she should have taken Colin's offer of his CastleAir. Knowing how much it had cost him to risk crashing it, his selfless action had touched her beyond words. But this had been Kurt's dream, and she had to fulfill it for him his way.

One of her hands crunched into a fist. They'd guard the hangar day and night. No one would get to the Castell again, and Colin flew expertly. She trusted him to give his all to cross the finish line. Billy had miscalculated this time. He couldn't get to the airplane. He couldn't buy Colin. But she couldn't let him see the hole in his offer.

"Everything," she said calmly, evenly. "Because a snake like you probably still has a trick or two tucked under his slimy belly. How do I know you won't cheat?"

"I give you my word of honor." He placed a hand over his heart and smiled brightly at her.

She swallowed her bitterness. "And we all know how much that's worth."

"Now, Lise, that's no way to treat the man who holds your future in his hands. It's time to make nice. Do you want the material or not?"

She wanted to strangle him but made her hands lie still in her lap. "Yes."

"Then we've got a deal?"

"Yes, damn you. We've got a deal. Put it in writing."

"What's the matter, sweet Fräulein, don't you trust me?"

"No."

He laughed heartily. "Honesty. I like that in a woman."

"I admire it in a man."

"I'll have to keep that in mind."

Billy left his office and came back a moment later, taking up his position perched on the edge of his desk. "Jessie'll type up the contract for us."

Liesl looked deep into his perfectly sculpted face. "What happened, Billy? You used to be my protector against Kurt's pranks when we were kids. You were such a sweet boy."

"And look where it got me. Kurt got you, and I ended up knee high in the debts my father left me." He walked away from his desk, then back again. He didn't sit on the edge. He rested his hands on her chair's arms. "Sweet boys get trampled, Lise. And sweet men end up losers like my father." He pushed himself off. "I can't die the same way. I've got the power my father never had. I can buy everything I want. *Everything*. Even you."

"You can't buy love, Billy."

He shrugged. "The jury's still out on that one."

"Don't you get lonely, alone with your power?"

He looked at her, silent, unsmiling. For a moment in his forlorn expression, she saw the boy in the man.

"I'll go check on Jessie," he said and left the office.

Take away the leather-trimmed chairs, the expensive wood furniture and the office's glossy trimmings, take away the fancy clothes and the tough talk, and there still stood the little boy who'd stared longingly at the penny candy jar in her father's store. She'd slipped him pieces then. He'd accepted, but in his eyes Liesl had seen that one piece wouldn't offer contentment. She understood now what had happened to him all those years ago. Tired of secret handouts, shamed by his father's debts, he'd gone out for the whole jar, except now the penny candy had grown to deals worth dollars in amounts she could only guess at. Liesl realized she didn't feel any anger toward him anymore. What she felt was pity.

Billy returned and handed her the neatly typed contract. Her heart sank at the chance she'd taken, but she couldn't see any other way out. This time she was prepared. This time she'd keep Kurt safe.

"There you go, Lise. All neat and legal so you can rest your pretty little head easy."

"Thank you." She rose and accepted the document. A quick glance assured her he'd outlined their contract as agreed. She would read it more thoroughly out of his scrutinizing gaze.

"When can I get the aluminum?" She folded the pages and placed them securely in her jacket pocket.

"Any time you want."

"I'll send someone."

As she reached the door, Billy spoke. "If you change your mind, I'll still take your promise of marriage."

"I won't."

"I can give you everything you want, Lise."

"Except what I need."

As she came out of Billy's office, she practically ran into Max and two of his friends.

"*Oma* told me what happened," Max said, glancing with hatred at Billy's building. "I wish . . ." He grit his teeth so loud, Liesl heard the crunch.

"He's not worth it, Max. We've got a lot of work to do, but we'll be all right."

"I brought Stefan and Anton to help out."

"Good." Back in her organizational mode now, Liesl drew up mental lists of things to do. As she hurried down the hill toward the airport with the boys flanking her, she put her plan of action into motion. "Stefan, is your truck in working order?"

"Yep. Got it back on the road last week."

"Would you drive to Dallas and pick up supplies for me?"

"Sure thing."

"I've called ahead. They'll have everything ready."

One down, a million to go! She wouldn't sleep tonight, but she knew she wouldn't be alone.

"Anton, do you think you can round up a couple more people to transport the aluminum I need from Billy's yard to the airport?"

"I'll ask Karl to lend me his truck. We'll get it there for you. Be back in a flash." With a wave of his hand, Anton trotted back up the hill toward the German side of town.

"What do you want me to do, Liesl?" Max asked.

"You can help Colin with the Castell."

Once at her office, Liesl handed Stefan the supplier's address and sent him on his way. It still riled her that she had to go so far to get what she needed, when the supplies were available so close. Max disappeared into the hangar, leaving Liesl alone.

Her heart filled with joy. Billy might be able to buy everything, but Liesl had something infinitely more precious. As interfering as her family was, when she needed them, they stood behind her. Why hadn't she realized this before? They were part of her strength, just as she should have been part of theirs.

And Colin, how quickly he'd become a part of them! The picture of him bouncing her nieces and nephews on his knee had shot a deep, long arrow of regret. By now, one of those babies should have been hers. Would Kurt have looked so comfortable playing with their child? She'd never know. Little Sophie, who clung to her mama like glue, had fastened herself naturally to Colin's chest. As he'd rocked her, she'd fallen asleep, her little fist wrapped around the collar of his shirt. The pang of envy still hurt.

Liesl shook her head. Her dream of bearing Kurt's children would never come true. No sense dwelling on it. But she still had Kurt's dream, and it would have to do. She truly believed they would get the Castell put together in time.

Quickly she changed into Levi's, a work shirt and boots, and rushed to the hangar.

The day had grayed. Rain-scented wind whipped at her face, blowing her hair into her eyes. The cool air stung her skin, leaving a chill that went soul-deep. They could fix the airplane's broken wing, but she had a bad feeling that Billy hadn't played his last card.

Thursday

Colin marveled at the way her family had rallied around Liesl even though they didn't believe in her goal. It seemed as if the entire community had shown up to help. Food and plenty of hot coffee appeared as if by magic. As he refilled his cup, Colin smiled. Liesl was right. Any excuse was good for a get-together. The destruction didn't seem quite as bad amid their good-hearted laughter. Why couldn't his father have stood behind him like these people? Just once. That's all he'd ever asked.

Rain drummed with machine-gun rapidity against the hangar. Colin warmed his cold fingers on the hot mug. The air had grown positively frigid, but no one would have guessed it by the warmth generated by these people.

The hangar had stood silent for only one awkward moment when Sandy Blackwell, who owned a clothing store on the Anglo side, arrived bearing a plate of sandwiches. "I'd like to help."

No one answered him for a moment. They all stared at the man, who grew more uncomfortable by the minute. It was as if no one knew what to say, so Colin stepped forward, accepting the plate Sandy offered. He wasn't part of this town's feud, and they could use all the help they could get. "All you need is a broom to join this party."

"I'll be right back." Ten minutes later, he returned with Tom Moore, Matt Longway, two brooms, a shovel and a wheelbarrow.

Liesl's extended family took shifts coming and going all day, working on cleaning and organizing, freeing him to concentrate on the airplane itself. Max assisted him like a well-trained surgical nurse while Liesl supervised the entire operation. Even a few more Anglos drifted in to share the task.

At times, Liesl's perfectionistic streak got in the way, but she drove herself harder than anyone else, and work had advanced at a pace Colin would have thought impossible.

By nightfall, as the need for them lessened, the help trickled away to tend to their own chores neglected at home. After charging ahead full steam for over twenty-four hours, even Max's energy had flagged. Amid yawns and half-hearted protests, Colin had sent him home to rest.

As Colin drained the rest of his mug and placed it on the table, Liesl reappeared from the adjoining room, handwritten manual in hand. Wisps of hair, loosened from her ponytail, flew wild around her face. Dark smudges underlined her eyes. Her peaches-and-cream skin had faded to an ashen white. But her step hadn't slowed. Stalking purposefully toward the plane, she spied him by the coffee table.

"Colin! How can you stand there doing nothing when we still have so much work to do?"

"I need an energy break," he said, attempting levity.

"You've already had at least a gallon of coffee." She dropped the manual on the table, rattling the scattered mugs in the process. "You'll be lucky if you can fall asleep and rest before the race."

Hands on hips, she scowled at him. Her attempts at fierceness made him smile. "I think the effect is fading."

He reached up and twined a loose strand of her hair around his index finger. The silk stirred memories. They came fast and furious like flecks of paint thrown against a canvas by an inspired artist.

"Maybe a kiss would help." The words slipped

out before he could stop them. He hadn't meant to say them, hadn't meant to let her know he wanted her.

Loaded silence and a magnetic pull vibrated between them like a gyro gone crazy. And heat, so much heat in this cold hangar. His hand curved into the warmth, cupping her cheek. It slipped down the creamy column of her neck. The pad of one finger rested for a moment against the silver chain bouncing at her neck. Her pulse jolted and scrambled fast against his hardened skin, shooting shards of electricity straight into his bloodstream.

"Liesl?" The word came out a supplication.

Her breath puffed in quick, hot bursts against his chin. His breath labored in his tightening chest with every one of her short blasts. He moved his hand to twine his fingers in her ponytail. As if they had a will of their own, they buried themselves deep into the silk and pressed against her nape, drawing her forward. His free hand skimmed her waist. It moved slowly up until it cupped her breast. Her nipple bloomed against his palm. Her mouth parted with a sigh. He heard its echo on his soul, and groaned.

"Liesl!" It was no longer a question, but a demand. He pressed his mouth against hers. The world disappeared. It held only her. Like water to a thirsty man, like food to a hungry man, her answering kiss quelled and fired a basic need. Her scent enveloped him. Her taste addicted him. Her feel, soft and warm in his arms, overwhelmed him.

He deepened the kiss, needing more. She arched against him, sliding her hands up his chest, around his shoulders. The trail of her fingers sent a shudder of delight rippling through his body. In his ears, the sound of their hearts beat to the same rhythm, awakening an echo from another time.

No! This was his. This was now. He didn't want some misty vision blurring his pleasure. The fog thickened. He didn't want to share. He fought the fog, bringing Liesl closer, tasting her with panicked intensity. *This kiss is mine!*

A train whistle shrieked into the night.

"Liesl . . ." It was a prayer. It was an apology. It was everything, and nothing.

Still dazed, he lifted his head, ripping himself from her like a Band-Aid from sensitive skin. It hurt. The pain came again when her soft fingers slid back down his chest and her arms fell to her sides.

She looked at him, eyes wide and bright. He reached for the wisp of hair flattened against her pinkened cheek and pushed it gently behind her ear. Her swollen lips still shone from his kiss. He traced the scratch he'd made with the stubble of his beard, circling his gaze back to her expectant eyes.

"Do you know your eyes have a navy ring around the light blue? Like night curving around day. Absolutely beautiful." One of these days he would learn to speak intelligently to her. Regret sighed deep inside him. He wouldn't be around that long. In two days he'd fly through Jakob's time window and go home.

"We've got work to do, Colin." The words raced out in a gush. Her gaze darted all around him, never once landing on his eyes. When she turned from him, he saw her step falter. She recovered quickly, grasped the manual, and disappeared behind the airplane.

He licked his dry lips, and regretted the action. He could still taste her heady flavor, still feel the heat of her thrumming along his skin, still hear the echo of her racing heart in his ear. And when he moved to join her, he had to fist his hands to keep them from shaking visibly.

Never again, he silently vowed. But already his craving for her sang with feral intensity through his veins.

Two more days.

The mask. He had to remember the mask, or he wouldn't survive.

Chapter Eight

Friday

As dawn creased the night sky, the Castell's engine rumbled loudly in the hangar. Liesl smacked Kurt's handwritten manual on the wing and flipped pages to find the right set of data. She needed sleep. She needed food. What she didn't need was any more aggravations.

Through the long night, Colin had frayed her patience to its end. If she lived forever, Liesl didn't think she'd ever understand him. One minute he kissed her breathless, sending her senses flying in a dizzying spin, the next he pretended that nothing had happened, snapping jokes that didn't even begin to lighten the heavy air around them, and now, to make matters worse, he toyed with the engine's perfect tuning.

"But the specifications say—" she shouted over the engine's roar, pecking a finger at the data to prove her point.

"Forget the book, Liesl. Sometimes perfection gets in the way. Sometimes you've got to trust your gut." He smiled that teasing smile of his, cranking her frustration to a new high.

"An engine is like a woman," he continued. "You want it to purr when you turn it on. Listen . . ." He cupped a hand over his ear. "That sounds like a woman who's had good sex." He stuffed both his hands in the open cowling and tinkered with something out of sight. "Now, this . . . this sounds like a woman who's been made love to and satisfied completely. Hear the difference?"

She rolled her eyes heavenward. He would have to pick a totally inappropriate analogy—one that brushed much too close to the wanderings of her overtired mind. But listening to the engine's noise, she was forced to admit she did hear the slight change of tone from a rolling purr to a contented murmur.

He shut the engine down, then looked at her from the open cockpit. The naked light from the bulbs on the ceiling cut harsh shadows across his face. Dark stubble shadowed his jaw and tired lines jagged near his eyes.

Then he smiled, and the lifting of his lips transformed his whole face. His eyes twinkled like bright stars, and oh, how she wanted him to kiss her senseless once more.

"Want to go for a ride?" he asked.

Her heart pounded in her chest with anticipation. "Me?"

Colin roared with laughter. "Why not?" He lifted his eyebrows in a teasing challenge. "Unless you don't trust your own work."

"I'd trust it with my life."

"Maybe it's me you're afraid of?"

"I'm not afraid of anything." *Except the way you make my head spin, my heart ache, and my soul bleed.*

They rolled the airplane onto the apron. After a thorough walkaround, Colin helped her into the pilot's seat and climbed into the co-pilot's seat.

"Ready?"

She nodded, fingers self-consciously tangled in her lap. She rounded her shoulders forward to keep them from touching his in the narrow confines of the cockpit.

"Ground rules. When I say 'I got it,' I want to see your hands up in the air like so and off the joystick. And if you feel like you're going to puke, please don't do it in my lap."

She snapped her head in his direction, panic streaking through her unexpectedly. "What are you planning to do?"

"I'm gonna show you how to make love to the sky." His voice lowered to a gritty drawl and his teasing smile could have lit a small country. It was Kurt all over again—the endless teasing, the excitement, the illogical attraction.

If Colin was going for the shock factor, he was doing a good job. Her insides responded with a vicious pang of buried needs. Making love with Colin in any capacity would surely drive her into insanity. No way out now without admitting to more than she dared. She strapped herself in.

He meant nothing to her, she reminded herself. He was just a pilot. He couldn't mean anything to her; tomorrow he'd be gone. And damn him, he didn't have the right to bring back everything she'd shared with Kurt. She was strong, competent, self-sufficient. She'd show him. No matter what he did, he couldn't get to her.

Liesl swallowed hard and concentrated on the instrument panel in front of her. Far better that than the mischievous look in Colin's eyes. She knew them all—the tachometer indicating the crankshaft rpms, the manifold pressure gauge showing the load on the engine, the oil pressure gauge, the oil temperature gauge, the cylinder head temperature gauge. During the race those would be the most important features of the cockpit. Like a symphony conductor, Colin would orchestrate a fine line between maximum speed and engine endurance, using their readings as a reference.

There, she could handle this. She could handle him. Just concentrate on the airplane, not his appealing profile softened by the early morning light. She shot him a sly glance. He winked at her and started his takeoff checklist. She closed her eyes and tried to stem the fire burning her cheeks.

Using his own set of controls, Colin taxied to

the end of the grass strip. He pushed the throttle forward, revving the engine. Sensing excitement in the air, she opened her eyes once more. Needles bounced on instruments. Her heart followed suit. Hands on the edge of her seat, she unconsciously leaned forward.

"Here we go," Colin said.

The Castell rolled down the strip. Straight as an arrow, Colin guided it down an imaginary center line with the rudder pedals. She felt the airplane's awkwardness on the ground. It picked up speed. She felt the wind on the wings. The whole airplane came alive. She felt it strive to fly. And she wanted it, too. The engine strained. It shuddered. The noise grew deafening.

Then it happened.

Colin eased back the stick. With a sigh, it lifted off the grass and into the air. With an answering sigh, her heart lightened. Colin smiled at her and laughed so freely his joy vibrated through her like the echo of a Sunday church bell. She smiled back. Silver nose to the lightening sky, they climbed.

When Colin leveled off, lowering the nose to the horizon, Liesl gasped at the sight. Gold painted the bottoms of lavender clouds in a pink sky. She'd never seen anything so beautiful. Checking his instruments, Colin made small adjustments and pulled the throttle back to cruising rpms. It seemed as if they stood still and the glorious spectacle of day birthing took place all around them—just for them.

"So, you want to learn to dance, Liesl?"

Choked by the beauty of the morning, she nodded.

"The horizon is your partner. The airplane becomes part of you. You become part of it. Put your hand on the stick."

Imitating Colin, Liesl wrapped her left hand tentatively around the joystick between her legs.

He laughed at her. The skin around his eyes crinkled. "Come on, hon. Hold it like you mean it."

As she tightened her hold around the stick, fire burned her face once more.

"Good. It's your connection to the airplane." His voice fanned her like a caress. "Feel it. Feel the vibrations in your hand. Feel the life."

She groaned inwardly. Why did everything he said seem to take on sexual overtones? His voice, of course. Slow and seductive, it buffeted her nerve endings like a tropical breeze. For a brief, mad moment, she felt an insane jealousy toward the airplane.

"That's it. Move it around a little. Feel it respond."

She shifted the stick to the right and felt the airplane turn and dip.

"Good. Move the stick back a little bit and apply a little right rudder. You're doing great. Now look at the horizon. When you dance, you look your partner in the eye. Let the feel guide you. Let the horizon guide you."

Pressure vibrated in her hand. Gravity pulled at her seat. Simple joy lifted her heart. The airplane skimmed along the line where blue sky met brown earth. The music of wind on wings, of purring engine, of Colin's voice in her ear sang into her muscles, into her blood, into her soul.

Her hand jerked back at the thought, upsetting the airplane's delicate balance. Crazy. He was driving her crazy.

"Easy now," Colin said, guiding her to a level attitude once more. "Try it again."

She turned left this time.

"Now increase your power a little and climb at the same time. Easy, not too steep. Level out." She did. "You're a natural."

The compliment pleased her more than it should have, sending a small thrill to the pit of her stomach. A wave of warmth spread from it, disturbing her.

"Okay. Loosen your grip and follow me."

He showed her then how to dance with the sky. The airplane rose and dipped, turned and leveled. In a series of lazy eights, they waltzed, they actually waltzed with the ground! He streaked the sky in a burst of speed and practiced a pylon pattern, injecting a massive dose of elation straight into her. She followed his every move with her hand, followed the sensual murmurs of his voice with her heart, followed the dance with her body until there seemed to be no barrier left between the sky, the machine, and the humans inside it.

They were one.

Time ceased to exist.

Then panic set in. She teetered on some invisible line where past, present and future blended. And as glorious as this moment of perfect union was, Liesl had never felt so lost. Where did she belong? In the past with Kurt? In the future with Colin? In the present alone?

As if zapped by lightning, Liesl snapped her hand from the joystick. Colin gave her a quizzical look, but didn't speak. Moments later he turned the airplane around and headed back toward the airport.

"She's as ready as she'll ever be," he said, adjusting the power for a steady descent.

All she could do was nod. She couldn't trust her voice.

Turning away from Colin, she looked out the side of the canopy. Her vision blurred. She was falling in love. She hadn't thought it possible, but her heart nearly burst from it. And he wouldn't even be born for another twenty years. She wanted to cry bitter tears for the pain to come when he left, for the unfairness of it all.

She'd failed. Without lifting a finger, he'd made love to her as deeply, as thoroughly, as if their bodies had joined intimately. Without touching her he'd gotten to her.

The lacy white impression of the moon decorated an otherwise pale blue sky. A perfect day for the competition. Below them, the small squares of houses stood like crooked pieces of a mosaic along the curving highway. The white dots of cows milled about greening fields, their barbed-wire boundaries almost invisible from this height. As they flew by, Lake Schönberg reflected the Castell's silhouette on its mirror-clear waters. The peace of the passing scenery made a stark contrast to the violent storm of emotions swirling inside her.

Colin entered the airport pattern and started his descent. When the wheels kissed the grass, Liesl felt the weight of the world return.

After shutting down the engine, Colin sat silent in his seat. The tired lines reappeared on his face. His shoulders slumped.

"I want you to get some sleep," Liesl said. "You won't be able to fly this tired."

"I'm fine." He closed his eyes and circled his neck with his hands.

"You're one stubborn mule."

Half a smile creased his cheek. "Yeah, so I'm told."

"If you won't sleep, then rest and plan your strategy."

"Aye-aye, Captain." He slid the canopy back and extricated himself from his seat, then offered her a hand. She tripped a toe over the canopy lip, landing hard against Colin's chest.

The ghost of the man she'd loved hovered in the hazel of his eyes. In the smoky look of his gaze, she saw that he'd felt the perfect union of their spirit as they'd flown. He wanted her now in the flesh as he'd had her in the air. And the thought that she wanted him just as fiercely frightened her to the marrow. She'd never been able to resist him. Not then. Not now. His arms tightened around her.

"You didn't puke." As he spoke, his lips barely brushed hers. "You were wonderful."

Her fingers dug into his shoulders. She'd

meant to push him away. "Colin, please don't."

Her skin zinged with awareness. Her body ached with need. Her heart broke with conflicting emotions. If he kissed her now, she wouldn't be able to resist. And she couldn't give in. She couldn't risk the pain of losing him a second time.

He eased her to the ground. "You're right. I think I need some sleep."

To distract herself, to connect with reality, Liesl ran her hand along the Castell's skin. "Too bad we don't have time to paint it."

"It wouldn't make much difference. But if it makes you feel better, you can have the boys rub a coat of wax on it. Be ready to leave after lunch. I want to have time to scope out the competition."

"All right."

She helped him roll the Castell back into the hangar. By the time she'd secured the airplane in place, Colin had fallen asleep on the cot in Kurt's room. She hitched a blanket over him. Giving in to an impulse, she bent down and gave him a quick kiss. As she pulled away, her breath quivered.

Hand pressed to her mouth, she turned and left. She ran into the morning, pumping her arms and legs up the hill. Out of control. Her feelings had gone out of control. She couldn't afford to lose control this close to her goal.

She slammed the gate closed and savagely shoved the rusted iron tongue into its clasp. How could life be so cruel? Finding the past in the future would still leave her alone in the present.

But the past and the future didn't exist, so she'd have to concentrate on the present—on the race.

It was all she had.

"Will she be all right?" Liesl asked Wenona. She'd taken a detour to her aunt's house to check on the bird's condition before going home.

"She will be fine." As she bent to croon at the bird, Wenona's thick black braid fell forward. She handed Liesl an eye dropper and showed her how to feed the bird. The sparrow's outlook on life seemed to have brightened since Liesl had asked Wenona to look at the glassy-eyed creature. "I don't think the eggs will be as lucky."

"Does she know?" Liesl asked.

"She understands the circle of life."

Tante Wenona's house had always fascinated her. Life here seemed to flow at a different pace. The peace she'd found in Wenona's kitchen had been lacking in her own home, where an uneasy tension always hung in the air. Unlike the cinnamon and soup scents of *Oma's* kitchen, Wenona's smelled of herbs which hung from the rafters and fragrant mesquite smoke which burned from the wood stove.

Liesl closed the cage's rickety wooden door and sat on one of Wenona's time-polished chairs. "It doesn't bother her to lose her family?"

"Death is a passage, child. Just like birth. She will have a new nest and a new batch of babies to take care of soon." Wenona set a cup of steaming tea before her and offered her a thick slice of bread spread with butter and wild honey. The thick honey dripped on one side of the crust. Liesl licked her lips imagining Colin's taste on them.

"But death . . ." Liesl lifted her shoulders in a helpless gesture and let them fall again. "It seems so final."

"No, little one. Death is only a beginning."

When Liesl was a child, Wenona's midnight black eyes had frightened her. They seemed to read minds and souls with unerring accuracy. Liesl had learned over the years that they could also comfort. Wenona stared at her now, and though Liesl twisted restlessly in her chair, she was thankful. There would be no need to explain. Even if she couldn't find the right words, Wenona would understand.

Liesl tightened her hand around the glass eye dropper, frustration screaming along her nerves. She'd used the sparrow as an excuse, she realized. All along she'd meant to talk to Wenona, to ask her about the crazy thoughts driving her insane.

"How . . . where does a soul live when the body dies?" The glass tube shattered with a ping in her hand. Liesl looked down numbly at the broken pieces littering her palm.

Wenona swept the pieces onto the cradle of her apron and dumped them in a wastebasket.

She filled a cup with tea and joined Liesl at the table.

"It goes into the Mysterious Center and inevitably circles back to life." With a weathered finger, Wenona traced a circle in the crumbs beside the round loaf of bread on the table. "Death occurs so that life might occur. Without death there would be no change. And change has no meaning or purpose unless it relates to the changeless Center."

"I don't understand."

"Sometimes we get a second chance. What was left undone the first time?"

Liesl took a tentative sip from her cup and tasted chamomile in the tea. A thousand questions flew and squawked like a disturbed flock of crows in her head. She looked up from the dark amber liquid in her cup and stared quizzically at her aunt. "As much as I love you, *Tante*, sometimes I think you speak a different language."

"You feel the part of Colin that is Kurt. You feel it and you fear it."

Liesl held her breath, and felt her heart drum against her ribcage.

"Can they both exist in one?" she asked on a long, shaky breath.

"The grass is part of the cow." Wenona traced the circle in the crumbs once more. "The cow you eat for dinner becomes a part of you." She swept the crumbs into her hands, walked to the open window, and threw them on the ground. "The chickens eat the crumbs. We eat the chickens. The soul, too, follows the circle. What was left undone the first time, Liesl? What regret weighs your conscience?"

So many things. Liesl sighed wearily, closing her eyes. Too tired to care, she let the tears pressing against her lids slip down her face. She'd never told Kurt how much she loved him. He'd held her in a separate compartment. They'd loved each other, but they'd both been afraid to give themselves completely—because she hadn't been perfect; because he'd lost too many people he'd cared for. "But he's leaving tomorrow."

Wenona seemed to understand how far Colin would travel. "Then I say, child, you waste precious time. Go to him. Don't be afraid."

Liesl watched, shading her eyes from the bright sun with one hand while Colin hopped on the Castell's wing and slid the canopy back.

"Change your mind?" he asked, looking hopefully at her.

"No, I'll take my father's car. I'll meet you there."

"Suit yourself."

No, it didn't suit her. Not at all. Molding herself to him, feeling his hands on her, tasting him on her tongue. That would suit her. Highly impractical. Wholly illogical. But suit her it would, as nothing had in a long time.

If only she wasn't so afraid.

She wasn't ready yet. Despite her talk with Wenona, or maybe because of it, she needed more time. Time to sort out her feelings, time to make sense of the impossible happening all around her, time to phrase her words.

Time. Always time. She'd run out of it before. She'd have to make her decision soon.

She hoped she wouldn't reach it too late.

The Trinity Air Show was a three-day affair with a varied program of aerobatic demonstrations, military fly-bys, landing contests, and of course, the Trophy Race—a forty-five-minute all-out sprint around four pylons on a thirty-mile course, ten laps in all.

Colin had landed at Trinity Fields, on the northwest side of Fort Worth, two hours earlier and immediately got caught up in the excitement surrounding the air show. The airport grounds buzzed with activity. Dozens of airplanes stood chocked or tethered to makeshift ground anchors. Hundreds of people milled around. The scent of hot dogs and avgas filled the air, along with the drone of engines and the cacophony of voices speaking all at once. Here, he didn't feel so far from home.

With the sun low in the sky and black shadows stretching over the airport, Colin grew worried about Liesl's whereabouts, and his distracted gaze kept searching for her in the ever-shifting crowd. He'd staked out a cozy little corner for the Castell and now struggled with pitching a canvas tent beneath its wing. He'd take no chances. If anyone tried to harm his craft tonight, he'd be right there to protect it.

"Need help?"

He looked up from his work and smiled. When he saw Liesl standing there, a ridiculous sensation of warmth spread through him. He'd missed her. More than he should. "Sure."

She'd swept her hair back into a neat twist at the back of her head. The dying day's light fired the gold of her hair and gave her skin the look of rich cream. Under a black jacket, she wore a white blouse of some soft material with a series of small tucks running down the front and a pale blue scarf knotted at her neck. Her black pants revealed the gentle curve of her hips, arousing his hunger for her once more.

He gestured to the wooden stake. Her fluid movements had him swallowing when she took the stake from his hand. She held it in place while he hammered it into the ground.

"It's been a long day," she said.

"Yeah, a long one." His tongue seemed to tie itself in knots and his hand to grow ten thumbs. "Guess you found me all right?" He groaned, feeling like an idiot. "I thought you'd gotten lost . . . or something."

He was afraid the "something" might have been her decision to steer clear of him after their flight this morning. He shouldn't have done that to her. But he'd been caught up in the freedom of sharing the sky with her.

She'd felt it too, the thrill, the cessation of time, the perfect oneness. She'd felt it and understood it. And he'd known then he'd made a terrible mistake. For a moment, their souls had connected on another level, and sheer panic had zapped through him because the future suddenly seemed so bleak without her in it, and the abysmal sadness brought by the thought had made him want to kiss her one last time—to capture the pure perfection of the moment and treasure it forever.

But he belonged to a different time, and she belonged here. He couldn't take her with him any more than he could stay here.

"I stopped by the race office to make sure everything was set," she said, her voice as unsure as his.

They tiptoed around each other. Like strangers, Colin thought. He wanted to apologize. He wanted to scream. He didn't know what he wanted anymore. He didn't like the feeling.

Once the tent stood, Colin tested it for solidity. "Should do for the night."

Miserably uncomfortable, Colin leaned against the Castell, crossing his feet at the ankles. He needed to walk, to run, to move—to hold her, to kiss her, to love her. Planted here with her so close didn't do much for his overtaxed nerves. "Did Max come out with you?"

"No, *Tante* Wenona wouldn't let him skip school. He should be along shortly with Stefan and Anton."

"Oh." He shoved his hands in his pockets to keep them from reaching for the wisp of hair that had loosened from her twist.

When Max and his friends appeared down the line of airplanes, he sighed with relief. Checkered shirts with tails untucked worn over a white T-shirt, jeans with the cuffs rolled up and army boots seemed to be the uniform of the time. Max's dark looks and the flight jacket he wore distinguished him from his blond friends.

As they walked, each worked on eating a hot dog. They jostled each other and joked, growing silent as a pretty girl went by.

Had he ever been that young? Colin wondered. At seventeen, Max and his friends still looked like boys. At seventeen, he'd already lost the love of his life and often woke up feeling a hundred years old. The boys reached the Castell in high spirits. Seeing someone they knew, Stefan and Anton excused themselves and left.

"Why'd you park so far?" Max asked, popping the last of his hot dog in his mouth. "We had a devil of a time finding you."

"I'm hoping *everyone*'ll think we parked too far," Colin said.

"Oh!" Max said, understanding dawning on him. He rolled the napkin he held into a ball and stuffed it in his jacket pocket. "Didn't see Billy, but we did see the Mustang and the Lightning he's got entered." He turned to Liesl. "Guess who's flying the Mustang."

"You know I don't like guessing games." Liesl flipped the loose strand of hair behind her ear. What's eating her? Colin wondered at her sudden change of mood.

"Matson."

Like a puppy who'd just brought back a stick, Max waited expectantly for her reaction.

"It doesn't surprise me at all." Anger shimmered in her voice. "Billy had to bribe the pilots with *something*."

"Who's Matson?" Colin asked.

"One of the better pilots around," Max said. "Most of these fellas come fresh from the Air

Force or Navy and haven't flown pylon races. Matson has—and won. He's got a reputation for being super aggressive. He pushes his plane to the limit just for the fun of it."

Max peeked inside the tent. "Do you have any food around here?"

"No time to get any yet."

"You'll have to keep your eye on Matson," Liesl said, kicking a stone with the toe of her boot. "He's known for his dirty tricks. He's been known to force opponents to cut a pylon."

Colin wanted to reassure her and gave her his most confident smile. "Maybe I can teach him a trick or two."

"This is no laughing matter, Colin." Her hands flew to her hips and her voice dripped with irritation. "This is serious. Flying for me, he was an asset. Flying against me, he'll be a liability."

"I'm a good pilot, Liesl." He wrapped an arm around her shoulders and squeezed gently. Mistake. Tortured pulse scrambled along his veins. "I won't let you down. Have you had dinner yet?"

"No." She eased away from him as if she, too, had heard the rushing of his blood.

"Great. I'm starved. I'll let you treat me to a hot dog or two while Max babysits."

Max groaned his protest, but pointing out the significance of the task bestowed on him gave him a new sense of importance. The bribe of more food didn't hurt, either.

Here among this crowd of people, Colin was safe. He relaxed and let himself enjoy Liesl's excitement at the show, seeing everything in a fresh way through her eyes. Hot dogs had never tasted so good. Coffee had never smelled so fragrant. Colin sized up his competition and assured Liesl the Castell was up to the challenge.

Accepting his hot dog bribe, Max skipped out on them as soon as they returned, promising to be back bright and early the next day.

Night had fallen. Soft light from stars and a near-full moon gleamed off the metal birds lined in rows. Silence, except for an occasional human noise disturbing the nocturnal peace, permeated the grounds now that they were closed to the public.

Awkwardly Colin hitched an elbow on the Castell's wing. "So, ah, are you going home, or staying at a motel nearby?"

"I'm staying here. With you." She gave him a look as if this had been understood all along.

Colin straightened. Her? Here? All night! "That's out of the question. The temperature's supposed to dip in the low forties tonight. You'll freeze." *I'll burn.*

"And you won't?" Her gaze narrowed, her chin lifted.

"I've got a sleeping bag." Her mouth opened to speak, but he cut her off. "*One* sleeping bag, Liesl. Not two."

It didn't faze her at all.

"You need sleep, and someone needs to stay awake to watch over the airplane."

"I can't let you do that." He scrubbed a hand through his hair.

"Why not? It's my airplane."

Her nose puckered when she got mad. He liked the way it marred the too-perfect composure of her face, making her seem human and approachable. Too human; too approachable. He wanted to reach out and smooth the wrinkles over the crooked ridge with his finger. "I want to know you're safe."

"I'm not leaving." To prove her point, she parked her pretty little butt right in front of his tent and crossed her arms over her chest.

Rolling his eyes skyward and lifting his hands in a helpless gesture, Colin gave up. He hadn't planned on much sleep anyway. Maybe having company wouldn't be so bad. "Come inside, then, away from the wind."

He scooted in ahead of her, unrolled his sleeping bag, and set the digital alarm on his watch for six.

Liesl eyed the process with curiosity, but he didn't explain the beeps. Let her wonder. He removed his boots and dropped them with a thump. Let her understand they belonged in different worlds. He rolled his jacket into a pillow. Let her know he could resist her. He stretched out on the sleeping bag, reached beneath his pillow, and extracted a blanket which he tossed to Liesl.

"Good night," he said, and closed his eyes.

"Good night."

Minute after endless minute ticked by. Colin shifted and reshifted, trying to find a comfortable position. This wasn't going to work. Her gentle breathing drove him crazy. Her soft shifts shouted her presence. The chattering teeth she tried to hide completely undid him.

"You're shivering," he said gruffly, lifting his upper body and leaning his weight on an elbow.

"I'm fine."

She shot him a brave smile but huddled beneath the gray blanket, and illuminated by the moon's light, she looked pitiful.

"Come over here."

She shook her head in quick, short strokes. "No, you sleep."

"I won't be able to sleep with your teeth chattering. You want me to fly rested tomorrow, don't you? So stop arguing with me and come over here."

She stared at him, hesitating, debating. With a defeated sigh, she capitulated.

"I won't bite. I promise." He tried to laugh away her fear. It came out in an awful rumble. What was wrong with him? He was acting like a damned kid on his first date.

He slipped out of the bag and unzipped it all the way. After smoothing out the surface, he lay back down, inviting her to join him. She stretched out beside him with careful precision, making sure no part of her touched any part of him. She wasn't doing him any favor. The distance only added to the agony. He drew the blanket up around them both.

"Are you nervous about the race tomorrow?" he asked, seeking to ease her discomfort, seeking to forget her proximity.

"Yes." As his knuckle accidentally brushed the top of her thigh, he heard the almost imperceptible stagger in her voice. "I didn't think we'd make it."

"Neither did I." Her flowery fragrance drowned his senses in pleasure. "You're lucky to have such a supportive family."

"Yes, I am." She fidgeted, pulling half the blanket off him. "I-I'm sorry. You . . . you need to sleep."

He took the well-worn edge of the blanket from her. Her fingers' nervous fumble had his stomach doing a loop. "I'm too keyed up."

"Do you have a strategy planned for tomorrow?"

"Pretty much." Lifting his arms to cradle his nape with both hands, he accidentally grazed her temple with his elbow. She took in a shaky breath. He forced himself not to soothe the spot. "I'm hoping to qualify with good enough speed to start on the inside. It'll give me a psychological edge if nothing else. I'm planning on wide, easy turns, and—"

Her head snapped in his direction. "Won't that put you behind?"

"No, in tight turns the additional induced drag from the centrifugal force would pull down the speed maybe twenty, twenty-five miles per hour. In a wide turn, I'll travel a bit further, but lose only one or two miles per hour. Doesn't look quite as flashy, but in the end it'll leave me with more engine to go for it when it counts."

"What else?"

"Well, I promise I won't cut a pylon." He

laughed, trying to lighten the tension swirling around them.

"Be serious! If Matson maneuvers you into cutting one, you'll be penalized a lap or disqualified. It could mean the difference between winning and losing."

"You've got to trust me and let me fly the race my way, Liesl."

"I do." She moved again and stared at the tent's ceiling. The ends of her hair teased his cheek. "It's just so important to win."

"I know." He'd spent most of his life obsessing about the concept. For what? Where had it gotten him? He'd lost everything he really cared for.

One more attempt at shifting the conversation, his thoughts, into neutral territory. "What do you for fun?"

"For fun?"

She tucked and retucked the loose strand of hair behind her ear. He stilled her hand and removed the pin from her hair, fanning the silk around her head. As he dragged his fingers through the softness, a sigh of pleasure escaped him. He didn't want to resist anymore. He could have her, get her out of his system without involving his heart. He could do that, but not to her.

"Yeah. You know, Saturday nights when people go out and have fun?"

She shuddered. "Mostly I spend them at the airport. Sometimes I go with my cousin Emma to Fort Worth and catch a movie."

"What kind of movies do you like?"

She licked her lips. "Musicals. MGM puts out some good ones." The tone of her voice hiked up a few octaves. Her words rushed out like a waterfall, tripping over each other. "Do they still have musicals in your time?"

He fought back the need to turn to her and release the heated tension she'd stirred. "Some. Different. Mostly you have to go to the theater to catch those. Action adventures are big now. Blood, guts and violence. But you can rent videos and catch all the classics. Karen used to love—"

He stopped himself mid-sentence, his feelings suddenly twirling into a hurricane. And as hard as he tried to deny the fact, he still wanted Liesl.

"Karen?"

"A friend." He turned away from Liesl's warmth, trying to rescue the last vestiges of his control.

"Is she why you want to go back?"

Colin took a deep, long breath. "Karen is dead."

Liesl trembled against him.

"You're still cold," he said, capturing one of her hands in his. It shook. "It's like ice." He placed it over his heart, letting her feel the increasing beat of his pulse, feeling hers at her wrist. She snapped her hand away. "How am I supposed to keep you warm when you won't lie still?"

"I'm fine." Her voice wavered.

"Well, I'm not." Cursing, he wrapped one arm around her waist and slipped the other beneath her shoulders and spooned her tight against his body. If he didn't touch her, if he didn't feel her against him, he'd explode.

Nose in her hair, he drank in her scent. She felt like home. Ridiculous, of course, this fantasy of his, but he could almost imagine holding her like this every night, falling asleep snug in the comforting cocoon of her heat.

"You know you drive me crazy," he said, his voice rasping painfully in his constricted throat. Paradoxically, his admission gave him back an inch of control.

"Ever since I saw you through my windshield," he continued, "I've had dreams about you. Disturbing dreams. It's like I've known you forever, waited for you all my life. And it's so crazy, because you and me, we literally come from different worlds."

"I know," she whispered unevenly.

"Liesl . . . this isn't going to work."

"I know."

Chapter Nine

Liesl struggled to turn around in Colin's arms and face him. When his arms had grabbed her with such need and snugged her against him with such ferocity, something had shifted in her. Her fear of the past, of the future vanished, leaving her with only now.

Now was all she ever had, she reminded herself. Tomorrow would take care of itself, and yesterday would live forever in her mind.

It wasn't disloyalty, it was life—Wenona's circle of life.

She knew that by sunset tomorrow he'd be gone, but today, now, he was here, and he was hers, if she wanted. His words, his shaky voice, his trembling body told her so, and the ache deep in her soul needed the soothing only he could give, because in him the past and the future came together in the present.

"I know," she repeated. She reached out to touch him, trailing a finger along his temple, following the curve of his jaw, his skin smooth, then stubbly beneath her index finger. "I want to be near you, too. The things I feel for you are too strong to be real. I-I don't know if it's just an echo from the past or something new. All I know is that it's strong." She brushed her thumb along his lips, feeling his hot breath stroke her skin. "Kiss me, Colin."

"You're asking for trouble," he said, his voice low and gritty against her finger.

"I know."

He stared down at her. In the low light of the moon, his eyes shone black with desire. "I don't want to hurt you."

Tentatively she pressed her lips against his. "You won't." He was a gift to herself, and to life meant to be lived, not pined away.

"You deserve love, Liesl. I can't offer you that. My heart died a long time ago."

"I'm not asking for love. I'm asking for you, for now. You'll be gone tomorrow. Let me have tonight." Experimentally she ran her tongue along the soft curve of his lower lip. His body stiffened and his breath jittered against her. "Please."

His body relaxed and slowly, fluidly, he shifted to answer her kiss. "One night, then. For you."

He pulled her against him. She lifted her arms to circle his neck. His slow, deep exploration of her mouth had her senses swirling like

a bird caught in an updraft. Leaving her insecurities behind, she let herself fly upward. His
heat and hers mingled, banishing the night's
cold air. She tasted him in return.

"You taste so good," she said. "Wild and sweet
at the same time."

His low growl rumbled in a sensual flutter
against her. Needing to touch him, she plunged
her hands beneath his shirt and felt the swift
tightening of his stomach muscles. Her study
of his ribs had barely begun when he removed her hands and brought one palm to
his lips.

"No," he said. "You wanted a night, let me
give you a night."

He pressed her to the sleeping bag, his long
legs tangling with hers. His hand started at the
round of her hip and moved up, slowly, deliciously, resting for a delirious moment on her
aching breast. She lifted to meet his touch, and
as his hand moved on, she moaned her protest
in his mouth. "Colin . . ."

"We have time. We have all night."

Yes, they did, she realized. For now, time
seemed to have stopped. They could taste and
feast at their leisure, the cosmos would wait for
them. For once time would wait for *them*.

He kissed her again with lazy ease, taking her
higher and higher into the breathless heavens.
With lingering torture, he shifted to play with
the thumping pulse at the juncture of her neck
and shoulders.

He removed the choking scrap of scarf from
beneath her collar and attacked the row of tiny

buttons with excruciating slowness. Each patch of newly freed skin received a warm welcome which burned along her veins like a burst of solar heat. His hands lingered on her breasts, but his mouth bypassed their aching need for it, trailing down to her stomach instead, leaving behind a quivering mass of flesh.

Liesl reached for the buttons of his shirt, but he captured her wrists and held them near her head. "Oh, no. Not yet, Liesl. Not yet."

A needy, helpless sound vibrated in her throat. "I want you, Colin."

His devilish smile did nothing to suppress her need. "I know."

As his mouth found the pulsing nipple beneath her white cotton bra, she gasped and arched against him. When he continued to flick the straining peak with his tongue, she squirmed beneath him with delicious agony, rubbing herself against his swollen need, silently begging for release. Her hands flexed hard in his from the desperate ache he aroused. "Colin . . ."

He released her hands and straddled her hips. The heat of him transferred with swift intensity through the material of their clothes. His hardened need seemed to have no effect on him as he peeled away the layers of her jacket, shirt and bra, his eyes appreciating the flesh he exposed.

"Beautiful," he whispered before lowering his mouth to hers again. He teased her throat, her breasts, her nipples, her stomach with feathery kisses and fiery breath, sending a devastating pleasure surging like a rudderless airplane through her.

Her hands reached for him, pulling him down on her, assaulting him with the same kind of savage longing he'd rained on her, letting his hunger feed hers. She thrilled at his helpless moan, at his greedy answer. Her senses were buffeted in the turbulent wake of his heat-stirred musk.

Body against body, lost in space, boundaries disappeared.

Suddenly the discordant rhythms of their drumming hearts fell into cadence. They both froze, hearing echoes of the past. The pulse at his throat bounced in time with hers. The tempo of his short breaths matched hers.

Frightening.

Intriguing.

They stared at each other across the moonlit darkness enveloping them in the tent. Recognition hummed from somewhere outside time and space, outside comprehension, outside belief. Then it flared, hurling them to a higher altitude.

Their bodies came together again. Old. New. The same. Different. As they gave in to the pulse of desire strumming between them, dream and reality merged. The barrier of clothes fell away. Awareness heightened.

She felt every brush of skin on skin, every breath, every trembling of needy flesh on needy flesh with this new, almost painful sensitivity. "Colin?"

Hard and pulsing, the satiny length of him

pressed against her. "Yes, Liesl?"

"Now, please." Her hands pushed against the dip at the bottom of his spine, urging him to her.

"Yes, now."

He eased himself into her, slowly stroking her inner ache. Blood pounded in her ear. She couldn't catch her breath. The whole world narrowed to one point of unbearable pleasure. He took her higher still, lifting, soaring, hurling her across a galaxy of impossible bliss. When she opened her eyes, her gaze latched on to his and took him with her on her fantastic journey.

His rhythm assumed a new urgency, a fervor that took and gave, tantalized and possessed, pushing them both to the edge of the universe.

For one breathless moment, she felt weightless, suspended in this timeless apex of heaven.

Then the whole world exploded around her in a burst of a thousand stars.

Fighting his uneven breath and the pulsing shivers still racking his body, Colin held her tucked hard in his arms. He held on to her with fear and longing. Her ear rested softly against his heart, her hand on his heaving chest, her ragged breaths fanning his skin. As gray fog overtook his mind, nightmare blurred with reality.

"Forever, Liesl." A voice not his own echoed in the night. Where had that come from?

Her blue eyes turned up to his and rounded with question.

His grip on her tightened.

"Colin?"

"I'm sorry. I don't know what happened."

His mind screamed with pain and joy, with fury and ecstasy. He pried himself from her out of sheer terror that his mouth would utter more promises he couldn't keep, more phantom memories from a past he'd never lived. Concentrating his attention on the task, he dressed.

"I have to use the facilities," he said, and all but ran out of the tent.

Cold wind slapped his cheeks. He drank it in with wide, thirsty gulps.

He'd meant to give her what she wanted, not open the lock to his closed heart. One evening to make her smile like the memories haunting him. One evening to wean his system from her incredible pull.

No! Cursing, he slammed his fist on the airplane's side, and rejoiced in the throbbing pain shooting to his elbow. He couldn't love her. Choking for breath, Colin stretched his neck, offering his face to the heatless moon.

So many stars. How bright were those pinpricks of light without the haze of city pollution to dull them. Bright, like Liesl's eyes as she'd drawn him into her pleasure.

God help him, he loved her. Even in his all-consuming teenage love for Karen, he'd never imagined a love so deep, so full. It swelled his heart and filled his mind, but he couldn't allow himself the feelings. He sure as hell couldn't tell her how he felt.

Tomorrow, he'd leave.

They had no future together. His future was fifty years away. Hers was here.

He stuck his fists into his jacket pockets and strode out to escape his thoughts, his feelings, himself. But Liesl swirled in and out of his mind. The feel of her, warm and soft against him. He groaned. The scent of her, flowery and tantalizing. He hunched his shoulders forward and hurried his pace. Her taste, intoxicating and sweet. He bit his lower lip. Her soft sighs, her gentle touch, the violent explosion of her body beneath his played and replayed themselves in his mind, already haunting him like some sort of vaporous ghost.

She'd given herself to him, made love to him with a passion he'd never expected, never known existed. She'd made him feel. She'd made him forget. She'd filled him with an overwhelming sense of completeness.

And for a moment, he'd been tempted to give in to the feeling, to believe the two of them together would be enough. But he knew his failure would always hang between them. If he didn't go home, if he didn't finish what he'd started, he would regret it. And regret would surely taint whatever bond fused them.

When he reached the chain-link fence bordering the airport, his aimless flight ended abruptly. He paced from one metal pole to the next and back again, trying to convince himself he'd made the right decision. She wouldn't fit in his world. He couldn't stay in hers.

He wasn't in love with her. He scrubbed a

hand over his face, over his hair. He wasn't in love. Because loving her would make him too vulnerable.

Standing still, he stared at the far horizon where navy skies met black hills. He had to concentrate on the race.

Tomorrow, he'd be going home.

With Colin gone, the night's cold assaulted Liesl with a vengeance. Shivering, she put the layers of her clothes back on, wishing she could cover the raw emptiness in her heart with the same ease.

She sat cross-legged on the sleeping bag, the blanket wrapped around her shoulders, waiting for Colin to return. The tent's sides flubbed in the wind. Nothing had ever sounded so lonely.

She'd asked for this night, knowing there would be no tomorrow. Their time together had been glorious, magical. She would savor it over and over again. She had no regrets.

But she'd made the mistake of falling in love with him. Not just the part of him that was Kurt, but the part of him that was Colin, too. She loved all of him with a depth and a fullness she hadn't thought possible.

With a jerky yank she tucked a strand of loose hair behind her left ear. She hadn't felt this alive in two years. She was in love and she wouldn't apologize for it, not to him, not to herself.

When she heard his footsteps, her heart sped up and her mouth went dry. She knew he'd left to escape. But was he running from her or from his own feelings? As he lifted the flap to enter, she held her breath.

"You're still awake," he said, crawling in and closing the flap behind him. A crack of dim light from the moon filtered through the space where the flaps didn't quite meet.

"I'm guarding the Castell while you sleep, remember?"

He sat beside her, knee brushing knee, connecting. She swallowed her sigh of contentment.

"I guess I should try to sleep," Colin said, pulling off his boots.

"Colin?" Liesl worried the frayed edge of the blanket with one hand.

"Yes?"

He looked at her over his shoulder, straight and level. She couldn't read his thoughts or guess at his well-guarded feelings. Doubt trickled in. Had she done anything wrong? She'd loved him with all her heart, body and soul. There was nothing wrong with that.

To close the circle, she had to finish what she'd left undone. Her heart jittered unsteadily. The words she needed to tell him stuck to the back of her throat. She wanted to close the circle, but she'd have to take the long way around. "I . . . I want to thank you for tonight."

"No regrets?" He nervously tucked the ends of the blanket around her knees. His fingers trembled slightly against the material of her pants. She recognized his fear and it gave her courage.

"None. You?" She looked hopefully into his

eyes, but the thick walls hid the mirrors of his soul.

"No." He refolded his jacket, punched it once, and stretched out on the sleeping bag.

Now that she'd found him, she couldn't let him go again. She took a deep breath before blurting out her forward idea.

"I love you, Colin. Take me with you when you leave."

He stared at her, not moving a single muscle. In the deep silence between them, Liesl was sure he could hear her heart pounding, the bones of her knuckles cracking from the force with which she held the blanket's edge.

Slowly he flowed up. On his knees before her, he reached for her shoulders. He licked his lips and shook his head. "I have nothing to offer you. I live alone in a hangar. I never know where my next meal is coming from. I have no security, no home, no family that cares for me. You have all those things here. How can I take all that away from you?"

"Because I love you," she whispered, keeping her gaze steady, her voice level.

He shook her shoulders. His fingers, digging into her flesh, hurt. "When you're alone in my tiny room while I'm out scrounging for survival, what do you think'll happen to that love? It'll die, Liesl. It'll die, and you'll have no way of getting home again. I can't do that to you."

"I'd have you." The blood seemed to freeze in her veins.

A painful frown creased his forehead. "What

about your dream, Liesl? Could you give it up so easily? What'll you do to occupy your days?"

"Take care of you. Of the family we'll make together."

He shook his head. "That wouldn't be enough for you. I can't afford a family right now."

She shrugged, but the ice wouldn't leave her body. "I could get a job. They still have post offices and stores where you live, don't they?"

"It's a world of technology—computers, faxes, modems. You've got no marketable skills."

The last vestiges of warmth drained out of her. Her hold on the blanket's edge tightened. "I'm a good mechanic."

"With outdated engines."

Trying to tamp down the swirl of dread forming in the pit of her stomach, she pried his fingers from her shoulders and squeezed his cold hands. She knew he loved her. It showed in his care when they'd made love. It showed in his fear. "What are you afraid of, Colin?"

"Nothing. I'm not afraid of anything." He pulled his hands from hers and turned his back to her to lie down again.

She gripped the blanket once more with her stiff fingers. The dread vanished, leaving acceptance in its wake. "I see."

To keep him from seeing her body shake, her eyes tear, she retreated to the front of the tent. She'd done her best. She'd tried to close the circle.

She'd told him she loved him, offered herself

to him, and he'd told her she couldn't fit into his world.

She wasn't good enough. She wasn't perfect enough.

Even though she'd said, "I love you," the words she'd never dared tell him two years ago, he'd rejected her. A part of her had known all along this would happen.

But she couldn't take the words back, and she wouldn't beg for his love.

She couldn't be perfect, and he couldn't accept her as she was.

So that was that, she thought with a shuddering sigh.

"Are you cold?" he asked.

"No." She was numb, completely numb. "Try to get some sleep. You've got a race to fly soon."

She cracked the flap open and looked at the Castell, gleaming in the moonlight. At least she still had a purpose. She'd start her center. She'd learn to fly, too, and waltz with the sky and the ground, the way Colin had taught her.

She wouldn't cry. Not this time.

Somewhere in the restless night, Colin slept. A fitful sleep, riddled with nightmares. Nightmares he couldn't escape no matter how hard he tried to fight them.

He was six years old, driving to the store with his mother. School would start in a few weeks and she wanted to get him some new clothes so the teacher wouldn't think he owned only rags. He hated shopping for clothes. They were so stiff when they were new, and just when he got them feeling right, his mom kidnapped his old ones and hauled him off to buy new ones.

"Be my good boy, Colin, and put on your seat belt."

The words fluttered somewhere in his brain, but didn't stay long enough to register. A balsawood airplane in one hand, a plastic model in the other, he flew a mock dogfight in the sky of his imagination.

He heard the click of a seat belt unfastening. But the Red Baron was coming in for a final dive at the enemy. He felt his seat belt drawn tight around his stomach. Rat-a-tat, rat-a-tat, *the Red Baron loosed his guns. The enemy spun out of control.*

His mother screamed. He looked up. A truck, rounding a curve, charged right at them. As she'd fastened his belt, his mother had drifted to the wrong lane. She jerked the wheel to the right. Horn blaring, the truck racketed by.

But the car didn't turn the curve.

It plunged down the hill, bouncing down and down. It stopped sideways against a fence post. As it settled, the mashed metal popped and creaked. His mother lay over the steering wheel, the windshield a crazed halo around her head. Colin couldn't move. He held on tight to his airplanes, and watched mesmerized while blood poured down his mother's crushed face.

My fault. My fault.

Colin tried to claw his way out of the nightmare, but the gray mist only shifted.

He was seventeen and Karen begged him to fly her to Houston. She'd missed the bus to cheer-leading camp because they'd been too busy making out in the cab of his truck. The day was clear, but the wind gusts blew strong. He'd never flown in such high winds before.

"Come on, Colin, be my hero."

How could he refuse her when she cocked her head like that, when her lower lip pouted so enticingly, when her amber eyes flashed with so much trust?

"You've got your license," she continued, teasing the lobe of his ear with her teeth, driving him crazy. "Your father would let you borrow one of his planes. Come on, Colin, it's the only way I'll be able to get to camp. And I've got to get to camp."

"All right. I'll do it."

Without asking, he'd borrowed his father's old Cessna 172. Feeling on top of the world with Karen's ebullient thanks gushing all around him, he'd taxied to the runway and taken off.

At the most vulnerable time, just as the airplane made its transition from ground to air, a vicious cross wind blew him right off the runway. He struggled to recover, but he didn't have the skill. He crashed, crumpling the airplane on its right side, crushing Karen beneath him. As he tried to breathe life back into her, her blood flowed onto his hands.

My fault. My fault.

He fought the suffocating fog, but it thickened around him. Karen wouldn't leave. Her bloody face danced around the dark, dimensionless cave

235

of his nightmare. Colin, Colin, *she called.* Help me! *She twirled and her brown hair turned to gold. When her face reappeared, she was Liesl. Liesl with a bloody gash on her temple. Liesl screaming, and screaming, and screaming.*

With a feral growl, he wrenched himself from the mist and jerked to a sitting position, his heart stuttering, his breath ragged, his forehead slick with sweat. He wiped a hand over his eyes, swallowed hard, and mopped the moisture from his upper lip.

Silence.

No screams.

No Liesl.

A nightmare. That's all.

He'd been right to discourage her love, to make her stay in her own world. His love had already killed two people. He wouldn't have her death on his conscience, too. She'd get over him, forget him. With time. Wasn't it supposed to heal all wounds?

The blanket, still warm with her scent, rested pooled around his middle. He brought it to his face and drank her warmth. He'd made the right decision. He couldn't bear to see her hurt.

He looked at his watch. Six-thirty. He'd slept right through the alarm.

Already the hubbub of ground crews and pilots at work filtered through the canvas. Colin pulled on his boots and hurried outside.

With a hand shading his eyes, he looked for Liesl. Where was she? To keep himself busy more than because it needed to be done, he slowly tracked around the Castell, making sure everything was in order.

"Beautiful day for a race, isn't it?"

"For some." Clear and a shade lighter than Liesl's eyes, the sky sported not a single cloud. The wind didn't puff hard enough to blow a ripe dandelion apart. Perfect flying weather. Horrible weather to say good-bye. Colin rounded the tail to face Billy.

Dressed in a black Stetson, black jacket, gold brocade vest, black pants and black lizard boots, he looked like a fancy gunslinger from an old western movie. All he lacked was the gunbelt. And he'd probably have that on, too, Colin thought sourly, had the race officials not forbidden it.

Billy's mouth widened to a toothpaste-commercial smile. "I'd be worried, too, if I were in your boots. I've got two entries and two of the sharpest pilots around. But I didn't come to brag." He motioned to the two stooges standing behind him. They held a wooden crate between them, and at Billy's signal, they dropped it at his feet.

"Here you go," Billy said, beaming. "As promised, one set of Curtiss three-blade constant-speed propellers."

When ethics had been handed out, Billy must have been absent, Colin decided, shaking his head with incredulity. "After what you did to Liesl's plane, do you really think I'd accept them?"

"I did nothing wrong."

237

"Of course not." Colin made a rude noise and turned to leave.

"Pop the top, boys."

One assistant drew a small crowbar from his back pocket. As he pried the teeth between the cover and box, the nails groaned and squeaked. With the top pulled off, Billy dismissed his men and crouched down beside the crate.

"You know," Billy said, shifting the packing straw to reveal the contents, "it's really better for everyone concerned if you just go on home now."

"Is that so?" The shiny silver blades sparkled in the morning sun. He didn't need Billy's bribe blades. Liesl had promised him hers after the race. But oh, it was tempting, so tempting to accept. With time ticking by so fast, and the window threatening to close, the thought of leaving this mess behind held a strong allure. In less than an hour, he could be on his way home.

But he'd promised her.

"There's a lot more ridin' on this race than Liesl's win." Billy propped one of the blades up and caressed it as a lover might a woman.

"What, yours?" Colin didn't bother to hide the sarcasm. It didn't faze Billy in the least.

"No, Mr. Castle." Billy rose, dusting his hands of the few bits of straw clinging to them. "A whole town's future depends on Liesl's loss."

"Why should I care what happens to the town?" Colin leaned against the Castell's side. He didn't care, couldn't care, even if Liesl was concerned.

"Do you care about what happens to Liesl?"

As they stared at each other, airplane engines buzzed around them, people hurried down the makeshift taxi way, someone tested the public address system.

Drawing his jacket aside as if showing off imaginary guns, Billy stuck his thumbs in the belt of his pants. "Do you really think winnin' will make any difference to what happens to her airport? She's a woman, Mr. Castle. No self-respecting businessman is gonna invest in a woman's venture."

He was up to something, but Colin couldn't figure out what. What, other than the airport, did Billy expect to gain by Liesl's loss? "She's got guts, she'll find a way."

Billy raised his black Stetson, smoothed his greased hair, and settled the hat on his crown once more, shading his eyes with the brim. "Do you know how she paid for the repairs?"

"Why don't you go ahead and tell me?" Colin crossed his arms over his chest to hide the tension strumming a warning through his body.

Billy raised a booted foot and placed it on the crate's edge. One hand rested on his hip, the other supported his chin as his elbow braced against his raised knee. "She came to me for a loan."

"She wouldn't do that." The back of his neck prickled with alarm.

"Well, she did." Billy leaned forward and grinned. A coyote's self-satisfied smile, Colin thought with contempt. "She put her airport up as collateral."

His fingers flexed hard against his elbows. "I'll

have to make sure she wins, then."

"That's no guarantee." The smile widened until the creases in the tanned skin reached almost to his ears. "I can call the loan back at any time."

The threat hung unspoken between them. He planned to call it back before the race, and have Liesl lose everything. Colin's hands closed into hard fists.

"Knowing how you operate, she wouldn't sign a contract with that clause."

"She was desperate."

Colin sprang forward, clamping one hand around Billy's collar, holding the other poised to punch the smile right off his face. He wanted to hit him, wanted to see that pretty smile disfigured permanently with a broken jaw and missing teeth. But he wouldn't give Billy the satisfaction of knowing how close he'd come to losing control. He shoved Billy away. "You're a real pig."

"Now, now, there's no need for that." Billy straightened his shirt collar and jacket, brushed away imaginary dirt. "I'm a shrewd businessman. I've wanted that airport for a long time. She gave me a legal way to get it. I take advantage of the cards that are dealt to me."

"No matter who it hurts." Colin sneered and walked away. He turned and faced Billy. "Why does it mean so much to you?"

"A man's allowed to have his little obsessions."

Vague images vaporized in front of him. Memories. About to brush them away, Colin concentrated on them instead.

Kurt and Willy walked into the general store. Kurt winked at Liesl. She blushed. They pretended to look over the goods displayed on the shelves, but their gazes kept returning to the girl with the golden braids.

"She's beautiful," Willy said.

"She's more than that," Kurt answered. "She's sweet, and she doesn't mind getting dirty, and so much fun to tease."

"She's beautiful," Willy said.

The image faded and fractured. Colin understood that Billy had never been able to see that Liesl's true beauty lay inside, not in the peaches-and-cream perfection of her skin, the periwinkle of her eyes or the gold shining in her hair. Billy didn't see that. He saw only the outside—of everything.

Suddenly another of Willy's little obsessions came to Colin's mind. Billy had never gone through Grüber's woods after the horse incident. Hadn't crossed to the German side of Schönberg since his father's death. Hadn't walked onto the airport since Kurt's death. Colin backed Billy up, caging him against the Castell. Billy's hat hung sideways on his head, then fell to the ground.

"Are you still afraid of ghosts, Willy?" Colin said in a harsh whisper. "Aren't you afraid I came back to get even?"

Billy's face blanched, then reddened with anger. "You don't scare me anymore. Once the airport's mine, I'll burn your ghost away, Kurt, like I've done with all the others, and I'll let the land rot like your soul."

"Kurt? Do I detect a guilty conscience?" Colin enjoyed tormenting Billy, watching the seams of his image come apart, seeing the insecurities surface.

"You can't hurt me. I'm stronger than you. I've got the power now, not you. And I'll have Liesl, too. How do you think she'll feel losing everything?"

First she lost him, then she lost his dream. Jakob's words echoed in Colin's mind. His heart pounded in his chest. Blood whooshed in a deafening roar past his ears.

"But, kind soul that I am," Billy said, taking advantage of Colin's stunned condition to shove him back with the heels of both his hands. "I'll give you one last chance to play the hero for your lady."

Hero. He was no hero. Didn't want to be. Someone always died.

Billy extracted a sheaf of paper from his inside jacket pocket and held it up. "This is a copy of Liesl's contract. Leave now and you can take it with you. She'll keep the airport, and her people'll take care of her, as they always have, and the town'll have a chance to heal its wounds. Everybody wins that way."

"Except you. What do you get out of it?"

Billy picked up his hat and brushed the dirt from it. "A chance to start fresh with Liesl. A chance I never had with you or your ghost around. So what'll it be, the race or the future?"

Colin stood toe to toe with Billy, staring down at him, watching each shift on his feckless face.

"How do I know you won't go back on your word?"

Billy crammed the hat back on his head. The brim poked at Colin's nose. "Without the contract in my hands, I can't call it back."

Colin raised the brim. "What guarantees me that you don't have another copy tucked somewhere in your office?"

He smiled crookedly. "My word as a gentleman." His smile faded. "For the friendship we once shared." Billy slapped the folded contract to Colin's chest. "Come on, be her hero one last time."

Leaving now would give him a greater time leeway to find the window. He had less than a day to go back through Jakob's window before it closed. After the race, time would be short. He'd pushed the window as far as he could. He couldn't let Billy call back the loan. And Liesl, he could do this last thing for her, guarantee her she'd keep her airport and another chance at building the center she dreamed about in the future.

It was all he could do for her.

As he reached out for the sheaf of paper, he heard a gasp behind him. He turned to find Liesl standing there, mouth wide open with incredulity.

"Colin?"

A passing airplane disturbed the crate's packing, drawing Liesl's attention to its contents. She spotted the propeller blades shining in the sun.

"I'll have my boys take this crate to Schön-berg." Billy said.

Colin didn't comment. As Billy's footsteps faded away, Colin watched Liesl's eyes become shiny with tears. He watched her mouth tremble. He watched her shoulders sag. The helpless sound coming from her throat had him rushing to her in long strides.

"Clear!" someone yelled from the side. The Corsair's engine roared to life, then settled into a mutant kitten's purr.

The cardboard tray she held wavered and fell to her feet. Black coffee spilled from the waxed paper cups, sloshing wet stains on both their pants and drowning the sugar-covered donuts squashed beside them.

"How could you!" Her whole body went rigid. Her head shook in denial.

The Corsair's engine sputtered, coughing blue smoke, then roared again, shaking the ground. The propeller's backwash blew Liesl's loose hair forward.

Colin grabbed her arms to keep her from fleeing. "There's a reason. Listen—"

"No!" She jerked her arms free. "I don't want to hear."

"It's hard for me—"

"Hard for you!" Her arms flew wildly around her. Her face twisted with pain and betrayal. "How easy do you think it was for me to ask you to fly for me? To see you every day? To trust you?" One hand went to her heart, and the shattered look in her eyes ripped his insides apart. "I fell in love with you, Colin."

He was doing this for her. Because he cared. She had to know that. "You don't understand!"

"I understand." He'd never seen her face so devoid of color, so hard and unyielding. "You've got to get back to your world and leave me to mine." She took in a hurried breath, and the blue scarf at her neck quivered. "You're right, Colin Castle. You're no hero." She spat out the words, her anger unmistakable over the rumbling engine's noise. "You're a first-class coward."

She stalked away, pounding her heels into the grass. The Corsair pulled out of its parking spot with a lurch and zagged sideways.

As if he viewed a film in slow motion, Colin saw the inevitable. He raced forward, slogging through the viscid air with all his might to save her.

"Lee-ee-sl-l!"

His voice sounded thick and heavy. Liesl didn't pause.

The tip of the Corsair's angled wing clipped her head.

As she fell in a heap to the ground, Colin watched helplessly, paralyzed.

In the cavern of his mind, he heard shouts. He saw people turn and gawk, then gather around her fallen body.

"Someone call an ambulance!"

Colin knelt beside her and turned her over. Her eyes were closed. Blood poured from a gash on her temple. He gathered her in his lap. As his hand fumbled up to brush her hair from the wound, he saw his palm smeared with a red streak. He stared at it, and couldn't stop the uncontrollable shaking overtaking his body.

It was Karen all over again.

Chapter Ten

Blood poured from Liesl's wound at an alarming rate. With stiff and shaking fingers, Colin unknotted the scarf at her neck and pressed it to the wound. The pale blue turned dark.

She didn't stir. Not once. No matter how Colin pleaded with her, she didn't move. Ghost-white and so still, Colin couldn't stand to see her so lifeless. *My fault. My fault.*

"Wake up, Liesl, please wake up."

He stared at the closed lids, translucent blue and as fragile-looking as Wedgwood china, and silently begged them to open. They didn't.

Small and frail, her hand in his, and oh so cold. He hung onto it with fierce determination, connecting, willing her to live. He couldn't let her die. Not this time. He couldn't let go. Not when they lifted her onto the stretcher. Not in the ambulance.

"Faster! Can't you go faster?" Colin yelled, feeling more helpless than he ever had. She was so pale, so still. And all that blood, surely she'd spilled every drop in her body by now.

"Can't risk a bumpy ride with a possible brain injury," the paramedic said as he monitored Liesl's vital signs.

Brain injury! No, God, no. Liesl, please!

He didn't let go when they wheeled her into the emergency entrance and down the sick-green hall with the garish lights.

As they reached an examining room, a burly attendant dressed in white held him back. "End of the line, fella."

"I'm going with her." Colin refused to let go.

"The sooner you let go, the sooner we can take care of her," the attendant said in a low and calming voice. He lifted his hand and signaled to someone behind Colin.

"I'm staying with her."

It took another attendant and a man in a beige security uniform to separate him from Liesl. "Please," he begged as she disappeared into the room.

"What seems to be the problem here?" a be-spectacled, gray-haired man with a stethoscope hanging around his neck asked. The badge on his pocket read "Dr. H.R. Wright."

"This gentleman won't let the patient free to be examined," the attendant said, brushing his bang back into place.

"I need to know she's all right." Colin shook

off the restraining hands holding him back.

The doctor laid a reassuring hand on his shoulder. "We won't know until we take a look at her, and we can't do that with you hanging onto her."

"I have to stay." Colin looked forlornly at the metal door hiding Liesl. "I can't let go. She can't die."

"I understand your concern, but you must let us do our jobs."

The doctor led him to the nurses' station. "I'll let you know what I find as soon as I can. Nurse Henderson here will need to ask you some questions."

The doctor walked back down the hall into the holding room with Liesl. Colin watched the door sigh closed. She was going to be okay. She had to.

Clipboard in hand, Nurse Henderson, in her starched uniform and starched, winged hat, extracted a pen from behind her ear and poised it over the form. He gave her the pertinent information in an automaton-like voice.

He focused on the door, on Liesl lying so still behind it, and willed her to wake up.

"Nature of the injury?" The nurse's strident voice pierced his thoughts.

Colin pounded his fist on the counter, taking his eye off Liesl's door for a second. "Aren't you supposed to tell me that?"

"Take it easy, mister. What happened to her?"

His gaze snapped back to the door separating him from life and death. "She got hit by an airplane wing." *My fault. My fault.*

"How long has she been unconscious?" the nurse's droning voice continued.

"I don't know. Twenty minutes. So much blood. Is she going to be all right?"

"I can't tell you that right now. The doctor will let you know."

He ran a hand through his hair and drew in a long, shaky breath. He had to stay calm. Losing his cool wouldn't help her. The nurse wanted information to help Liesl, to save her. He closed his eyes, relived the experience, and answered the nurse's questions as best he could.

A phone shrilled in the background. A cart squeaked down the hall. Voices whirred all around him in dream-like repercussions. He forced his breathing to slow, his heart to calm.

Whatever you do, God, don't let her die. My conscience couldn't take it. I promise. I'll stay. I'll go home. Whatever You want. Whatever it takes. Please, let her be all right.

After what seemed like the millionth question, Colin cut the nurse off in mid-sentence. "Please go in there and tell me how she is."

"We'll need a family member to sign these forms to authorize treatment."

Colin signed the forms without looking at them. "I need to know how she's doing."

Nurse Henderson looked up at him and seemed to take pity. "I'll see what I can do."

The stiff skirt of her uniform swayed in time to her efficient steps. The door opened and sighed closed.

Resigned to waiting, Colin faced the closed door, and prayed as he never had before. The security guard stood by the door while Colin paced a tight half moon around the door, peppering him with questions.

"Is this a good hospital?" Eight tiles up. Stop. Turn. Eight tiles back.

"The best."

"This doctor, what kind of doctor is he?" Walk. Stop. Turn. Walk.

"Dr. Wright is a general surgeon—"

Colin pivoted on his heels to face the guard. "Does he know anything about head injuries? Shouldn't a neurologist examine her?"

"Relax, fella." The guard offered him a reassuring smile. "Dr. Wright is one of the best. If he thinks she needs a different kind of doctor, he'll get one in there."

So many advances in technology had been made since 1946. "But do they know enough?"

"Look, fella, you've got to relax." The guard shook his head. "She's getting the best care she can possibly get."

"Yeah." But he didn't believe it. He wished he could spirit her away and get her to the technology of his time.

He couldn't save her.

Again.

Colin continued his pacing—three white tiles, one dark gray, three more white, then back again. One of the white tiles had a ripped corner where dirt painted a dark triangle. He hoped the examining room was kept in a more sanitary condition. What was taking them so long?

An eternity of gut-wrenching madness passed

before the doctor finally reappeared. Colin grabbed him by the arms before he had a chance to speak. "How is she?"

"It took twelve stitches to close her wound. Most of the scar will be hidden by her hair."

Colin shook him. "Is she awake? Can I talk to her?"

"She came to for a short while, but I am a bit concerned. The extent of her injuries doesn't warrant her lack of response. So far there's no sign of pressure on the brain, but—"

"What does that mean?" Air rasped painfully through Colin's constricted lungs.

"Head injuries are always a bit tricky. I've ordered a series of X-rays—"

"What about a CaT scan? Shouldn't she have an MRI?" He couldn't breathe. His head started swimming. They didn't know enough.

"Cat scan? MRI?" The doctor looked at him as if he'd gone completely crazy.

"Never mind." Taking a deep breath, Colin relaxed his hold on the doctor's coat and resumed his pacing. "Tell me she'll be all right."

"We won't be certain until she comes to again. She'll be going down to X-ray, and then to a room. We'll keep her overnight for observation."

Overnight. Might as well be a hundred years. He couldn't stay. He couldn't go. He was trapped in the middle of a horror script with no ending. "I want to see her."

"Once she's settled in a room, I'll send someone down for you." Dr. Wright pointed down the hall. "The waiting room is around the corner."

"Yeah." Colin had no intention of following orders. He stayed by the door, trailed the gurney down to X-ray, then to her room.

In the dimly lit room, Liesl looked close to death. The white sheets and white bandage wrapped around her head swallowed her small body. An IV tube trailed from her arm to a post where liquid dripped with nerve-wracking regularity.

Colin dragged the lone chair in the room close to her bed. He took up her cold hand and warmed it in both of his. As she breathed, he watched the small rise and fall of her chest and urged the movement by matching it with his. His forehead dropped onto the hand he held with both of his.

"Wake up, Liesl. Please wake up."

He rubbed her wrist, feeling her pulse bleep slowly under his thumb. He started talking to her, the words pouring out because he couldn't bear the silence. He pressed his nose to her skin, drinking in her scent to keep out the antiseptic hospital stench. He'd had too much of that in his life, and it only meant one thing. His mother, Karen, his father, they'd all come to a hospital to die.

But not Liesl; he wouldn't let her.

"You've got to wake up, honey. Who's going to build that training center you've dreamed of for so long if you're not there? Max is counting on you. He's got the sky in his blood. Just like you, he's a natural."

He raised his head and looked at her face for signs of life. So still. Where had she gone? He brushed away the strand of hair caught on her cheek and tucked it gently behind her ear. His heart cried, but he forced his voice to remain light. He spoke of anything, of nothing. Every word became a plea, a command, a connection with her.

Still she didn't wake. A nurse came in, assessed Liesl, made notes on a chart and left.

Each passing minute loomed ominously over him. He'd have to make a decision soon.

Either way, part of him would be trapped in time forever.

Liesl felt herself rock back and forth between the past and the present. Kurt and Colin. Love and loss. Life and death. Pain, so much pain. It ripped at the tissues of her brain and pounded like a hammer wielded by a wild man. Questions came like shouts across the dulled edge of her consciousness. A touch felt like a burn, a pinprick like an ice pick.

Leave me alone, she shouted, but no one seemed to hear. They prodded and poked and yelled at her, and when she opened her eyes they shimmered and wavered like some obscene monsters in a circus side show.

Who were they? What did they want with her? Couldn't they see she needed to be alone, needed to rest? She was so tired.

"Go away," she croaked. The sound of her own voice exploded in her head, reverberated along her bones, and seemed to split her in two.

Bright lights burned into her eyes. The over-powering smell of copper and disinfectant nauseated her.

Her senses on overload, she closed her eyes again, thankful for the bliss of darkness, for the silence descending once more over her.

Then she floated weightlessly in a colorless soup, free from pain. She wanted to stay here in this nothingness forever. She didn't want to hurt anymore. She didn't want to feel anymore. Just float into nothing. So much better than pain. She was tired, so tired, and life hurt so much. For a little while, couldn't she just stay? She let herself drift freely in the blessed nothingness.

A balmy heat enveloped her and she turned her face to its brilliant heat.

"It's not your time," said a clear, vibrant voice. "You must go back."

Surprised, Liesl opened her eyes. The sun blinded her and filled her with joy. "I don't want to. I'm so tired. I don't want to fight anymore. I want to rest."

The sun didn't speak again, it grew bigger, then faded. The clouds overhead shifted to silver and filled with moving images. Her life was playing itself on this panoramic screen. Time began and ended in the same moment. She saw everything, understood everything. Bits and pieces of other journeys showed her the dozens of broken circles she'd left behind over the life of her soul. They twined and intertwined, sometimes brushing, sometimes missing the circles made by Colin's soul. He'd been a part of her forever, and always they'd parted before the circle could be closed. From fear—fear that love wouldn't be enough, that love would be too much. And that fear had cost them the loss they'd tried so desperately to avoid. Why hadn't they learned?

"It's time to close the circle," said the heavenly voice, gentle as a caress. "It's not too late."

"It is too late," Liesl said, shaking her head.

"There's still time. Go back. Trust your heart."

Gentle hands turned her around and urged her back toward the pain.

"It hurts too much." Liesl balked, wanting to hold on to the comforting nothingness of the colorless soup, wanting to float away from the pain, from the familiar voice she heard calling to her across the mist. His strength, his will tugged at her. She hesitated.

"I'll help you," promised the voice, and warmth and peace suffused her.

Slowly Liesl became aware of the hard mattress beneath her, of the pain pounding in her head, of the bruise throbbing on her arm, of Colin's hoarse voice speaking to her.

"So you see you're being very selfish," he said. "A lot of people need you. Come back, Liesl. There's so little time and so much . . . Liesl?"

Selfish? What was he talking about? He was the selfish one, breaking his promise to her, leaving before the race. Her eyelids scraped over her tender eyeballs. The race! She had to get to the race.

"Liesl? Can you hear me?"

"Stop shouting!" she managed over the crushing grasp of his hand on hers. "Let go of me!"

The sound of her groggy voice surprised him so much, Colin obeyed and loosened his grip.

She was back! Relief rolled through him in a giant wave. *Thank you!* He closed his eyes and lifted his face to the ceiling, sending up a brief prayer of thanks to the heavens, then searched her face. Her eyelids fluttered, and a touch of pink brightened her cheeks.

"Welcome back, Liesl!"

As she opened her eyes, she snatched her hand away from his. "Go to hell."

"Where do you think I've been? I thought I'd lost you." He reached for her again. She turned away from him.

He deserved that, he knew, but the simple rejection cut deep. His hands twined listlessly on his lap. "Are you feeling all right? Should I call the nurse? The doctor?"

"Go away."

"Listen, Liesl, you—"

"I'm not listening." To prove her point she covered her ears with her hands and scrunched her eyes closed.

"I'm trying to explain."

"Save it for someone who cares."

She started to move her head sideways, then stopped as if the movement hurt. He wanted to run to her, to hold her, to take her pain from her. He wished he'd been the one clipped by the Corsair.

"You care. I know you care," Colin said gently. She was hurt. He couldn't blame her. "It wasn't what you thought."

"What's there to think? You needed propellers and there was a box with shiny new propellers. Go away, Colin. I've got a race to win."

She pulled the blankets off and tried to sit up. Colin jumped from his chair and steadied her. "I don't think you should move before a doctor sees you."

She twisted from his grasp, evading him. Colin let go. He wasn't going to hurt her again. Not ever. But he had to explain that he'd done what he thought was best for her. She had to understand that much before he left. When she refused to lie back down, he propped several pillows behind her and tucked the sheet and blanket around her.

The room's door exploded.

"What's going on here?" A nurse rushed in and started poking and prodding. She frowned at Colin sitting on the bed's edge.

"She came to," Colin answered, settling back in the chair.

"I can see that." The nurse picked up Liesl's wrist and took a pulse. "Do you know what your name is?"

"What kind of stupid question is that? Of course I know what my name is."

"Do you know where you are?" The nurse flashed a light into her eyes.

"In a torture chamber."

Colin hid his grin. If her foul mood was anything to judge by, she'd be just fine. Again, he offered a silent prayer of thanks.

"Who's the president?" the nurse continued.

As the nurse prodded the tender flesh around

Liesl's wound, Liesl swatted away her hand. "Truman. Ouch, that hurts."

"Do you know what date it is?"

"March 23, 1946." Liesl's head sprang forward from the pillows. "Oh my God, what time is it?"

"Now, Miss Erhardt, if you're going to get overexcited, I'll have to sedate you."

"Colin?" Liesl's hand reached blindly and found purchase on his blood-stained shirt sleeve.

The nurse turned a cold, hard stare in Colin's direction. "You'll have to leave, Mr. Castle."

"No, I want him to stay." Liesl's fingers bit into the flesh of his forearm. "I promise I'll calm down." Her body physically relaxed onto the bed, but her grip on his arm didn't lessen. "If he goes I'll get really upset."

"If I hear anything louder than a whisper from this room, he leaves and you get a sedative. Is that understood?"

Liesl and Colin both nodded.

"The patient needs rest," the nurse admonished.

"I'll make sure she does." He smiled his best smile.

The nurse seemed unconvinced. "The doctor will be in to see you soon." She made a final entry on her chart and left.

"You've got to get me out of here!" Liesl whispered harshly.

Colin picked up her hand and pressed a kiss on her knuckles. "No. You need to stay here and rest. You took quite a blow to the head."

She ripped her hand away from his touch. "I've got qualifiers to fly, a race to win! How could you leave me without a pilot so close to the race?"

Colin leaned back in the chair, crossing one ankle over the opposite knee. "Because of the contract. Liesl, how could you deal with Billy after what he'd already done to you?"

"I had no choice." As she brought her free hand up to rub her temple, the IV tube followed her movement. "But I don't understand. If you know about the contract, then you know that if you don't fly I'll lose everything."

Colin shook his head, trying to sort out the words into something that made sense. "No. Billy said if I flew, he'd call in your loan before the race. Then you'd have nothing at all. At least if I didn't fly, you'd still have the airport."

"And you believed him!" She thumped the side of the bed with a closed fist. A flush of anger reddened her cheeks. "If I win, I owe him nothing. If I lose, he gets the airport. That's all I agreed to."

Colin bent forward, slapping his foot back to the floor, reaching for her hand, and stopping himself before she could reject his touch once more. "Except for the clause giving him the right to call back his loan at any time."

"What?" Her head shot forward, and Colin gently settled her back onto the pillows. "Do you think I'm stupid enough to sign a document like that? I know Billy well enough not to trust him. I read every single word on those papers. You've got to fly, Colin. I'd rather take a chance on losing the airport than not fly. What time is it?"

"Half an hour to the qualifiers."

"Then what are you doing here? Get out there and fly for me. You promised."

The pink in her cheeks brought on by the anger receded, leaving her skin pasty white. Pain wrinkled her forehead and furrowed her brow.

"Is that what you want?" he asked.

"Yes." Her eyelids drifted down. She pried them up again, fighting their heaviness. "Colin, you've got to fly."

"You rest." Colin rose. She lost the battle with her lids. He pressed a soft kiss on her too-pale cheek. "I'll win your race for you. I promise."

"Yes, win . . ." Her voice was low and sleepy. She turned once, a question on her lips, but it faded unasked. Her head shifted sideways, a strand of dull golden hair falling across her cheek. Gently Colin pushed it aside.

"Circles," he thought he heard her mumble. "Close the circles."

I'll win for you, and I promise, I'll go away and I won't ever hurt you again.

Billy took the shortcut between two hangars on his way to check on his pilots. Jenkins tagged along, apprising him with his latest report on Liesl and her pilot. Matson trotted up to meet them.

"He's flying," Matson said, lighting up a Camel. "I saw him heading for the fueling station." He casually leaned against the hangar wall.

Billy stood in the shade, leaving Matson to

squint up at him. "Nothing to worry about. It's taken care of."

"What did you do?" Matson smiled and puffed on his cigarette.

"Made sure all you have to do is keep enough engine for the end and you're a shoo-in."

"I can handle him either way."

Billy got right up in Matson's face. "That's not the point. The point is I expect you to win. If that means flying him into the ground, that's what you do. Is that understood?"

"Yeah," Matson said, blowing a ring of smoke in Billy's face. "I got it. But I don't need to fly anybody into the ground to win. Even some hotshot war pilot."

"You just make sure you do."

Matson flicked down his cigarette and left.

"I don't think he's a happy pilot," Jenkins said, sneaking up beside Billy.

"I don't pay him to be happy." Billy swung around to face Jenkins. Damn pilots and their egos. "You paid off the judge like I asked you to?"

"Taken care of, Mr. Ackley. On the last lap, he'll miss a pylon, no matter how he flies." Jenkins's nose twitched with delight.

"Find Walters and make sure he can back Matson up. I don't want anythin' to go wrong this time."

"Liesl?"

Liesl opened her heavy lids and saw her father sitting at her bedside. "Papa? Where's Colin?"

Her father nervously patted her hand. "At the airport."

She breathed a sigh of relief. "Did you come to get me out of here? I want to leave."

"No, the doctor says you must stay the night." He shifted from side to side in the chair.

A slow thumping had taken residence in the right side of her head. It kept tempo with the itching of the stitches below the bandage. "Is the race over?"

"No, it starts in one hour."

Liesl reached for the blanket's edge and pulled it up. Her feet dangled from the side of the bed and the room seemed to spin around her. "I've got to see the race."

"Max will tell you all about it." Her father swung her legs back onto the bed and smoothed the blanket back into position.

"It's not the same." She shifted forward again, but her father's firm hand held her in place. "Papa . . ."

A wave of sadness swept through her. Tears bubbled from deep inside, but wouldn't fall. Her eyes were too dry to cry. As the dry sobs racked her body, her shoulders shook.

"Liesl, what is it?"

"I've lost him, Papa. I wasn't good enough. I didn't try hard enough, and I've lost him just like I lost Kurt."

Awkwardly, her father sat next to her and put an arm around her shoulders. She let her head fall on his chest. "You were right, Papa."

Liesl felt her father's sigh warm against her hair. "No, daughter, I was wrong. I should have accepted your choices. Kurt. The airport. They made you happy. I should have trusted your feelings. I wanted to keep pain from you, but instead I pushed it onto you."

He squeezed her harder, hugging her as he never had before. She melted into his embrace. How often had she wished for it as a child?

"I know what it's like to lose someone you love," her father said in a strangled voice. "When your mother died, a part of me died, too. I was . . . devastated."

"I know," she whispered. "You resented me for living while she died."

"Liesl, no!"

Her father pushed her away at arms' length. At the pained expression on his face, she wished she could take back the words, but now that she'd started, she had to finish. "You were always asking me to do better. Nothing I ever did was good enough for you. I thought you didn't love me."

"Oh, Liesl!" He shook his head sadly. "I loved you too much. I was afraid if God knew how much I loved you, He would take you away from me, too. I wanted you to grow up strong enough to stand on your own. I never dreamed you thought I didn't love you."

"I thought if I could be perfect enough, you would forgive me for killing my mother."

"Oh, Liesl! Your mother's death was an accident. An error on the doctor's part, not yours. Losing your mother was bad enough, but the thought of losing you, too, would have been more than I could have borne. You are my daughter and I love you. All I've ever wanted for you was to be happy."

"I was happy with Kurt. I was happy at the airport making his dream come true. I was happy with Colin." The sobs caught in her throat, strangling her breath. "He's leaving, Papa. I never thought a heart could hurt that much."

Tears wrenched straight from her soul burned her eyes with their salt and fell, darkening the front of her father's black suit jacket.

"I couldn't give love a second chance," her father said, brushing away her hair from her damp cheek, his eyes oddly soft. His bottom lip trembled slightly. "I wasn't strong enough. But you are. There's still time."

Liesl shook her head. How could she explain to her father that Colin's travel would take him to a different time, not a different place? "He must leave after the race. He can't ever come back."

"Liesl, look at me." Her father shifted until she had no option but to look him straight in the eye. "It's life that matters. I've wasted all of mine mourning. Don't let that happen to you, daughter. Don't make the same mistake I did. You've got a second chance at happiness, don't let it slip from you. Fight for it." He smiled weakly, tears making his own eyes shine. "Like *Oma* always says, life is meant to be drunk by the cupful—"

"Not tasted with a coffee spoon," they both finished together, laughing amid the tears.

"But, Papa, how will I reach him in time?"

He got up and paced from the window to her bed and back. Suddenly he veered toward the closet and came back out with a black skirt, white blouse, and her favorite white cardigan. "*Oma* sent these for you. Get dressed. Sometimes the best medicine doesn't come in a bottle."

Against the protests of the nurses and the doctor's advice, Liesl's father signed her out and led her into the sunshine.

As he carefully maneuvered *Onkel* Aldo's Packard along the Fort Worth streets, she knew he wondered at the wisdom of his decision. Worry filled his frequent sidelong glances. Every few minutes he asked her how she felt.

"I'm fine, Papa. You don't have to drive so slow."

When she saw the speedometer reading inch up, she smiled, and turned to hide the ripple of dizziness sloshing in her brain. She'd never loved her father as much as she did at that moment. For her he had put aside his every apprehension—Colin, the race, the wound beneath her bandage.

He cared. He'd always cared.

They reached the airport with half an hour to spare before the race. A crush of spectators milled around the grounds cordoned off for public exhibitions. A baby screamed in its mother's arm, sending the ache in Liesl's head throbbing. When she accidentally knocked someone's arm, a spray of Coke stained her white shirt. Using her father's arm to steady her, she rushed to the Castell's parking spot, and found it missing.

"He's probably gone to fill the gas tanks," Liesl said out loud, as much to reassure herself as to inform her father. "Or on his way to the starting line."

She urged her father to split up to look for Colin, and promised to meet him at the grandstand in twenty minutes. He hesitated, but finally agreed.

As fast as her aching head would allow, Liesl made her way to the fueling area.

"Liesl! Liesl!" Max came running toward her from the maze of parked airplanes. "Wait up!"

Huffing and puffing to catch his breath, Max bent forward and leaned his hands onto his knees. "How's your head?"

"Good as new." Her fingers gently massaged the nagging itch below the bandage.

"Have you seen Colin?" Max's gaze darted all around, searching the sea of airplanes.

Max's unnatural agitation made her nervous. "No, I was going to ask you the same thing. Is there anything wrong?"

"We've got to find him." Max straightened. "The race is fixed."

The thump of her heart against her chest matched the booming pulse in her head. "What do you mean?"

"I heard Billy talking to Jenkins. Colin will get disqualified no matter how he flies."

No! Not this close. "Are you sure?"

Still puffing, Max swallowed and nodded. "He

bribed one of the pylon judges. He'll say Colin cut the pylon."

"No!" Liesl started to leave, but Max stopped her.

"That's not all. Matson's got orders to fly him into the ground."

Liesl closed her eyes and wearily rubbed her temples. Her fear for Colin's safety increased the screaming throb in her head. Billy was pulling out his last card, and she couldn't let him get away with it. "You keep looking for Colin. When you find him, tell him exactly what you've told me. And for heaven's sake, make him understand that Matson is dangerous."

"Liesl, where are you going?"

She strode away toward the grandstand. Billy would want an audience for his triumph. "To crush a cockroach."

Chapter Eleven

Liesl rushed toward the temporary grandstand erected midway across the main runway. Her steps fell in rhythm to some unseen clock ticking her precious time away. Her head hurt, the stitches itched. And Colin was nowhere in sight. Where had he disappeared to?

Airplane noises, excited voices, the crackling public address system filled the air with a strident cacophony. The smell of fuel and food didn't do much for the nausea roiling in her empty stomach, either. As she moved, a riot of colors whirled by her, adding to her dizziness.

She found Billy in the grandstand exactly as she'd imagined she would, front row center, drink in hand, surrounded like a halo by a group of people whose favor he'd bought. Their heads bobbed in agreement with his every comment; their brittle laughter followed his on cue.

Without any preliminaries, she marched right up to the front railing. The red, white and blue decorative flounce fluttered around her ankles like an oversized skirt.

"How do you think the NAA Contest Board is going to feel when they hear you've bribed one of the race officials to throw the race?" she asked, hands on the railing to steady the wooziness floating in her head.

The group quieted all at once. Billy swiveled from his admiring audience to face her. His beaming smile didn't dim one bit.

"Well, sugar, that's no way to say hello," he said, amusement tingeing his voice.

She crisped at the sound of his oil-smooth voice, but she didn't have time to waste on her personal dislike for him. She had the race and the risk to Colin's well-being to worry about.

"I'm not here for a lesson in etiquette, Billy. I want to know what you're going to do about that bribed pylon judge."

"What are you talking about?" His eyebrows rose in mock consternation.

"Max heard you and Jenkins discussing how you fixed the race." A silent growl rumbled deep in her chest. The pounding in her head increased.

"Now, sugar, I wouldn't exactly call Max a reliable source." The twinkle of sport in his eyes was hard to miss. Like a cat with a cornered mouse, he thought he could play with her. "I know it's been a rough day for you with your accident and all, but you can't go around accusin' good citizens left and right like that."

"He also heard you order Matson to fly Colin into the ground if he got the chance," Liesl barreled on. Her fingers tightened around the railing.

"I think your pore little head got hit a little too hard." He shook his head with short, derisive strokes. "Do you think it's wise to leave the hospital before you're fully recovered?"

Her poor little head might be pounding and splitting, but she still had enough sense to realize that Billy was trying to intimidate her.

His companions seemed to understand his tactic, too. Their glances darted from each other to their leader. Some fidgeted. Some concentrated on their drinks. Most chuckled nervously, following his lead, knowing it could just as easily be them who suffered her fate. She felt sorry for them, and for Billy. His power no longer scared her.

It took all her willpower to keep focused on her objective. She would not let herself fall prey to Billy's verbal abuse. She didn't have time. "I'm feeling perfectly well. And I'm not going to stand by and watch you cheat your way to success once more."

Billy angled forward and waved a regal hand to his court of jesters. "You're embarrassing yourself. Are you sure you want to discuss this in public, darlin'?"

Liesl leaned into the railing, meeting his gaze without a flinch. "Are you afraid your court of clowns will lose respect for you? I'm on my way to let the officials know about your little tactics."

"Who would believe you?" His smile twitched on one side. "The judge certainly won't brag about it. You'll sound like a sore loser, Lise."

He rose with snake-like fluidity, handed his drink to a neighbor, and swung over the railing. Grabbing her elbow, he dragged her out of his group's earshot, hopscotching her across the crowd of people seated on the lawn waiting for the race to start. "You'll have to learn to lose gracefully."

Liesl stopped short, forcing him to halt and look at her. "No, you'll have to learn you can't always get your way."

"But I do." He cocked his head sideways, bringing a hand up to shade his eyes with the brim of his hat. "You can't win, Lise. When are you going to learn that?"

"When I've exhausted every breath in my body," she said with all the venom she could muster.

"Don't push your luck too hard." His smile dulled. His eyes narrowed beneath the brim. "Even my fancy for you has its limits."

"Are you going to kill me, too? The way you killed Kurt? The way you're trying to kill Colin?"

Billy straightened with a jerk, momentarily taken aback by her accusation. "I didn't kill either of them." His voice held no sweetness now. No glittering humor in his eyes, either, as they darkened with anger. "Rumors killed Kurt. Rumors started by his own best friend. All I did was fan them a little."

"Like the fire in my hangar. Like my butchered airplane."

"I had to."

His admission so stunned her, she couldn't keep the incredulity out of her voice. "Why? Why, Billy?"

"It's the last piece of property my father owned that I haven't gotten back."

"For that, you'd kill!"

"My father died for less." Hardness creased Billy's face. His grip on her elbow hurt. "Because of his name he lost everything. The bank didn't care that he wasn't a Nazi. They called back all of his loans, took over all of his businesses." Liesl pried his fingers from her elbow. Billy didn't seem to notice. "He lost everything. He was the first to venture out of your cozy little community. The first to take a risk. And because of his name, he lost everything."

Billy turned to look at her. Mouth wide open, Liesl could only stare at the man before her, a stranger in every sense of the word. "But he died by his own hand, Billy, not someone else's. There's a difference."

"I had to, Liesl. I had no choice. You didn't leave me any. If you'd said yes, then all of this could have been avoided."

His gaze drifted to the airplanes taxiing to line up for the racehorse start. "As for Colin, he'll fall victim to his own pride. Every man has his weakness. All I do is exploit them."

"For your own benefit. And you know what? That makes it your weakness. Your own power will be your downfall."

273

The public address system crackled, and Billy smiled like a coyote with a caged prey. "Pretty words from a pretty Fräulein. But you're too late, sugar. They're calling the race."

The Castell stood near the fueling station, fueled and ready to go. Colin slouched against the wing, finishing his coffee and studying the course map. When you're zipping around 100 feet above the ground, landmarks tended to blur into one another, but Colin thought he had a good handle on the situation. The railroad curve, the lake's fingered bay, and the red barn in the cow pasture would give him good reference points to turn for the pylons. The grandstand itself made an impressive marker for the home pylon.

He still found it hard to believe he'd be racing in the first postwar Trinity Trophy race. In prestige, it ranked right next to the Thompson Trophy. Winners often became instant heroes. The $10,000 first-place prize didn't hurt either. And though Colin had performed circuits as part of his show act, studied the pylon race performance, strategy, and results as part of his research into the CastleAir, he'd never actually flown a pylon race.

A mixture of nerves and excitement filled him. He glanced at his watch. Fifteen minutes before the start. He ought to get going. To ease his jitters, he performed yet another walk-around. The full extra tank mounted behind the pilot's seat worried him. The extra weight would shift the center of balance back, making the aircraft less stable on takeoff, but he needed the extra fuel to cover the 300 miles of the race.

Because of the scramble of signals with radios during the qualifiers, the officials had banned them for the race itself, making communication a precarious thing. Colin rigged a lap board he could see from the air. Each time he would head for the home pylon, Max would indicate the number of laps he'd flown.

The racehorse start would be madness, but once in the sky, Colin knew he would be in his element.

If he could keep his mind off Liesl, he should do just fine.

And that was his biggest problem. Try as he might to concentrate on the map or the fueling or his strategy, his thoughts of Liesl kept interfering. It didn't take much to lose a race. One moment of inattention could send him in a high-speed stall on a turn, make him mush too far in on a turn and cut a pylon, or give a less than honest pilot the opportunity he needed to fly him into the ground. None of which would help Liesl. But her bloodied face kept haunting him.

My fault. My fault.

He rubbed his eyes with the heels of his hands, squashing the lurid image.

Had she woken up again? Had her brain swelled and needed emergency surgery? Knowing she would be all right would free his mind to race, but the worry that he'd killed yet another loved one nagged him incessantly.

As the public address system announced the

first call for lineup, Colin climbed onto the wing.

"Colin!"

Colin's head snapped back to see Liesl hurrying in his direction. "Liesl?"

He stumbled off the wing and caught her on the fly. The white of her shirt did nothing to improve her pallid complexion, but the warm, solid feel of her against him sent a wave of relief flooding through him. She'd be all right. "What are you doing here? Shouldn't you still be in the hospital?"

He hugged her close, loath to let her go.

"We don't have time." Liesl pushed away from him. "Did Max find you?"

Colin couldn't completely sever his hold and supported her elbows in the cups of his hands. "No, I haven't seen him since the qualifiers."

"Billy bribed a pylon judge," Liesl said in a rapid jabber. "On the last lap, they'll say you cut one of the pylons and penalize you."

"Are you sure?"

She nodded, then reached a hand to her temple as if to steady an ache. She shouldn't be here; she should be at the hospital resting.

"Max overheard Billy and Jenkins talking. Billy's also ordered Matson to fly you into the ground if he gets the chance."

Colin had had a chance to meet Matson earlier. The man strutted about like a peacock and bragged as raucously as a crow. The other pilots called him wild and crazy, shaking their head in admiration. Everybody envied Matson his success, and especially the flock of pretty women tailing him.

Colin had dealt with his kind before. They usually ended up sabotaging their own successes. Which didn't mean Colin could ignore him. On the contrary, if Matson's ship started sinking, he'd be the sort to take as many people down with him as he could. No, Matson would deserve careful attention.

As for the pylon judge, the only way to disapprove his claim would be to make sure there was no doubt.

Colin trotted to an oil barrel used as a garbage can. He plucked out three empty cups with matching lids. Inside the hangar, he grabbed a can of oil from the work bench.

"What are you doing?" Liesl asked as she watched him line up his supplies beneath the airplane wing.

"There's only one way to prove I didn't cut a pylon, and that's to mark it."

He popped a hole into the oil can's top and poured the thick liquid into an empty paper cup. He fit a cover on, handed the filled cup to Liesl, and repeated the procedure three more times, one for each pylon.

"You can't do that," Liesl said, placing the cups on the wing's foot path.

"Why not?"

"There's probably a rule against it."

"Haven't read one."

"Colin! Be serious."

She tucked a strand of loose hair behind her left ear, making Colin smile. She was irritated—

a good, healthy sign. If she had the energy to get angry, she wouldn't die on him.

"I am," he said. "You want to win, don't you?"

"Yes, but . . ."

Colin rose and wiped the greasy streak off his hand with his handkerchief. "Max'll run the board, and you can complain to the race officials about Billy's threat and his bribe."

"Colin . . ."

Colin reached for her and held her snug against him, kissing the top of her head. "Everything is going to be all right. I promised you I would race. And I am. I promised you I would win, and I'll do my damnedest. You shouldn't get this worked up after the blow you took to your head."

"My head is fine." Her arms twined around his waist and her ear settled over his heart, speeding its rhythm. "I'm worried about you. How are you going to fly and play bombardier at the same time?"

"I'll take Max along." He stroked her back. "You can man the board."

Liesl edged out of his embrace enough to turn her face up and look at his face. "There's no time to find Max."

"I'll figure something out."

With a hand at the small of her back, he curved her into him. She pushed him away firmly.

"No, it's my airplane. I want to go."

"Are you crazy?" Colin yelled at her, then turned away, running a hand through his hair. "I can't risk harming you."

The public address system announced the final call. Liesl raced past him, onto the wing and into the co-pilot's seat.

"It's not for you to decide. You're a great pilot. I've seen you fly, remember? I trust you. I'm not leaving, and you don't have time to argue with me."

Damn her to hell and back. Having her with him would put her straight into the jaws of danger. Especially if Matson lacked the conscience he seemed to. Not after what had happened this morning. He couldn't risk her life.

"No, you're not dressed for it." *As if that would convince her!*

"I'll hike up my skirt so it won't get in the way." She smiled a teasing smile and exposed a length of thigh.

Colin rolled his eyes skyward. "You'll add extra weight."

That threw her off for a moment and she hesitated as she settled herself into the cockpit. "I don't think at this point that a hundred and sixteen pounds will make that much difference. You were willing to take Max, remember? And he weighs more than I do."

The public address system crackled a vivid biography of each of the pilots as his plane paraded into position in front of the grandstand.

"You don't have time to argue, Colin." She pulled on his shirt sleeve. "They won't delay the start for you."

Colin gave in. He had no choice. "Scoot over to the pilot's seat." He handed her the slick cup bombs. "All the turns are to the left and you'll need to lob your bombs from there."

Colin pointed out the small window above the instrument panel shroud on her side. His last turn around the pylons would cost him a lot in speed to turn steeply enough for Liesl to lob her bomb without hitting the wing. He'd need to have a healthy lead to win.

He climbed into the cockpit and strapped himself in. "Ready?"

"Ready!"

A flush of excitement colored her cheeks and shone in her eyes. Colin swallowed and shifted his gaze to his instruments.

As he slid the canopy closed, Max jumped onto the wing and knocked on the plexiglass.

"The race is fixed," he said, fighting for his breath.

"I know. Go mind the board."

"Liesl?" Max questioned as he spotted her in the pilot's seat.

"Not now, Max. Find Papa. He's in the grandstand. Tell him to find the race organizer and tell him about Billy's bribe—"

"Then man the board," Colin added.

Max nodded and left, running.

With the start of the Castell's engine, Colin's blood took on a different rhythm. It raced with the engine, revved the adrenaline, and had his body humming with anticipation even if he couldn't quite shake his fear for Liesl.

He turned to her. "I promise I'll keep you safe."

She smiled at him with so much trust, it hurt. "I know."

While the announcer prattled on about the competition and the competitors, Colin taxied to the start/finish line, taking his position second from the post. His qualifying speed of 344 miles per hour put him behind Billy's Mustang, flown by Matson, by two miles per hour and ahead of Billy's Lightning, flown by Walters, by one. The field consisted of ten airplanes in all: four Mustangs, three Cobras, one Lightning, one Corsair, and one Castell.

The first flag of the two-flag pre-start fell. Five minutes to air time. Colin went through his starting checklist. As the ten airplanes stood nose to nose, the noise level increased.

"You okay?" Colin shouted over the din of engine and P.A. noises.

"Colin, if you use even one brain cell to worry about me, I'm going to hit you. Your job is to fly. Let me worry about me. Clear?"

"Aye-aye, Captain."

But he couldn't help worrying. He couldn't help the dread of having her seated next to him in a potentially dangerous situation. He couldn't help thinking of the deaths already weighing his conscience.

The second flag fell. One minute to go. Colin slowly revved the engine. Even if he had to lose, he'd keep her safe.

"Hang on!"

The green flag fell.

Ten planes gunned their throttles together. They accelerated, heading for the single pylon turning point less than a mile away.

With his throttle wide open and his stick full

forward, Colin glanced left and right and noticed the Mustang and the Lightning pulling slightly ahead. His tail wheel skidded hard against the ground with the extra weight from the fuel tank. The Castell wanted to lurch from side to side, forcing him to use more rudder to keep a straight line.

As expected, Matson took the lead. Snapping his landing gear, he pulled ahead of the field down the first straightaway. Brown's Cobra followed close behind, but a stuck landing gear caused him to drop out within seconds of the start.

Colin held his breath as he passed the airport's midpoint with no signs of lifting off the ground. Five airplanes had now beaten him to the air. He glanced at his airspeed. One hundred and ten. The main wheels bounced off the ground, but the tail wheel still stuck to the ground.

Just as he thought of aborting his takeoff, the nose rose and the tail cleared the ground. The airplane's wings started to shudder, close to a stall.

No! Not again. He chased away thoughts of Karen's body crumpled beneath his, of Liesl's bloody face this morning.

With his heart hammering in his chest, Colin defied the stall. Pure luck, he thought as he regained control. He shot Liesl a glance, and she smiled at him, totally unaware of how close he'd taken her to death. Swallowing hard, he returned his attention to the race.

Prop wash from the other entries made the air turbulent, pitching the Castell up and down. The controls responded sluggishly to his commands. He was barely flying, but getting there. With silent encouragement, he urged the plane on, gaining rapidly as the airplane took to the sky.

"Crank the gear up," he ordered Liesl, wishing he sat in his CastleAir with its electric gear motor. As if she were an extension of himself, Liesl had already reached for the lever.

After the first pylon, along the railroad's curve, the Castell held seventh place. On the straightaway, Colin trimmed the plane and jockeyed for position, watching in every direction for other planes. He pulled ahead of Edmund's Mustang and Turner's Corsair, putting him in fifth place.

He shot Liesl another sidelong glance and found her face radiant with excitement. "You okay?"

"Fly, Colin, fly!"

The second pylon loomed straight ahead to his left at the bottom of Eagle Mountain Lake. Following his plan, Colin turned wide and kept his speed. On the downwind leg, he climbed to 300 feet.

The third pylon stood in the middle of a cow pasture. Colin eased around the turn while dropping 200 feet of altitude, gaining speed and racing past Raymond's Mustang down the straightaway.

Approaching the home pylon, he saw Max's lap board marked with a big number one. Rosewell's Mustang cut the pylon and had to circle back. The crowd was on its feet shouting.

Pylon flying, Colin soon discovered, was more an art than a science. All the numbers and strategies he'd learned served him well, but the seat of his pants and instincts now had him in third place behind Matson's Mustang and Walters's Lightning.

Having Liesl next to him turned into an asset. She kept him apprised of the other aircrafts' positions, leaving him free to orchestrate the instruments for optimum performance.

On lap five, they heard an explosion behind them. Liesl craned her neck back to find its origin.

"Dead engine on a Mustang," Liesl said. "I think the pilot walked away."

Colin nodded, concentrating on his instruments and his path around the pylon.

Lap six saw Harding's Cobra trailing smoke. He made an emergency landing in the cow pasture, scattering cattle right and left. Colin passed Walters.

Turner's Corsair backfired on lap seven, blowing part of his cowling off and forcing him to land.

On lap eight, Colin and Matson alternated in the lead. Matson maneuvered close, trying to intimidate Colin into backing away.

Lap nine had them playing chicken. Loath to risk injuring Liesl, Colin played conservatively and allowed Matson to pull ahead.

"Why did you let him get ahead?" Liesl yelled, punching his arm.

"We have plenty of time."

"No!" She pointed to the big ten written on Max's board. "This is the last lap. Give it all you've got!"

Rounding the home pylon saw him ahead of Matson by barely a length.

"Get ready," he said to Liesl. "Open the window. When I say 'now,' drop the first bomb."

"Ready," Liesl said after she'd complied with his instructions.

Colin banked the first pylon at a steep angle, losing precious speed. "Now!"

Liesl dropped her bomb. "I can't tell if it hit or not."

"Doesn't matter. Get ready for the next."

Matson pulled ahead on the straightaway.

"Now!" Colin yelled.

"Yes!" Liesl said punching her fist in the air in victory. Oil slicked the far side of the pylon. "Direct hit!"

With plenty of fuel to spare, Colin pushed the throttle forward and caught up with Matson. Matson crowded him. Colin banked for the pylon, deftly avoiding Matson's press.

"Now!"

Liesl dropped her last bomb. "Hit!"

Matson overshot the turn. Colin could hear him forcing too much power out of his engine to pull ahead of the Castell.

Throttle full forward, Colin gained over Matson. As they passed him, Matson's engine quit dead.

They edged over the finish line a foot ahead of Matson.

"We did it! We won!" Liesl screamed with joy, jostling his arm with both her hands.

He'd done what he'd promised; he'd won and he'd kept her safe. But the win felt bittersweet. Somehow he'd lost as much as he'd gained. Having her beside him during the race had shown him the power of partnership.

But he couldn't stay. He had to leave. He had to prove his worth to his father.

He landed the Castell, taxied straight to the fueling area, and killed the engine. As soon as she'd hopped over the canopy's lip, Liesl jumped into his arms and kissed him.

"We did it!" she said, light shining in her eyes. The flush of victory colored her cheeks with life. He fixed his gaze on her smile and memorized it. He wanted to remember her smiling.

Helping Liesl down from the wing, he barked orders to the attendants. They rushed around to comply. Ignoring Liesl's jubilation, he closed his mind to all the feelings he couldn't understand rumbling through him, and prepared for his flight back to Schönberg. He didn't need feelings; he'd lived most of his life ignoring them.

"Colin?"

His gaze grazed her face, then sheared away. He didn't want to see her brows furrow that way. "I don't have much time. If I don't hurry, I'll miss the window."

"Yes, of course."

At the defeated note in her voice, Colin closed his eyes and took a deep breath. Turning back to her, he gathered her in his arms. "I have to."

The uneven patter of her heart drummed against him.

"Take me with you."

His heart labored with pain. "I can't."

"Please."

"Your friends, your family, your life is here. I have nothing to offer you."

"I don't care."

"I do. I love you, Liesl." How natural those words felt. If only. . . . He kissed her, memorizing her taste, her feel, etching her into his memory. It would have to last him a lifetime. "I want the best for you. You have to stay, and I have to go."

"I'll never see you again, will I?" Her voice cracked, and as she spoke her lips brushed his neck. His stomach fluttered with need.

"No." A drop of moisture wet his shirt. His throat constricted. "Don't cry."

"I won't." Her lips trembled up into a brave smile. Her fingers played nervously with his collar. "Am I allowed to miss you?"

He snared her errant strand of hair around his index finger, felt the silk of it one last time, and tucked it behind her ear. "Not for long. I don't want you to. . . . Promise me . . ."

But he didn't know what he wanted her to promise. He wanted her never to forget him. He wanted her to forget they'd ever met. He wanted her to be happy and didn't know how to tell her, how to show her.

"Liesl . . ." The word escaped him on a painful breath.

"Shh." She put a finger on his lips. "I'll be all right. I promise."

With his heart shattering in his chest and his breath straining into his lungs, he felt lost. No matter what he did, he'd never be all right.

People swarmed around them, offering congratulations, asking questions, begging for autographs. The crush of bodies separated them. Liesl sniffed back her tears.

Funny how winning the race no longer seemed to mean so much. Colin would take a part of her when he left. But this time, she wouldn't fall to pieces. Like the sparrow, she'd mend and learn to accept the circles of life. This time she'd survive. He'd given her the sky, and she would pass on his gift to a generation of eager pilots. He'd given her the means.

This time, she had nothing to be sorry about. She'd given her love, she'd said the words. Her circle was closed.

Colin would have to close his own.

Liesl watched Colin climb into the Castell's cockpit. As he reached up to close the canopy, he glanced down at her. "I love you, Colin. Forever."

She couldn't read the expression on his face. The headache she hadn't felt during the race came back with a vengeance. She concentrated on the pain there, rather than the raw one building in her heart.

Who was she trying to fool? She'd miss him every day of her life. She wouldn't die, but she wouldn't be whole, either. With him, Colin would take an important part of her heart, leaving behind the fresh, new pain she'd feared all along. Numbness froze the intensity for now, but when she was alone once more the tears would come, and so would the emptiness, and the gnawing grief. They would haunt her days, and especially her nights.

The canopy slid into place with a click. Without a backward glance, he started the engine and taxied away. Tears clouded her vision, but Liesl forced herself to smile and wave.

Loving and losing again hurt so much, she wasn't sure she could emulate the sparrow and start new dreams as easily as the bird could make a new nest.

"Good-bye, Colin."

When her father and Max walked up behind her, she leaned into their support, swallowing back the constriction in her throat. Colin had shown her all the love she had around in the community she'd taken for granted. With its strength she could do anything—even fight Billy's power and unite their divided town.

She could do anything, except fall in love again.

If *Tante* Wenona was right and souls did outlive their earthly bodies, they would meet again.

Maybe next circle, they would get the timing right.

Chapter Twelve

Colin pushed the CastleAir's throttle forward, feeling the airplane's engine surge to life. The newly installed propellers worked perfectly. He released the brakes and the airplane launched down the grass runway. Keeping his attention on procedures, Colin gained altitude.

The blue sky above him, the yellow-green earth below him, the live power in his hands calmed his frayed nerves, but where was the joy, the freedom that came with flight? To his left a hawk floated in a thermal. He wasn't tempted to follow.

Something ate at him, and he didn't know what.

In the sky, he could be himself. He didn't have to pretend. He could relax.

But the muscles of his hands clenched the

joystick with skin-whitening tension. His jaw hurt from grinding his teeth. The muscles in his back ached from being held rigid.

What was happening to him? Why did he feel so disgusted with himself? Why did he feel he'd somehow lost again?

The window, of course. He'd pushed finding it and might not reach it in time. Because of Liesl. He'd let his attraction to her make him linger far too long out of his time.

He hadn't asked to travel through time, but he had.

And now he was leaving the woman he loved behind, knowing full well he'd never find the strength to love again.

Colin headed in a beeline toward the place where Traders Field would not appear for another quarter century or so, and retraced his flight from a week ago. He danced with the sky and teased the earth, seeking the pleasure he found in the freedom of the sky.

It escaped him.

Inspecting the land below him, he saw no reason for his desolation. He loved the land, the cruel harshness of it. It had often seemed as lonely as he'd been. Things changed, but not the land. The seasons could be counted upon to happen no matter what. It was a constant in time. Yellow in the summer, brown in the winter, fleetingly green in the spring. These flat acres of land, punctuated by hills softened by age and miniature canyons carved by drenching storms on heat-parched soil, were part of him. This sky where he found freedom was his home.

A timeless part of him.

He found himself glancing sideways, wishing he'd see Liesl's smiling face beside him. Her delight at discovering the joy of dancing with the sky had thrilled through him, taking his love for the sky to a new, unexpected height. If he closed his eyes, he could even recapture the feeling when time had ceased to exist, when they'd been one with each other and the universe. The connection had been so intense, both of them had turned away from it.

Gaining altitude over Lake Schönberg, he cleared the area, checked his instruments, and picked a reference point. The same one he'd taken in 1996. Still there. Constant. Like the revived ache in his heart—for his mother, for Karen, and now, a new raw layer for Liesl.

Pretending to do a steep takeoff, he moved the stick rearward. He shook his head and sneered. The worst part was that he could disappear right here, right now, and no one would know. No one waited for him anywhere.

His father would die. If not tomorrow, then in a week or a month. How far had the disease ravaged him? Would he even recognize his own son by his bedside? Would his father understand the victory that had cost Colin so much?

Jakob, old, alone, and weighed down with regrets wouldn't be around much longer, either. He'd already formed plans to move on. He wanted to die in the old country—Berlin, where his career as a metal worker had started.

And Liesl had said her good-byes, setting him free to find his success.

The stall warner sounded. Colin applied left rudder and moved the stick full back to get a break. The left wing dipped while the right wing rose. The nose fell, inducing the plane into a spin.

Success, what did it mean anyway? And whose definition was he using?

Success had meant standing on his own, being his own boss, living and breathing flying every moment of the day. Proving to his father that he could follow his own calling and make his mark in the world. Making up to his father for the mistake of taking his beloved wife away from him. His father had rarely laughed after the accident. Alone and lonely, he'd poured all of his energy into his burgeoning freight business.

Success for Colin had meant the sky and the excitement it provided. Failure had been the earth and the stress he'd found on it. He wouldn't have been happy pushing papers for his father, or for anyone else.

What did success mean now? He didn't know, and the frustration of it ate at him.

Even if he succeeded, what would he have to look forward to? He'd be alone with his success. Like his father.

The earth beneath him spun its mosaic pieces of blue water, brown and spring-green fields, and blacktop ribbons into a wash of blended colors. And in the spinning colors, he saw Liesl. Her gasp of horror when she saw him that first night. Her hatred turning into love. Her unselfish giving.

If she'd fought him, if she'd begged him to stay, if she'd tried to cage him, then leaving her would be much easier. But no, she'd looked at him with her big blue eyes filled with love and set him free.

She wasn't really in love with him, Colin tried to convince himself. She wanted the part of him that was Kurt.

Idly he counted the spin's turns.

Why hadn't he taken her with him? She'd have willingly left everything she had to come with him. He shook his head. She had so much here. He had so little there.

He was doing the right thing. For her. For him. She'd be hurt for a little while, but she'd get over the feelings she thought she had.

It would take him a lifetime to forget her.

He didn't like the emptiness widening into a giant chasm inside him.

The airplane spun in ever tightening circles. His feelings followed the same path, blending one into the other until nothing remained except a strong sense of urgency.

Life is meant to be drunk by the cupful, not tasted with a coffee spoon. *Oma's* favorite maxim suddenly exploded with meaning.

Tasters were afraid and took life in tiny little lukewarm sips. Gulpers took chances, risking to burn their palates in the process. But what rewards they reaped for their efforts. A life full of flavor and all the nuances in between.

Come on, Colin, be my good little boy. Come on, Colin, be my hero. I love you, Colin. Forever.

His mouth went dry. Beads of sweat formed

along his brow and slipped down the side of his face into his shirt collar.

She'd never asked him to be her hero. She'd given him her love unconditionally, knowing he'd leave, knowing she'd opened herself to pain. And he'd thrown that love back at her as if it were a Christmas gift that didn't fit.

If she truly loved him, he was the world's greatest fool.

The sound of his beating heart pounded in his ear. He couldn't hear the engine. He couldn't hear the wash of wind over the wing. He couldn't hear the click of the instruments spinning in front of him.

With a defeated calm, he moved to his spin-recovery checklist. How could his life have changed so much in just one week?

Success was relative, he decided. With no one to share it with, what meaning did it have?

He'd found his someone; couldn't he simply make new dreams?

He felt the window's tug.

No, he decided, he wasn't the earth's greatest fool. He'd have to travel clear across the universe to find a bigger one.

Everything he'd ever wanted, ever needed, was right here.

He hooked his finger on Jakob's black button near the throttle. And then he made up his mind.

From his mansion on Schönberg's highest point, Billy Ackley stared at the hangar far below. Copper burnished the evening sky, making the steel building appear as if it were on fire. But this illusion wouldn't cleanse the ghosts from his life. They danced around him now, mocking him.

The land on which Liesl's airport stood would never be his. He swirled the hundred-year-old brandy in the crystal snifter, and turned from the view outside. He looked around at his finely appointed house.

His money hadn't been able to buy him what he'd wanted most—Liesl's love. He realized now that all he'd done was for her. To show her that he was better than Kurt. But for him she'd had only pity. Her heart had always belonged to Kurt, always would.

"Don't you get lonely, alone with your power?" she'd asked him.

He hadn't—until now. He'd been too busy dreaming and planning, anticipating the day when Liesl would share his life.

He'd worked so hard, so damned hard to win back everything that should have been his. But not once had his money and power come close to getting him the love he'd seen shine in Liesl's eyes when she looked at Kurt, at Colin. All his success had meant nothing to her. He'd tried to bribe her. He'd tried to break her. He'd tried to make her submit. But still, she'd remained true to her heart. She would rather have died alone than live with him. Even with all he could give her.

And her stand had cost him more than he wanted to admit.

He sank into the rich leather chair and gulped

down the last of the brandy. As the liquid burned down his throat, he could feel his power crumbling around him. His friends had never been friends. They'd stood by him because they feared him, and now that Liesl had shown them he could be beaten, his hold on them was slipping. How much would it take to buy them back?

Soon the train tracks dividing the town would mean nothing. Soon the rift he'd encouraged would be only a dim memory. He'd seen the signs already when some of his men had crossed the tracks to help Liesl rebuild her plane. He'd seen the signs again when few had vouched for him with the Contest Board.

Billy rubbed his neck as if erasing an invisible rope. He wouldn't take the easy way out. He wasn't a coward like his father. He might have lost for now, but it wasn't worth dying over. Money spoke loudly. If not here, then elsewhere. There were other places, other towns that would gladly welcome him and his money.

There were other women, too. One of them would surely love him and make for him the home he'd dreamed of sharing with Liesl.

He hadn't lost. Not really.

All he needed to do was reinvent himself.

He'd done it before.

He'd do it again.

The scenery sped by, but Liesl saw none of it. Max handled her father's car with precision along the narrow stretch of highway. She'd left the huge Trinity trophy to be engraved with her name and results by the race officials. In her hand she held the $10,000 first-place check.

Her father's complaint to the Contest Board had erupted an uproar of accusations and counteraccusations. By the time the Board had sorted through the mess, the bribed pylon judge had confessed to his weakness, Matson insisted he'd have flown the race the same way with or without Billy's instructions, both of Billy's entries had been disqualified, and Billy had been barred from racing any entries for two years. An enraged Billy had left swearing revenge.

But Liesl didn't care. Billy couldn't hurt her anymore.

She looked down at the check in her hand, wishing she could muster the joy she'd assumed it would bring.

"Are you all right?" Max asked, not taking his eyes off the road unfolding before them.

"Yes. I'll be fine." Her hands moved like startled birds, her voice felt much too bright, and the smile she painted on felt tight. "There's so much to do. I've already got a dozen offers to invest, and two pilots who've offered their services as instructors. I don't know when we'll get a chance to catch our breath."

"He's not coming back, is he?" Max's fists clenched and unclenched around the steering wheel.

Liesl stared at the check in her lap. "No."

Max's head moved in short strokes. His brow furrowed. "Why? I don't understand how he could leave."

Colin's departure was Max's loss, too, not just

hers. His hero worship for Kurt had trickled down naturally to Colin. She turned her gaze to the speeding scenery, wishing that somehow she could have frozen time in those happy moments when they'd all worked together on the Castell, frozen time the night they'd loved each other without reservation.

"Everyone has their destiny, Max. His is elsewhere." Unconsciously one hand went to her aching heart.

"I still don't understand."

She didn't know if she could explain what she herself didn't quite fathom. "He was a gift on loan to us." Her hand reached over to comfort Max. "After Kurt died, a part of me did, too."

"I know. I've been so worried about you." He fidgeted, nervous about his admission. "When it looked like we weren't going to find a pilot, I thought you'd shrivel up and die. I couldn't stand to see you that way. Nobody could. But we didn't know how to help you."

"I understand that now." Warmth flowed through her and she smiled. "Colin has taught me so much. I used to think this tight-knit community of ours was a prison. Everybody knows everybody's business."

Max chuckled, shaking his head in agreement. "Don't I know it!"

"I watched the way the whole community gathered around me to protect me from Colin. I watched the way they accepted him when they discovered he wasn't a threat. I watched the way he fit in and relished their acceptance. And I realized they weren't a prison, but a harbor."

Max nodded. "Someplace we can always find someone waiting with open arms for us." His face grew serious. "I never knew my father, but I never missed having one because I had a dozen of them watching over me."

"Yes, everybody's little brother!" Liesl was silent for a moment. "I thought if I was to love again, I'd have to give up what I had with Kurt. But loving Colin taught me my heart was big enough for both."

The pain was mixed with joy. With the pain, he'd given her memories she would treasure forever. Loving Colin had enriched her life. It had shown her she didn't have to lose her identity to become part of someone else's life. She could be herself and part of someone else, too. She didn't have to be perfect, she simply had to be.

And she didn't have to forget.

"I've found my heart." She smiled and held up the check, waving it in the air. "I have a purpose. And I have the support of the people I love. What more could I ask for?"

"Someone special to love you."

Liesl folded the check in half and slipped it into her pocket. "One of these days . . . you never know."

But she doubted it. She'd given her heart away twice. Once it broke. Once it healed. Now the spot reserved for loving a special man would remain empty. And maybe the pain would dull with time.

Max turned off the highway onto the side road that would take them to town. With the sun setting, a chill returned to the air. Liesl reached for the sweater in the back seat and put it on.

The car drove alongside the barbed-wire fence delineating her property. As Max neared the wooden gate with its peeling white paint, Liesl asked him to stop.

"Are you sure?" he asked, his forehead crinkled with worry.

She smiled. "Yes. I want to make sure everything is closed up for the night. I'll be along shortly."

"I can stay with you, if you like."

"I want to be alone for a little while. I'll be home for supper." She got out of the car. "Stop worrying, will you! You're too young to worry so much—especially about an old widowed cousin. Go on home."

As Liesl pushed the gate open, it creaked. She strode purposefully forward, then stopped at the crest of the hill. The sun's last golden light seemed to etch a halo around the hangar. Her mind rang with the memory of love and laughter she'd shared there with Kurt and Colin, and she sent a thankful prayer that she'd had the pleasure of both of them touching her life.

When she continued toward the small office beside the hangar, even the bluebonnets swaying in the dusk's breeze approved of the light step she struggled to keep. She shrugged out of her shirt, removed her skirt, and slipped into a pair of Levi's and an oversized man's shirt.

She crossed over to the hangar and slid open the corrugated door. The air felt strange tonight, light and spicy with the scent of spring. She filled her lungs with it, feeling alive despite the bruising ache.

Inside, the Castell stood, a dark silhouette against the hangar walls. She ran a hand over the cowling. It was still warm. Her mind drifted elsewhere, listening, waiting, wishing. . . .

Slowly, softly, a buzzing noise pierced her reflective mood. She knew that noise, had heard it a thousand times. Her head snapped up. Her hopeful heart stopped for an instant, then jabbered erratically.

As she made her way to the hangar door, Liesl forced her steps to remain slow.

A black dot appeared on the horizon.

Her stiff steps carried her to the oak tree beside the hangar.

The dot grew larger and larger. Liesl wrapped one arm around her waist. One hand went to her trembling lips. Her mind stayed blank, fearing to hope against hope.

The black dot entered the traffic pattern, glinting green as it turned into a final approach. Colin's CastleAir. As her heart hammered against her ribs and her breath came in erratic spurts, a sense of unreality, of foolish expectations, held her in place.

He flared a few feet above the ground, and the CastleAir's wheels kissed the grass with a satisfied sigh. He tracked straight down the mowed strip and taxied slowly to the apron in front of the hangar. The engine's rumble ceased, its echo rolling through the night air.

Tears burned her eyes at the sight of the canopy sliding back, of Colin's dark hair poking through it. Colin extricated himself from the cockpit and onto the wing. With a swift jump, he landed on the ground.

He couldn't have seen her standing there in the dark, yet his footsteps carried him surely toward her. He stopped suddenly, arm's length away.

"You're back," Liesl said, smiling tentatively, heart jolting painfully against her ribs. Her hands reached back for the solidity of the tree trunk's rough bark.

"Yeah, I had to find out if that bird's wing would heal properly."

She fought the smile turning the corners of her mouth. "Is that all?"

"Maybe I figured you might need a chief pilot to help you start your training center." He ran a hand through his hair, shifting his weight from one side to the other. "I'm a pretty good pilot, and I've got some experience as an instructor."

The smell of spent fuel from the airplane, the hint of leather from his jacket, drifted in her direction. The engine pinged as it cooled. The air tingled with the electric envelope she remembered from the first night she'd met Colin.

"Well, I've already had several solid offers from other pilots," she said, barely hearing herself over the pulse of blood in her ear. "Try again."

Any moment now, her voice would croak like a sick frog. She didn't know how much longer she could stay so close to him without launching herself into his arms. She wanted him more than she wanted her next breath, but she needed to know he'd come back for himself as much as for her.

He cleared his throat and shuffled the toe of his boot in the dirt along the base of the tree, missing the toe of her boot by a fraction of an inch. "Maybe I could be your business manager. You know, help you put together an investment proposal, help you run your school." He shoved both his hands into his back pockets and smiled crookedly at her. "I've got a business degree I've never used that could come in handy."

"Um. I suppose." She pushed herself off the tree trunk and with one slow step closed the distance between them. She slid her arms around his neck. Her lips curved all the way up. "But what I really need is a partner," she murmured against the crook of his neck. Her smile widened when his pulse jumped to meet her lips.

"A partner?" He gulped and pushed her firmly away. His eyes held such sorrow, it spread a wildfire of fear through her. "That counts me out then." He opened his arms wide. "This is all I've got to offer you, Liesl."

"It's enough."

He squashed her against him, holding her close, as if she would vanish if he let go, then just as suddenly he released her. "All of my love, Liesl. That's all I have to give you."

His forlorn expression had her gulping back tears. She grabbed his hands and squeezed them. "Don't you know it's everything?" She paused, gazing deep into the swirling green in the brown of his eyes. "What about your dream, Colin? Will you regret giving it up?"

He shook his head and smiled, lighting up his whole face.

"I love you, Liesl. Without you, it would have meant nothing." As he brought her hands to his lips, his eyes shone. "Any place without you would have been hell. I had to come back. We can make new dreams together. I belong here with you."

She couldn't stand the distance anymore. It yawned between them as deep and as wide as the time tunnel which had almost taken him away from her. He'd come back to her. The why didn't matter.

She twined her hands around his neck and stroked his hair, the words she wanted to say refusing to come out. She let her mouth slide over his, the hunger of endless open circles throughout time showing him what her choked emotions couldn't.

"Marry me?" he asked, his gritty voice rasping warmth into her ear.

"In a heartbeat." She didn't bother to wipe the tears of joy spilling down her cheeks. "You realize Papa and *Oma* will want to make a big deal out of this wedding."

"I wouldn't have it any other way."

She pulled the silver chain from beneath her shirt and drew it over her head. With ease, she unclasped the ends. The rings dropped with a tinkle into her open palm. She fit the smaller one onto her finger and the larger one on Colin's. "It still fits."

A pained expression flitted over his face. "I'm not Kurt."

Liesl grasped Colin's hand, touching silver band against silver band. Two closed circles joined by love. "I know. You're Colin Castle, the man I love."

He lowered his lips on hers and kissed her with a fierce possessiveness she reveled in. She returned his embrace with all of her heart, mind and soul.

The night was cool and filled with the joyous concert of life going on all around them. In the distance, a train whistle shrilled, disturbing the natural symphony. The backwash no longer called her name. Arm in arm they slowly headed back toward town, secure in the knowledge they had a lifetime of tomorrows left to share.

This time, they would get it right.

Epilogue

Traders Field, Texas, March 1996

The sun sank on the horizon, painting the fading blue sky with streaks of crimson and gold. As the show drew to an end, the mob below scattered and returned to the makeshift parking lots along the chain-link fence. Their feet slapped a tired rhythm on the trampled grass. A few looked over their shoulders with longing at the shiny airplanes parked in a row. As they recounted the feats they'd seen, their voices buzzed with excitement. The halogen lights blinked on, illuminating the ground with circles of light.

Jakob Renke watched from a safe distance. He gripped the side of the door, and didn't loosen his hold as he spotted two figures lingering on the apron. One lone airplane zoomed into the sky, ripping the dying day with a roar.

"It was a good show, wasn't it?" the man said, letting out a whistle of appreciation.

"*Ja*, a good show," Jakob answered without enthusiasm.

The man gripped his shoulder. "Next year, yours'll be up there."

Jakob turned to look at the man. In the face he saw Kurt's smile and Liesl's eyes. "*Ja*, next year."

Kyle had walked into his hangar this morning. At first glance, Jakob had mistaken him for Colin. Kyle had said his grandfather had sent him to help with the replica project. Jakob had known then that he would never see his airplane again, and that Colin was giving it back to him the only way he could. But he didn't need the airplane anymore; he'd accomplished what he'd set out to do.

He'd looked for Colin all day, thinking he saw him around every corner, thinking he heard his voice over the din of the crowd, thinking he felt his presence among the roaming throng of people.

"I vaz right to try," he said to himself, searching the dark for the two familiar silhouettes.

As they stepped into a pool of light, he recognized Liesl's laughter ruffling the crisp air. Sensing his gaze, Colin looked up. Gray streaked his brown hair. The wrinkles of time decorated his face. But life sparkled from his eyes. And love, love for Liesl. Colin waved and turned back to the woman at his side.

Liesl sported a new hairdo, her white hair cut short in a no-nonsense style. The lines gracing her eyes and mouth did not diminish her beauty. Her body curved naturally into Colin's, seeking his touch even after fifty years, the way a flower sought the sun. Her big blue eyes gazed at Colin in adoration.

A wave of relief swept through Jakob. Knowing the calculations were off, he'd been gnawed by worry all week. He hadn't slept. He hadn't eaten. He'd watched the sky day and night for signs of the CastleAir's return, for confirmation that a lifetime of work and repentance hadn't gone to waste.

A tear slid down his cheek. He removed his glasses and wiped it with the back of his hand.

"I'll be back tomorrow," Kyle said. "Then we can start on that CastleAir. I've worked on my grandfather's ever since I can remember."

"*Ja,* tomorrow." Jakob turned toward Kyle. "Tell your grandfazer he made zee right decision. Tell him Nick died last week." Colin had missed his father's funeral, but he'd found the life he was always meant to live.

"Who's Nick?"

"He vill know."

Jakob watched Kyle saunter down the apron toward his grandparents with the same spring that Colin's gait had had when they'd first met. As the trio disappeared, Jakob gave way to tears of joy. The screams of terror that had etched themselves into his brain fifty long years ago finally ebbed and vanished.

309

Sylvie Kurtz

She'd never been his. She was exactly where she belonged—in Kurt's arms.

He'd fixed his mistake.

Tonight he would sleep in peace.

Three captivating stories of love in another time, another place.

MADELINE BAKER
"Heart of the Hunter"

A Lakota warrior must defy the boundaries of life itself to claim the spirited beauty he has sought through time.

ANNE AVERY
"Dream Seeker"

On faraway planets, a pilot and a dreamer learn that passion can bridge the heavens, no matter how vast the distance from one heart to another.

KATHLEEN MORGAN
"The Last Gatekeeper"

To save her world, a dazzling temptress must use her powers of enchantment to open a stellar portal—and the heart of a virile but reluctant warrior.

__51974-7 *Enchanted Crossings* (three unforgettable love stories in one volume) $4.99 US/
$5.99 CAN

HEARTWARMING ROMANCE BY

ELAINE FOX

Hand & Heart of a Soldier. Emma Davenport has a mission: to smuggle medical supplies for the wounded Confederates. First she has to enter enemy territory—the Darcy residence. She knows her connection to the Darcy family supplies the perfect cover, but she doesn't count on William Darcy being armed for a battle of desire. His intoxicating kisses and passionate embrace threaten to shatter all of Emma's defenses. And though she is dedicated to her cause, Emma can't stop her virile foe from capturing her rebel heart.

_4044-1 $4.99 US/$5.99 CAN

Traveler. A late-night stroll through a Civil War battlefield park leads Shelby Manning to a most intriguing stranger. Bloody, confused, and dressed in Union blue, Carter Lindsey insists he has just come from the Battle of Fredericksburg—more than one hundred years in the past. Before she knows it, Shelby finds herself swept into a passion like none she's ever known, and willing to defy time itself to keep Carter at her side.

_52074-5 $4.99 US/$6.99 CAN

Dorchester Publishing Co., Inc.
65 Commerce Road
Stamford, CT 06902

Please add $1.75 for shipping and handling for the first book and $.50 for each book thereafter. NY, NYC, PA and CT residents, please add appropriate sales tax. No cash, stamps, or C.O.D.s. All orders shipped within 6 weeks via postal service book rate. Canadian orders require $2.00 extra postage and must be paid in U.S. dollars through a U.S. banking facility.

Name _____

Address _____

City _____ State _____ Zip _____

I have enclosed $_____ in payment for the checked book(s). Payment <u>must</u> accompany all orders.☐ Please send a free catalog.

High Energy/Whirlwind Courtship
Dara Joy/Jayne Ann Krentz writing as Jayne Taylor

High Energy by Dara Joy. Physics. Zanita Masterson knows nothing about the subject and cares little to learn. Until a reporting job leads her to one Tyberious Augustus Evans. The rogue scientist is six feet of piercing blue eyes, rock-hard muscles, and maverick ideas, and the idea that he is seriously interested in her seems insane. But a night of monster movies, cookie-dough ice cream, and wild love is almost enough to convince Zanita that the passion-minded professor is determined to woo her—with his own masterful equation for sizzling ecstasy and high energy.

And in the same heart-stopping volume...

Whirlwind Courtship by Jayne Ann Krentz writing as Jayne Taylor. When Phoebe Hampton arrives quite by accident at the doorstep of Harlan Garand's mountain cabin, he is less than pleased. Convinced that she is another marriage-minded female sent by his matchmaking aunt, Harlan would gladly throw her out. But Phoebe is a damsel in distress, and an attractive one at that, so against Harlan's better judgment he lets her stay—even though she wishes she were a hundred miles away! Grudging host and grudging guest will just have to put up with each other for a few days. After that, they'll never see each other again—or will they?

___3932-X **(two passionate contemporary romances in one volume)**

$5.99 US/$7.99 CAN

Dorchester Publishing Co., Inc.
65 Commerce Road
Stamford, CT 06902

Please add $1.75 for shipping and handling for the first book and $.50 for each book thereafter. NY, NYC, PA and CT residents, please add appropriate sales tax. No cash, stamps, or C.O.D.s. All orders shipped within 6 weeks via postal service book rate. Canadian orders require $2.00 extra postage and must be paid in U.S. dollars through a U.S. banking facility.

Name _____

Address _____

City _____ State _____ Zip _____

I have enclosed $_____in payment for the checked book(s).
Payment **must** accompany all orders.☐ Please send a free catalog.

Futuristic Romance

WARRIOR Moon
MARILYN JORDAN

"A gripping tale of forbidden love and cunning betrayal!"

—Nancy Cane, Bestselling Author Of
Keeper Of The Rings

Dedicated to upholding the ancient ways of her race, Phada is loath to mix with the men of her world—especially the hard-muscled brutes who protect her homeland. Yet despite her resolve, the young Keeper can't understand her burning attraction for virile and courageous Sarak. Although he is nothing more than a servant, he leaves her breathless with the stirrings of an emotion that can only be passion. But on a perilous quest to save her people from utter destruction, Phada must trust her very life to Sarak. And if she isn't careful, she'll find love, devotion, and ecstasy without end beneath a warrior moon.

_52083-4 $5.50 US/$7.50 CAN